D1637977

things I
should
have said
and done

COLETTE McCORMICK

Things I Should Have Said and Done

Published in the United Kingdom by
Accent Press
www.accentpress.co.uk

Paperback ISBN: 9781786150240
    eBook ISBN: 9781786150233

First Edition: November 2016
Category: Contemporary Women's Fiction

For Mum and Dad, I wish you could have been here to see this.

CHAPTER ONE

One minute I was fine and the next … well, I'm not sure what I'd call it exactly, but I'd never felt it before. I was shaking and I could hardly breathe and all I could think was, *Oh my God! What's going on?* To be honest, there might have been the odd expletive as well but, *oh my God! What's going on?* was the gist of it.

Surrounding me was an incredible light. It was like when there's been heavy snow and your eyes struggle to adjust to the sun shining off it. You know, like when your eyes can't really focus on anything because everything is so white. It was just like that, except even whiter. My eyes instinctively screwed up to protect themselves like they would do on a really sunny day but this light wasn't like a sunny day, not even a very sunny day. This light physically hurt my eyes.

I tried to open them a couple of times but it hurt so much I was forced to keep them closed. I was in complete panic.

I was breathing in short bursts which I took in and let out in stages. I didn't know what was going on but I knew I was panicking. I'd never had a panic attack before and I couldn't understand why I was having one now.

What on earth was that light? I asked the question over and over in my head. *What is that light? What is that light? What is that light?*

I also asked myself why it was so noisy. There were loud noises all around, like when I'm watching TV at my granddad's and he hasn't got his hearing aid in. People were shouting, and someone even screamed. I wanted to scream myself but couldn't. It was taking everything I had to breathe.

Oh my God, what was wrong with me? Why couldn't I breathe properly? Why were my teeth chattering?

The answer to all three had to be the same – I was scared. No, I was more than scared; I was petrified.

I tried to think.

Somehow I knew that no matter how much it hurt, I would have to open my eyes. I thought rubbing my eyes might help but it only made things worse. So now, as well as the light, there were circles flickering under my eyelids as if I had a migraine coming on. *Ah,* I thought, *that's it; I've got a migraine forming.* It would be worse than any other I'd had before, but that was the only explanation. Oh great, not only would I have a blinding headache soon but I'd have the vomiting later. Yippee!

That would have to wait. Right now, I had other things to worry about. Slowly, a millimetre at a time, I forced my eyes open and blinked rapidly in a desperate attempt to adjust to the brightness. They hurt like hell, but I'd managed to open them this much so I forced myself to hold my eyes wide open. My facial expression was probably freakish but I didn't care. Anyway, I doubt anyone noticed because when my eyes eventually opened properly I was able to see I wasn't the only one panicking.

To the left of me was a woman.

'Help!' she shouted. 'Someone help.'

'What's wrong?' I had to yell because the noise was deafening.

Apparently I didn't yell loud enough.

2

'What's wrong?' I said again, moving closer and shouting even louder.

But there was no response, so I turned around to look for someone else. There was a man running towards me and I held my hands up in a gesture that made it obvious I wanted him to stop, but he didn't. He kept on running and I had to jump out of the way as he passed by.

'Oh, thanks anyway,' I shouted, adding *ignorant bugger* under my breath.

I looked after him, standing on my tiptoes to try and see where he was running that was so important, but I couldn't see a thing. There were too many people in the way. Heads were bobbing up and down and the bodies were packed together too closely.

Everyone seemed too preoccupied even to notice I was there.

Hang on a minute, where was I? Now that I could see I needed to work out where I was. Maybe I'd be able to work out what was going on. How could I not know where I was? Oh my God, maybe I'd had a blackout. *Shit!* I knew I should've had those headaches checked out. I'd dismissed them as nothing but it looked like they might be something after all. OK, I'd ring the doctor in the morning.

What was the last thing I remembered?

I took a couple of deep breaths and tried to calm down enough to think straight. I remembered being at Mum's house. We'd popped round to check on her because she said she wasn't well. She'd looked alright to me and I was a bit huffed that she hadn't picked Na ... Oh my God!

'Naomi!' The scream almost burst my own eardrums but no-one else seemed to notice. 'Naomi,' I shouted, 'where are you?'

I whipped my head around, desperately looking for my daughter.

'Naomi,' I screamed again. 'Naomi, where are you?'

But there were so many people around and Naomi was just a little girl. I couldn't see her anywhere.

'Have you seen my daughter?' I asked anyone who would listen.

Nobody answered. No-one paid any attention to me.

That didn't stop me. 'Please, have you seen my daughter?'

Eventually, a woman noticed me. 'God help her,' she said. 'She never stood a chance.'

'Who?' I asked. 'Who never stood a chance?'

But the woman was looking off into the distance beyond the crowd and I realised she had been talking to herself more than to me.

So now I had another question.

Who never stood a chance?

Oh my God, please, anything but that. Please don't let it be Naomi.

I may have been panicking before, but now I was in overdrive. Thoughts of Naomi and what might have happened to her rushed through my head and a nightmare was starting to form.

Was she the reason for the pandemonium?

Had something happened to Naomi? I almost didn't want to know because part of me knew the truth might be more than I could bear.

But bear it or not, I had to know. I had to know what everyone was looking at and what had made the colour drain from the faces of people nearby. I had to know what had made a woman scream in the street in the middle of the day.

I had to know, but I was terrified.

I forced myself to take some more deep breaths. I pushed my chest out as I took them in and puffed my cheeks as they came out. I didn't do it consciously; it was like my body was working on autopilot and it did what it needed to keep me functioning.

I knew that the answer, whatever it was, was at the front of the crowd, and for the first time since the light thing happened, I was focused. I knew I had to get to the front of that crowd and I wasn't worried about who I upset to do it.

I expected that I would have heard at least the odd grumble as I barged my way through, but no-one said a thing. In fact, I met no resistance at all. It felt like everyone was moving out of the way so I could get through.

'Naomi,' I shouted again and I heard a sob in my voice, 'Naomi, I'm coming.'

And there she was.

CHAPTER TWO

'Naomi!'

I reached out my hand but my legs gave way beneath me and I fell to my knees beside her. I wasn't conscious of pain as I hit the concrete but then I wasn't really conscious of anything other than my daughter.

Naomi was still in the car, which was the last place I remembered being. She was still strapped into the back seat dressed in her red and white school uniform, just like she had been. She was facing me but her head was lolling to the side and her eyes were closed.

'Oh my God,' I whispered with a sob.

My eyes were drawn to the front of the car and I couldn't help noticing that it wasn't the shape it used to be. Our car must have been involved in an accident.

We had been involved in a car accident.

'She never stood a chance.' The woman's words echoed in my head.

No! Naomi couldn't be dead. Oh please God, no.

The crowd may have surrounded the car but they kept their distance. The nearest person to me was about six feet away. 'Help me,' I said. 'Please, help me get my daughter out of the car.'

But he didn't even look at me.

'What's wrong with you?' I shouted. 'Can't you see I need help?' I looked around from one person to the next but not one of them moved. 'Why won't you help me?' I screamed.

Sod them, sod the lot of them. I'd get her out myself.

I reached for the handle and pulled, but I couldn't move it. I couldn't even get a good grip on it.

'Phone an ambulance!' I yelled at the crowd as I ran towards the front of the car.

And that's when I saw … it.

There, on what was left of the bonnet of my car was … a man. At least, it looked like a man. It had a body with arms and legs, they were sitting at very unnatural angles, and the head … the head didn't look like a head. It was a mass of pulp and it was all over what was left of my windscreen.

My stomach turned over and as I heaved I was grateful that my lunch stayed where it was. I held my hand over my gaping mouth and took in a huge gulp of air and held it there. Only a cough forced me to release it.

'What's that?' I asked. OK, I know it was a silly question but at least somebody answered this time.

'It's me.'

I looked over the body to the other side of the car and saw the man who had spoken. I looked from him to what was lying on my car. They were wearing the same blue jeans and the same checked shirt but how could they be the same person? What did he mean? It couldn't be him. The man speaking still had his face in place, for a start.

'What do you mean?' I asked.

'It's me,' he said again, without taking his eyes off the front of my car. 'I'm dead.'

'What do you mean you're dead? You can't be dead. I'm talking to y …'

I moved my mouth and tried to form the words but my lips felt like they had been glued together. It dawned on me that he was the only one that had paid me any

8

attention. He said he was dead. Why would the only person to notice me be the dead man?

I felt like someone had poured a bucket of cold water over me and I felt myself starting to shake. I could feel my lips trembling as I tried to make them ask the question I didn't want answered.

He said that the person with no face was him and why would he say that if it wasn't true? But he also said he was dead and while I had no reason to doubt that the person with no face was dead, why could I see his ghost? And why was that ghost the only person talking to me?

Living people ignored me, a man almost ran through me, and now a dead guy was talking to me. I knew it could only mean one thing.

I stared at him, not daring to look to where I knew I had to.

Slowly, I forced my head to turn.

My stomach did another somersault, more than one, as I saw myself sitting in the driver's seat. I felt like there was a washing machine doing a fast spin in the pit of my stomach and at the same time it was like I had been kicked. I doubled up. My head was reeling and I started to retch though nothing was there. I'd only glanced at myself briefly but it had been enough.

He wasn't the only one that was dead.

The reason that the only person talking to me was a dead guy was that I was dead too.

'No,' I whispered, shaking my head hardly at all at first and then violently. 'No,' I repeated, louder this time. 'No,' I shouted, 'I'm not dead.'

Slowly, I forced myself to stand and looked at the man in the checked shirt. He didn't look at me. He couldn't take his eyes off his body.

I forced myself to look at my bo … At where I'd been sitting in the car.

There was another car, a red one, almost impaling me on the steering wheel. That must have been this man's car. I slowly moved around my car and the man, careful not to look at what was on the bonnet. I'd seen enough of that, thank you. The driver's window was broken and I could see myself clearly. From the way my cheek was resting on my shoulder it looked like my neck was broken and there was blood trickling out of my mouth and my ear.

I realised then that it wasn't Naomi who had never stood a chance.

CHAPTER THREE

'No.' I covered my eyes and whispered into the palms of my hands. I wasn't dead. How could I be dead when I could feel my heart beating in the base of my throat? How could I be dead when I could feel my feet on the floor? How could I be dead when I could feel the tears running down my cheeks? No, this was just a nightmare. I was going to wake up any minute.

Slowly, I spread my fingers. Nothing had changed.

Oh my God, I was dead.

But what about Naomi?

Well, she was alive, she had to be. She must be alive because she wasn't standing beside me; she was still in the car. If she was dead she would be with me. Wouldn't she?

I was basing that theory on nothing but hope but … Oh please God, let it be true.

I pulled myself away from my lifeless body and ran around the back of the car, hoping with everything that Naomi was still there and that my theory held water. She hadn't moved at all. Was she really alive? I didn't bother trying to open the door again. I crouched beside her with my face close to hers and held my hand near the pane of glass that separated us and started to whimper.

'Please don't let her die,' I prayed.

Eventually I heard the sound of a siren.

'At last.' I stood up and turned towards the sound. 'Hang on, sweetheart,' I said over my shoulder.

The siren stopped as the crowd separated and the ambulance pulled up a few feet away. Two paramedics hopped out almost before it had stopped.

'She's here,' I told them.

'I'll get the little girl,' one of them said. 'You see what we've got over there.'

I stood back as the first one rushed towards Naomi. He pulled on the handle of the door and it opened easily.

'What you got, Steve?' he asked.

I leaned in closer to hear Steve's answer and it came as no real surprise .

'Both dead.'

'Are you sure?' I croaked. 'Are you sure there's nothing you can do?'

He didn't answer – he just left the man and me where we lay and climbed into the back of the car to help his partner work on Naomi. I got the answer I needed. There was nothing he could do for me or the man.

My heart was in my mouth when Steve put his fingertips to Naomi's neck, as his partner appeared to check for broken bones.

'Strong and steady,' he said, and I let out the breath I'd been holding.

At the sound of another siren, I turned and saw it was the police. Their car stopped close to the ambulance and a female officer got out and walked purposefully towards us. She stopped a few feet away and stood with her hands on her hips, looking at the scene.

'Bloody hell,' she said.

Her male colleague appeared by her shoulder and asked, 'What's the situation?'

My voice cracked as I told him, 'I'm dead.' I laced my

fingers through my hair and added with a sob, 'And my little girl's still in the car.' I could feel tears on my cheek, big and hot and just ridiculous because they had never felt that way when I was alive. They were different now. Everything was different now.

The female officer gave him the official version which involved words like 'RTA', 'dead at scene', and 'injured child' but it amounted to the same thing.

How injured was she? Relieved as I was that Naomi was alive and that her heart beat was strong and steady, I needed to know what was wrong with her.

The police officers moved closer to the paramedics.

'How's she doing?' the policewoman asked, nodding towards the car.

'Looks like she'll be OK,' the one not called Steve said. 'Her pulse is good and there don't appear to be any broken bones.'

'Yes!' I squealed, clapping my hands together. 'Why is she unconscious?' I asked, but of course he didn't answer me. He did, however, answer the policewoman when she asked the same question.

'Concussion.'

My poor baby.

I leaned closer to the car and was whispering her name when I noticed Naomi's eyelids flicker. Then she blinked and when she opened her eyes she was looking straight at me.

I clasped one hand over my mouth to stop my heart popping out and held the other out to my daughter.

Steve the paramedic was now out of the car and standing near me. 'She's awake, Dave,' he told his colleague.

Steve and Dave, good solid names. I don't know why that comforted me but it did and God knows I was grasping at straws.

13

Dave touched Naomi's hand and used a gentle voice when he asked, 'Can you tell me your name?'

Naomi didn't answer so he asked again, giving her hand a little shake this time.

She didn't try to speak. She gave no sign that she had even heard him. She was still looking at me and for a second I wondered if she had gone to sleep with her eyes open. I know that might sound stupid but I know nothing about medicine so it might be possible. What am I saying? Right then, I knew nothing about anything other than that I was dead and my daughter had concussion.

'Naomi,' I said. 'Her name is Naomi.' My poor child looked so confused. 'Don't worry,' I told her, 'you're going to be alright. There's been an accident but you're going to be alright.'

Just then, the paramedics moved and it was clear they were preparing to get Naomi out of the car. Instinctively, I stepped back to give them room to manoeuvre. As I did so Naomi's eyes followed me. Now I needed both hands pressed against my mouth to keep my heart in.

Could she see me? No, that wasn't possible. I mean, I know you hear about living people seeing ghosts all the time but I'd always thought they were making it up. No-one else had seen me. No, it wasn't possible. It was a coincidence.

Or was it? I mean, I was still here. I was still wearing the same clothes I had been that morning. My feet were still on the ground. I was still walking around.

I was still here and maybe Naomi had sensed that.

Seconds later, Naomi was carefully lifted out of the car and placed onto one of those trolley things that hospitals use. She was just as carefully lifted into the ambulance and Dave climbed in with her. Steve closed the doors, climbed into the cab, and drove away. The siren whooped a couple of times to clear the crowd.

I hadn't noticed the second ambulance turn up. They hadn't arrived to the tune of sirens but they hadn't needed to, had they?

They were here for me and what was left of the bloke lying across my bonnet.

I looked across and saw that the ghost of the remains was still standing where I'd first seen him. He was still looking at himself.

I moved closer and eventually he lifted his head and looked at me. He tried to say something but couldn't. He couldn't look me in the eye either. He watched as they loaded his body into the ambulance and then he turned and walked away.

Within a couple of minutes, my body was in the back of the ambulance too. It had happened without me realising. I didn't feel a thing.

The second ambulance drove away in silence.

The police officers had turned their attention to the crowd of people that were standing close by. They'd started to ask if anyone had seen what had happened. One woman proved particularly helpful.

'I'd just come out of the bakers,' she said. 'I was going to get my bus. I was just standing there,' she pointed to pavement close to the cars, 'waiting to cross the road when that red car came racing down the road towards me at a million miles an hour. It's a good job I hadn't stepped out,' she said, 'or it would've been me.'

For a second I wished it had been, and then reprimanded myself for wishing that on anyone.

'The silver car had just come around the corner,' she said, pointing at the main road, 'when the red car came out of the junction and hit it.' Suddenly she started to cry. 'The poor girl didn't have a chance to get out of the way,' she said. 'She wouldn't have seen him coming. He just came out of nowhere.' She rubbed her eyes with a crumpled tissue she'd pulled from her pocket. 'She wouldn't have known what hit her.'

I hadn't.

Another witness, a man, coloured in a few of the details of what happened prior to the accident. He said he worked at a pub called The Golden Lion, about a mile away from where the accident had happened. This man, I think he said his name was James but it might have been Jake because he was very softly spoken, said that the man who had been driving the red car had been in The Golden Lion all day.

'He came in just after we opened,' James said.

'What time did he leave?' the policeman asked.

'About an hour ago.'

'And was he drinking all that time?'

'Yeah,' James confirmed. 'He had three or four pints and then started on the whisky. He'd had a proper skinful. In the end we refused to serve him.'

'But you didn't think to take his car keys off him?'

James could only shrug his shoulders.

'Are you sure this is the same man that was in the pub?' the policewoman chirped in.

'Positive,' James told her. 'I don't know his name but he works just round the corner from us. He comes in a lot. I know his car,' he said, 'and they were the clothes that he was wearing.'

So that's how it happened.

I had been minding my own business driving home from Mum's with Naomi when suddenly a drunk driver had come out of nowhere, hadn't stopped at a junction, and had hit me; quite literally, right where I was sitting in the driver's seat.

The woman had been right; I never had a chance.

More police arrived and started doing whatever it was that needed to be done after an accident so the two that

16

had been gathering information left them to it. I followed them as they walked back to their car, mainly because I didn't know what else to do. The male officer was shaking his head. 'Five seconds either way and it would have been different,' he said as he climbed into the driver's seat.

The policewoman stood with the door open and looked back to the scene of the accident. She nodded slowly and got into the car. A few seconds later they drove away too.

The crowd had all but dispersed. People had wandered away and only a handful remained.

I lifted my hands to my head and threaded my fingers into my hair. I closed my eyes and hoped that when I opened them I would find it had all been a bad dream.

To my eternal disappointment, things were just as I knew they would be. My car was still missing most of the driver's side, there was still blood and glass on the floor, and I was still dead.

There was no point closing my eyes again; it wouldn't change anything. Sometimes you had to face things head on.

I walked over to where a young policeman was tying blue and white tape between two lampposts. He passed inches away from me as he pulled the tape to a third post and then a fourth to make an enclosure around the cars.

I wasn't the only one watching him as he snapped the tape. There was a man standing by the fourth post as the policeman walked away to join a colleague who was directing traffic down a side street. The stranger looked at the car.

Who was he? I couldn't take my eyes off him. His clothes were odd and he seemed out of place. Well, not odd as such, but dated. He was clearly a fan of the retro look and he suited it.

I looked at my car for a minute. I loved that car. I

called her Daisy and now she was dead too. This wasn't like the dent I'd put in the boot when I reversed into the lamppost last year. There would be no repairing her this time. She was as dead as I was.

I turned and walked away. There was nothing here for me now.

I wasn't walking anywhere in particular; I was just walking, getting away from the scene of the crime. I looked in the odd shop window but my eyes were wandering and nothing caught my attention. That was until I looked into the window of the butcher's shop on Saddler Street.

It wasn't the special offer on sirloin steak that caught my attention, though I have to say it was very good. No, it was the reflection of the person standing behind me that made me stop and stare.

It was the man that had been by the lamppost watching the aftermath of the accident, the one in the retro clothes. He was a couple of feet behind me and he was watching me watching him.

He couldn't be looking at me, could he? I was dead and nobody could see me. Or at least no-one living, apart from Naomi, and I didn't dare hope her reaction had been anything other than a coincidence. So what was he looking at?

I turned around quickly. 'Can I help you?' I asked, more rudely than I meant to but what did that matter? He wouldn't be able to hear me.

'No,' he said. 'I think that's my job.'

18

CHAPTER FOUR

He'd answered me. He'd heard me

'You can see me,' I said.

'Yes.'

'W …' I'm not sure what I tried to say because I didn't get any further than that.

His hands had been in the pockets of his jeans but he took them out and held his right one out to me. My own hands, which had been on my hips, were now hanging limply by my side but I felt him take hold of my right one and shake it.

I pulled away. I looked at the hand he had shaken, and then at him, before looking back at my hand. I had felt him.

'I can feel you,' I said weakly.

He didn't answer straight away, but when I looked at him he was looking at me.

'I can feel you,' I repeated.

'I know.' We looked at each other.

'Are you dead too?'

'Yes.'

'Who are you?' I asked.

'George,' he said. 'Sorry I was a bit late but I'm here to help you.'

'Help me? I'm beyond help. How could you possibly

help me?'

He shrugged his shoulders. 'Don't know really, keep you company for a bit, answer a few questions, that sort of thing.'

'Answer a few questions?' Now I was having a conversation with someone I could feel anger building inside me and I could hear it coming out in my voice. 'OK, I've got a question for you. Why am I dead?'

His voice was calm, 'You're dead because some bloke had a bad day, got drunk, and tried driving home.'

'And why is that my fault?'

'It's not.'

'So why am I dead?'

'Unlucky, I guess.'

A thought occurred to me and I looked him straight in the eye. 'It's your fault, isn't it?' I said.

'No.'

'You apologised, you said you were sorry for being late. You were supposed to stop this from happening.'

'No.'

'So why apologise?'

'Because my mother brought me up to be polite,' he said with more than a hint of sarcasm. We stared at each other for a while. He sighed heavily and ran his hand over his hair. 'I was supposed to get here just as it was happening, but I got held up and by the time I arrived you were running about like a lunatic and I couldn't keep up with you. And then you were with your little girl and I didn't want to get in the way ... so I waited. I mean, by that time you'd worked out what was happening so it wasn't like you needed me to tell you.'

'Is that your job, telling people that they're dead?'

'Well, there's a bit more to it, but that's the first thing I'm supposed to do.'

'Nice job.'

'I've had better, but there's not a lot of choice on the Other Side so beggars can't be choosers.'

'I thought you sat on clouds and played harps all day?'

'That's just the angels.'

Thinking about it now, I can't believe we were having that conversation. I mean, it felt so natural. I was discussing job opportunities in the afterlife with a dead man who looked like he was on his way to a 1950s-themed party and it felt like the most natural thing in the world.

CHAPTER FIVE

He'd said it was his job to answer any questions I had.

'Where's my daughter?'

'Naomi is on her way to hospital.'

'You know my daughter's name.' It was a statement rather than a question but I was surprised by his answer.

'I know everything about you, Ellen.' He knew my name, which surprised me even more.

'Which hospital have they taken her to?'

He shrugged again. 'I don't know what it's called,' he said. 'I'm not from round here.'

'Then how are we going to find her?' I could feel a sob coming on.

He reached out and took hold of my elbow. 'Don't worry; we don't need to know what the hospital's called.'

In the blink of an eye we were in a hospital, though I didn't know which one it was either, not that it mattered as long as it I was the same one that Naomi had been taken to. Surely it had to be. What would be the point in appearing in a hospital that Naomi wasn't in? Not that it'd be the most pointless thing that had happened that afternoon – that prize went to me being dead.

I sniffed to hold back the tears and all I could smell was hospital.

George was at my side, still holding onto my elbow.

'Are you sure this is the right one?' I sniffed.

'Yes.'

'Where is she?'

I heard a noise and when I turned around I saw Dave the paramedic pushing a trolley. I could see Naomi was on it. I waited for them to come along side of us and then I pulled loose from George's grip and walked with them. There was no urgency to Dave's movements, which I thought must be a good sign and he spoke to his patient gently.

'Don't worry, sweetheart,' he told her. 'I've passed my driving test so you're perfectly safe.'

Naomi tilted her head to look at him before resting her head flat again and closing her eyes. She gave no indication that she knew I was there and my heart sank.

'Don't go to sleep,' paramedic Dave urged. 'The doctor's going to want to talk to you.'

'Where are you taking her?' I asked, but he didn't answer. Why would he?

I watched as Naomi was pushed through another set of doors and into an examination room.

A doctor and two nurses were already there.

Naomi lay on the bed in silence as the doctor moved her head first this way then the other. She followed his orders to look to her right then her left without making a sound.

The doctor mumbled something to her but from where I stood I couldn't tell what. He was a young man with floppy blond hair and he spoke in a voice that was slow and gentle and I noticed that Naomi looked at him with an expressionless face. That was unusual. Her face was usually so alive. But then I remembered that this was not a usual day.

Another nurse came into the room and she and the doctor discussed the charts he had been filling in. Their heads were together, only occasionally looking to their patient.

It was as I was standing away from her thanking God that she was OK that Naomi turned her head to me. She was looking right at me and when she smiled I knew for certain that she had seen me. My hand went to my mouth again to stifle the cry that I knew was about to pop out of it.

My baby could see me. I didn't know how it could be possible and it blew every theory I had ever had about life after death out of the water but I knew it was true.

The doctor placed the clipboard at Naomi's feet and gave instructions to one of the nurses who took the brake off the trolley and started to push it. Naomi didn't take her eyes from me until the doors to the examination room had closed behind her.

Naomi had seen me. I knew she had, I hadn't imagined it. I stood with my hands clasped together on the top of my head and cried.

George found me like that.

'Thought I'd better come and find you,' he said. 'You'd been here a while.'

Had I? Maybe. Who knew?

'You OK?' he asked.

I grabbed his arm excitedly. 'She can see me,' I said, tightening my grip as I spoke. 'Naomi can see me.' He didn't say anything and I realised what he must be thinking. I let go of his arm and stood up straight. 'It's true,' I said with more than a hint of a sulk in my voice. 'I'm telling you she can see me.'

'Then I'm happy for you.'

What did that mean?

I didn't get chance to ask because he had taken hold of my elbow again. 'Come on,' he said. 'Your husband's downstairs.'

The next thing I knew, we were in the corner of the most sterile room I had ever been in. The walls were painted white and devoid of any decoration. There was a window on one wall with a white blind across it.

'Where are we?' I looked around the room, moving around George as I did so.

'Morgue,' he said matter of factly.

'What?' I stopped moving and looked at him. 'What do you mean morgue?'

He gave a little shrug. 'I mean it's the morgue.'

'But ...' I was confused. 'Where are the bodies? There are those slabs and drawer things in a morgue.'

'That's down the corridor, this is ...'

Just then, the door opened and a man in a white coat entered, accompanied by the policeman who had been at the scene of the accident. There was no sign of his partner. Marc followed them into the room and I started to tremble at the sight of my husband.

Was it even my husband?

My husband was strong and tanned and always had a smile on his face. This man was pale and stumbled into the room. He looked around, taking in his surroundings.

'I don't understand, 'I thought Ellen would be in here.'

I wanted to shout to Marc that I *was* here, but I wasn't the wife he was looking for.

The man in the white coat moved to the wall with the window on it. 'Your wife is here,' he said.

What? Could he see me? I looked at George and he was shaking his head. He pointed towards the window.

The three men were standing in front of it. Marc's head was down and I could see that he was shaking. I wanted to hold him but what would be the point? I wouldn't be able to support him. All I could do was watch.

The man in the white coat mumbled something to Marc and he nodded his head very slightly. The man knocked on the window with the knuckles of his right hand and I saw the blinds move aside. Marc lifted his head slowly and he started to shake even more. He leaned forward and rested his forehead against the glass

Curiosity got the better of me and I moved closer. I knew what I was going to see and while I didn't really want to see 'it', well, me, I was pulled towards the window. I felt George try to grab me.

I stood next to the man in the white coat and looked through the space between him and Marc. On the other side of the window was one of those slabs, and I was on it. A white sheet covered my body but my face was there for all to see. There was a woman in a white coat standing beside me.

'She looks like she's asleep.' Marc's voice was slow and it trembled. I turned towards him and our faces were less than a foot apart.

'Yes, I do,' I agreed before quickly retreating back into the corner.

'Mr Reed.' It was the policeman but Marc seemed not to hear him. 'Mr Reed,' he said again, this time a bit louder. 'I'm sorry, Mr Reed, but I have to ask. Mr Reed, is that your wife?'

Marc's eyes concentrated on my image. 'She's ...' He didn't say what I was. Finally, he nodded. 'Yes,' he said, his voice choked. 'That's Ellen.'

'Thank you, sir.'

I noticed that the policeman had written something in his notebook. The man in the white coat shifted uncomfortably. 'Would you like to stay here for a while?' he asked.

'What?' Marc's eyes were wide and vacant.

'If you like,' Mr White Coat said cautiously, 'I could

try and arrange for you to spend some time with the body.'

Marc thought about it for a second. 'No,' he said with conviction. 'I would like to see my daughter.' Marc turned slowly and followed the policeman to the door. The policeman opened the door and Marc staggered towards it.

'There's one more thing I need to speak to you about, Mr Reed.' The man in the white coat pulled something from the pocket. 'We found this in your wife's bag.' He held out the organ donor card I had filled out and signed on my eighteenth birthday, much to my mother's annoyance.

It had seemed like a good idea at the time and, while I'm sure it still was, they were my organs and I didn't like the idea of other people having them. There was plenty of life left in my organs. I had a sensible diet and exercised regularly with the intention of keeping them healthy for a long time. It wasn't fair that I wasn't going to get the benefit of it and someone else was going to reap the rewards of all my hard work. It wasn't fair that I didn't need them anymore.

'It's what she wanted,' Marc croaked, and he was right.

'Thank you,' he said, returning the card to his pocket.

The door closed and they left the silence behind them. I stared at the door.

And I started to cry again. God, I cried more on that day than I did on any I'd been alive. Big, hot tears kept falling down my cheeks. I turned around to where I knew George was and let him put his arms around me while I cried into his chest.

After that particular bout of crying had stopped I pulled myself together, looked around, and wondered how this could be happening to me. I shouldn't be here in this strange, sterile place. I should be at home with my husband and my daughter. I should be doing normal family things like bathing Naomi and listening to Marc read her a bedtime story. I should be clearing up after tea.

I had no idea what time it was but I was pretty sure it was way past tea time and I wondered what would happen to the steak and kidney pie I had made that morning. I hoped someone would realise that it was in the fridge before it went off. It would be a shame to waste it because, and I know I'm blowing my own trumpet here, I do make a wicked pie.

Not any more you don't, I reminded myself, your pie making days are over.

I was suddenly light-headed.

I leaned on George more heavily.

Oh my God, Marc looked terrible, a shadow of the man I had kissed goodbye that morning. I wondered how he was going to cope without me because I knew, without needing to think about it, that I wouldn't know where to start if the shoe was on the other foot.

But the shoe wasn't on the other foot. I was the one that was dead. He was the one that was going to have to cope. I didn't know who I felt most sorry for.

I stared at the window, the one that Marc had seen me through and started to cry … again.

This 'life' sucked. I liked my other one.

I took a deep breath and asked George the one question that I really did need an answer to. 'Why me?'

'We all have to die.'

'Yeah, but why now? Why today? Why like this?'

He held me at a distance and looked into my face. 'It was your time, Ellen,' he said gently. 'We all have a time to be born and a time to die.' His eyes were the most glorious shade of blue and I hung onto them. 'There was nothing you could have done about it. It was always going

to happen. It wouldn't have mattered if you'd gone
straight home instead of deciding to visit your mum after
picking Naomi up. Not that you could have done that,
because visiting your mum was part of the plan.'

I wondered how Mum had taken the news.

CHAPTER SIX

I almost fell over when I saw my parents and I was glad George was there to hold me up.

They were clinging to each other and I felt completely helpless. I was the reason they looked the way they did.

My dad had adopted his default stiff upper lip but as I, with George's help, moved closer to them I could see the hurt and pain in his eyes. Mum's upper lip was anything but stiff and she leaned into my dad's chest and she was shaking as she cried.

'Don't cry, Mum, I'm OK,' I said, reaching out a hand but pulling it back before I touched her.

'Oh, Brian,' she sobbed. 'My baby.'

'I know Peg,' he whispered as he kissed the top of her head.

'Why, Brian? Why?'

There was no answer.

The despair they felt was there for all to see as they looked at each other. I was their only child and now I was lost to them.

Dad pulled Mum to him and she rested her head on his chest. She was staring straight at me but I could tell she didn't see me.

Like lots of daughters, there had been times when I had been unable to bring myself to talk to my mother. We'd had arguments and not spoken for a few days but I would have given anything to be able to talk to her at that moment. A few seconds would have been enough. I would have done anything to be able to speak to her one last time

'What are we going to do?' she wailed. 'What are we going to do?'

Dad forced her away again so he could look into her eyes. 'We're going to go on,' he said. 'We're going to remember our beautiful daughter every day of our lives and we're going to be grateful that we knew her.'

'But how can I?' she asked weakly

'I don't know,' Dad whispered, pulling her to him again. 'But you have to find a way.' He rested his cheek against the top of her head. 'We have to find a way.'

I saw Marc appear through the doors at the end of the corridor. He almost staggered towards them. Mum was the first to see him and she pushed herself away from Dad's chest and wiped her hands over her cheeks.

When Dad saw him he held out his hand to Marc. It looked like two old friends meeting for lunch, but instead of shaking his hand, Dad pulled Marc to him and held him like a child.

'Oh God, Marc.' Dad's voice was muffled as he tightened his grip around my husband.

Mum watched them from a distance but didn't move to join them.

After a few seconds the men separated and looked a little embarrassed by their intimacy. Marc ruffled his hair and Dad straightened his tie.

'Margaret.' I noticed how hoarse Marc's voice sounded.

'Marc.' Mum looked at him and saw the truth was written all over his pale face. 'It's true, then?' Mum said.

Marc lowered his head and stared at the floor. Slowly he lifted it up and nodded. 'Yeah,' was all he could manage.

'You've seen her? It's really her?'

'Yes,' he said. 'She looked like she was asleep.'

'She always looked beautiful when she was asleep,' Mum said with a distance in her voice, like she was remembering something from a long time ago.

'She looked beautiful to me all the time,' Marc said.

'Have you visited Naomi yet?' Dad asked.

'No,' Marc said as he rubbed the heel of his hand against his eyes. 'I went up earlier but the nurses were fussing over getting her ready for bed. I spoke to a doctor and said I'd go back after I'd seen Ellen.'

'How did she look?' Dad asked.

Marc threw my dad a look and there was an awkward silence.

'Oh, stop being so bloody stupid, Marc,' I chastised. 'He was talking about Naomi, not me, and you know it.'

Dad looked embarrassed when he realised the way his question had sounded. 'How's Naomi?'

I moved closer so I could hear Marc's answer.

He didn't answer straight away; he seemed lost in his own world. A movement from my dad brought him out of it and Marc took a deep breath as he struggled to gain control of himself. I'd never seen Marc like this before. He coughed to clear his throat. 'Naomi's fine, thank God. She's got concussion so they're going to want to keep her in for a few days, but considering what she's been through she's good.'

'Thank God,' my dad repeated.

'Why?'

We were all surprised at my mother's question.

'Why what?' Marc asked.

'Why are we thanking God?' she said, shrugging off my dad's attempt to put his arm around her.

'That my daughter is safe.'

'And mine is dead,' Mum said flatly.

Marc looked at her with a dark shadow over his eyes. He spoke slowly and deliberately. 'Your daughter was my wife, Margaret. My wife,' he repeated as I noticed tears forming in his eyes, 'and I wish with all my heart that she wasn't dead but she is.' He paused as he fought back the tears. 'She is and I thank God that *our*,' he emphasised the word, 'daughter has come through this relatively unscathed.'

Marc locked eyes with my mother. She was first to turn away.

'I'm sorry,' she apologised. 'I didn't mean it that way. Of course I thank God that Naomi is alright. It's just that ...' She broke down and shook with every sob. 'Marc, my baby ...'

Dad looked embarrassed. 'Is there anything we can do, Marc?'

'What?' It was as if he had forgotten Dad was there.

'Can we get you anything?'

'No, no thank you. I'm going to go spend some time with Naomi.' He was looking around in a confused manner. 'She might be asleep but I want to be with her.'

'I'd best get Peg home.'

My mother seemed oblivious to the conversation the men were having about her.

Marc went one way and my parents went the other.

I felt emotionally drained, if such a thing is possible in the state I was in, and once they had disappeared I leaned against the wall and let my head rest against it. I could see George out of the corner of my eye and I was glad that I wasn't alone.

After a few minutes I sensed someone approaching. I turned my head and saw a familiar figure, a man, walking towards me. There was a woman dressed in a blue trouser suit behind him and calling out but he was ignoring her.

George was now at my side and the woman spoke directly to him. 'Keep out of this, George,' she said sternly. 'I've told him I think it's a bad idea but he won't listen. This is between them and we'll be here to pick up the pieces when it's finished.' George and the woman stood together a few yards away and I heard her say, 'I need another job.'

I turned my attention back to the familiar figure. It was the man who had killed me.

Hadn't he done enough? What more could he possibly want from me? I had nothing to say to him.

'What do you want?' I asked with a croaky voice. I was still leaning against the wall.

'To speak to you.'

'Why?'

The man was looking at his feet. Then he lifted his head and stared one way then the other. I could see he was distressed but do you know what? I didn't care. He should feel distressed. He couldn't be more distressed than I was, anyway.

'Well?' I prompted

The man mumbled something I couldn't hear.

'Excuse me?'

The man coughed. 'To say I'm sorry.' He was looking into the distance as he spoke but then he turned to me. 'I'm sorry,' he repeated and I could see it was an effort for him to hold my gaze.

'Not as sorry as I am,' I said curtly.

He looked away uncomfortably. I felt the anger rising inside me. After fighting it for a few minutes, the effort was too much.

'What do you want me to say?' I asked. He didn't answer and I pushed myself to a standing position. My voice rose with every word I spoke. 'Did you expect me to say it was all right and not to worry about it?' I moved closer to him and he backed away until he could go no further. 'Did you expect me to say don't worry about it because you did me a favour? Did you expect me to say thank you for killing me?' I screamed the last sentence and I could see tiny beads of spit hit the man in the face. 'You killed me.' I poked his chest. 'You killed me.' I repeated, before having to turn and stifle a sob.

When I thought I was calm again I turned around, but as our eyes locked I could feel the anger return.

'I didn't mean to.' His voice was weak.

'Doesn't matter whether you meant it or not,' I said through gritted teeth. 'I'm still dead.'

'I know.' He looked away. By the time he looked back there were tears running down his face. 'So am I.'

I turned away again and took a couple of steps before turning on my heel and spinning back to him. He flinched.

'Why?' I asked.

'Why what?'

'Why did you do it?'

'It was an accident.'

'What?' I yelled. 'You accidentally poured God knows how much booze down your neck. Then you accidentally got behind the wheel of *your* car and accidentally cut *my* car in half.' I was screaming and waving my arms around. In any other world I would have been ashamed by my behaviour but now it seemed acceptable.

'I didn't mean to.'

'Really?'

'No.' His voice was breaking.

'What did you mean to do?'

'Get home,' he said. 'I wanted to get home and tell Gemma I was sorry.'

His sobs caught me off guard and I watched him struggle.

'I just wanted to tell Gemma I was sorry,' he repeated.

He stared at his feet and took deep breaths. He'd almost regained his composure and looked up. 'Look, if I could change this I would. Honest. If there was anything I could do to put you back with your family, I would. Trust me I would. But I can't, so all I can do is apologise.'

I pondered his words a moment and gestured with my head that he should follow me. Tentatively, he did and we walked a little way up the corridor. We sat on two plastic chairs.

Neither of us spoke for a minute or two.

'What's your name?' I asked eventually.

'Phil,' he said. 'Phil Webber.' For a second I thought he was going to offer his hand for me to shake and I was glad when he didn't.

'I'm Ellen,' I told him.

'I really am sorry, Ellen,' he whispered. 'I can't tell you how sorry I am.'

'You said.'

'It's true.'

'I'm sure it is but it doesn't change anything, does it?'

'No.'

'Who's Gemma?'

'What?'

'Gemma?'

'My wife.'

I nodded. 'What were you sorry for?' It appeared that his killing me made it all right for me to ask.

He sat back and lifted his head to the ceiling. 'Everything.' I watched his Adam's apple bob up and down. He continued to look at the ceiling as he spoke. 'I've been knocking off this woman at work,' he explained, 'Sharon ... Sharon Walsh ... nice girl.' He stopped looking at the ceiling and leaned forward, resting his elbows on his knees and turned to me. 'I went into work today. I'm an electrician ... was an electrician.

Anyway, I went to the office to pick up my work sheet and in with my list of jobs is a message from Sharon saying she needs to talk to me and I'm thinking she's finally got wind of the fact I'm married and she's going to tell me to piss off. So, I go to her office. She's the boss' secretary,' he added by way of explanation, 'and I ask her what she wanted.' He stopped and stared at his hands. They were shaking violently.

'What?' I asked.

He spoke slowly. 'She told me she was pregnant.'

'Oh.' The noise popped out without me realising it. 'Is it yours?'

'She says it is.'

'Do you believe her?' I had lost sight of the absurdity of this conversation.

'Suppose. Why would she lie?'

'What were you going to do?'

'Don't know. That was what I was trying to figure out.'

'At the pub?'

He said nothing. He lowered his head into his hands and pulled his hair. He made a noise deep in his chest as he gave one last yank at the little hair he had left before lifting his head and staring at the wall in front of him. 'She asked me if I was going to marry her ...' He stood up and started to pace. He started to pull on his hair again. 'Marry her? How can I marry her?' Then he was pulling at the skin around his nails. I winced as a long piece came away in his hand. 'I told her why I couldn't marry her. She called me a liar, said I was a coward who wasn't prepared to face his responsibilities. So I showed her Gemma's picture in my wallet. She started crying and screaming and said that could be my sister. I asked her why I would keep a picture of my sister in my wallet.' He moved his hand over his face. 'I told her I would face up to my responsibilities, of course I would, but I couldn't marry her. I could have strung her along,' he looked at me in desperation, 'but I didn't, I came clean. Anyway,' he was looking out of the window again, 'the boss came in and wanted to know what the hell was all the fuss about and why wasn't I rewiring some old biddy's house. Sharon tells him I've knocked her up and won't marry her.' I winced. 'He sent Sharon home in a taxi and told me to bugger off and sort myself out.'

He puffed out his cheeks and let the air out slowly. 'I didn't know what to do. I couldn't go home because Gemma's off this week decorating the back bedroom. I couldn't face her ... As soon as the pubs were open I went in. I was only going to have one, a bit of Dutch courage, you know. That's all I wanted. But I didn't feel any better after one. Things weren't any clearer so I had another ... and another. Eventually I realised I was going to have to go home.' He puffed out his cheeks. 'I wasn't going to take the car but I didn't have any money left for a taxi or even the bus and I live over the other side of town. It would have taken me hours to walk home.' He paused and looked at his hands that were still shaking. 'I remember getting in the car ... then the next thing I know I'm blind and she,' he used his head to point to the woman in the blue suit, 'was telling me to stay calm and everything would be alright.' He sat down again. 'You know,' I was surprised when he took my hands in his, 'I don't mind that I'm dead. I mean, I'd rather I wasn't but I brought it on myself. But you ...' Tears fell silently from his eyes. Eyes, I noticed, that were green.

'Yeah, well, it's done now.' I said.

Suddenly I found myself with my arms around this man who was responsible for my being dead, rocking him gently.

We stood at the door of Naomi's room and watched her. She looked tiny as she lay in the hospital bed and stared out of the window to her left. In her arms she held Jasper, the green teddy bear Marc had bought for her on the day she was born.

I heard the sound of footsteps along the corridor and I trod on George's foot as I stood back to let Marc pass. His eyes got a little of their brightness back when he saw our daughter. Seconds later I had to step back again to let another man pass. This time it was a grey-haired doctor, who looked at charts as he walked.

'Is everything all right?'

'Oh, yes, Mr Reed.' The doctor took a stethoscope from around his neck. 'Everything is fine.' He popped the earpieces into position and the flat end against Naomi's chest. 'My my,' he said. 'I've never heard a healthier heartbeat in my whole life.' Naomi started to smile, but stopped herself. 'Would you like to hear it too?' Naomi said nothing but didn't object as the doctor took the earpieces from his own ears and placed them in hers.

'I'm James Moran.' The doctor held out his hand to my husband.

'Marc Reed.' The handshake was brief but firm.

'You have a fine daughter, Mr Reed.'

Marc nodded.

'And a lucky one.'

'Will she be all right?' Marc whispered.

Dr. Moran looked towards my daughter, who was staring at the ceiling. 'Physically, your daughter is fine. There's barely a scratch on her.'

'And emotionally?' Marc looked at Naomi as he asked the question.

'Only time will tell. In my experience, children are resilient. They have a way of dealing with this sort of thing.'

'Has she asked where her mother is?'

Marc's question took me by surprise and I leaned forward to hear the doctor's answer.

Dr Moran looked grave for a moment.

'What's wrong?'

Dr Moran blew out a deep breath. 'Nothing is wrong as such,' he said. 'In fact, one could say it is a normal response. It's certainly a common one.'

'What is?' I asked the question along with Marc.

'Naomi hasn't spoken since she was brought here,' he said

Both Marc and I were silent.

'I wouldn't worry about it too much,' the doctor said. 'It's the body's way of giving Naomi time to come to terms with what has happened. I would have been more surprised if this hadn't happened. She's been through a lot.'

'How long will it last?'

'As long as it takes.'

Everyone looked at the child on the bed.

'I'm going to need that back,' Dr Moran said, holding out his hand. Naomi unplugged the stethoscope from her ears and held it out to him. 'I've got other patients to see but I'll be back soon, Naomi.'

'Thank you, Dr Moran.' Now it was Marc's turn to offer his hand.

'If you want some advice, Mr Reed,' he said, lowering his voice, 'just act as if this is normal.'

Marc nodded and turned towards the bed, forcing a smile onto his face.

I watched the doctor leave the room and was surprised to see a dark-haired girl of about nine skip after him. I hadn't noticed her but she must have been standing in the corner of the room all the time.

41

She waved her hand and I instinctively waved back. I tried to ask who she was but I couldn't get the words to form. Then she was gone.

Marc moved towards the bed. He sat by Naomi's head and they looked at each other. 'Hello, Munchkin,' he said, trying to force a smile.

Naomi just looked at him. He stroked her hair and brushed his thumb along her cheek.

'I am so pleased to see you.' He emphasised each word.

There was sadness and relief in the way he looked at her.

'Who was that little girl with the doctor?' I whispered.

'Mary,' George whispered back. 'She died twenty years ago when she was eight years old.'

42

CHAPTER SEVEN

George stayed at a distance as I walked beside Marc through the hospital car park. I thought that we must look like a couple of ordinary people who had visited a sick relative, until I remembered that anybody watching would only have seen one person. Only one of us was 'real' and that thought felt like a knife being pushed deep into my chest, a long, cold knife that pierced my soul. It was like realising I was dead all over again.

I walked with Marc anyway.

His hands were stuffed deep into his trouser pockets and he kept his head down. Normally, Marc had to slow his pace so I could keep up with him. This time it was the other way round.

'I'm sorry, Marc,' I told him, but I didn't know why.

Marc took me by surprise when he stopped walking.

'What's wrong?' I asked automatically. But then it occurred to me that he might be responding to my question. Had he heard me? Oh God, had my husband just heard his recently dead wife tell him she was sorry? No, surely that was too much to hope for.

But he had reacted to something.

He let his head fall back as far as it could so his face was to the sky. I couldn't see his eyes but suspected they were closed. I could see his chest heaving up and down under the white cotton of his shirt and he puffed his

43

cheeks out with every breath. He was struggling to control an emotion he didn't understand. Eventually he let out an extra-long breath and lowered his head.

'Come on, Marc,' I urged him.

He slowly shook his head before continuing his slow walk to the end of the deserted car park. The only other person about was a man sitting on a bench smoking a cigarette. He looked in our direction and moved his head in a brief acknowledgement.

I felt like my heart was breaking.

I suspected that the hospital's visiting hours had been over a long time because Marc's car was the only one left and, as we approached it, instinct sent me to the passenger side where Marc would normally have opened the door for me. That didn't happen this time. Why would it? I wasn't there. And the knife was pushed a bit deeper.

Marc started the car and I thought our moment had passed but then George was at my side and once again he put his hand on my elbow.

We were sitting in the back of Marc's car as he drove away from the hospital and I looked into his eyes through the rear-view mirror. Periodically he would look in the mirror right back at me but I knew all he saw was the traffic behind.

I wished that he could see me. I wished that he would notice me and smile at me the way he used to, but that was then and this was now and the two moments were a world apart.

I rested my head on the back of the seat, letting it drop to one side. It was raining and the window was covered in tiny drops of water that danced as the car moved. The street light shining through the drops created a rainbow effect against the darkness outside and on any other day I would have found it beautiful. Today it just made me sad.

Why was this happening to me? This time yesterday everything was different. This time yesterday I had a normal life. This time yesterday I was alive.

Why wasn't I alive?

It was because some random person I had never met in my life had driven his car into mine at precisely the wrong moment. Like the policeman had said, five seconds and it would have been different. But no, he had hit me at that precise second. Even so, I had a problem accepting it was an accident.

I mean, if he hadn't been in the pub he wouldn't have been drunk and probably wouldn't even have been on the road. He would certainly have had more control of the car. Going back even further, if he hadn't been having an affair with the girl at work, she wouldn't be pregnant and he wouldn't have spent all day in the pub. Or if he'd not got the job he wouldn't have met the girl in the office to start the affair in the first place. If … I stopped the train of thought before I sent myself insane. How far was I going to go back? If Phil had never been born?

If Phil Webber had never been born would that have meant I would still be alive? George had said it had been 'my time' so maybe I would have died anyway. I'd never know.

While I'd been thinking about the futility of my situation, my eyes hadn't really taken in what was passing me by. The night and the lights had just been a blur but suddenly I realised that something was wrong.

For the second time that day I didn't know where I was. I forced myself into an upright position and looked around trying to locate some landmark.

When the ornate Victorian Town Hall passed by I knew where we were.

The car slowed and pulled to a stop.

We were back in Silver Street.

Marc sat in the car and looked at the police markings. They were all that remained of the accident I had died in. Both cars and their residual debris had been removed, leaving white markings on the ground and a bollard leaning at a forty-five degree angle.

He sat for a while with his head resting on the glass. Then he slowly opened the door and got out. He staggered to the spot the police had marked. I watched from the car and sensed George watching too.

Marc stood for a while looking at the ground. His head was low and his shoulders hunched. Then he crouched. He put his hand on the road with his palm flat to the floor. After a minute he lifted his hand and put it to his mouth. I think he kissed it but I couldn't say for sure. He continued to crouch with his head bowed for several minutes. I watched him through the rain-streaked windows as the heavy rain bounced off him without him noticing.

I watched until Marc stood up. He turned slowly and, with his head still hung low, walked back to the car.

His hands were resting at the top of the steering wheel and he lowered his head onto them. He was soaked and as he leaned forward, droplets of water fell from his hair and into his lap. I inched towards him from my position on the back seat but there was nothing I could do to relieve his misery. It made my own misery all the more difficult to bear.

I felt so useless.

His shoulders were shaking and I knew he was crying again.

So was I. I lay my face against the head rest of the passenger seat and wept for what had happened and for what I had been forced to leave behind. I felt George's hand on my shoulder which gave me a little comfort.

Eventually, Marc's tears stopped and he sat up, using the palms of his hands to dry his face. He sniffed hard and pinched the end of his nose before lacing his fingers through his hair.

He sat for a while staring ahead and after a final look, he started the engine and pulled away.

He drove the long way home.

● ◆ ●

The house was in darkness as Marc pulled the car into the driveway.

When was the last time he had come home to an empty house? Naomi and I had always met him at the door when he came home from work. Not tonight, nor any other night.

He struggled to get the key in the lock but eventually he managed and opened the door. He walked in and I snuck in before he closed the door behind him.

George was already there.

So there I was – standing in the hallway I had left only a few hours earlier. Marc hadn't switched on the light but I could make out his shape against the glass of the window he was standing beside.

He looked lost.

He fumbled on the wall to his left and eventually managed to switch on the light.

I said 'Oh God,' and lifted my hands to my mouth, biting my thumbs as I saw, close up and fully illuminated, the desperation etched over his face.

I hopped onto the bottom step as he passed me on his way to the living room. He didn't bother with the light this time and heard him fall into the chair nearest the door.

I followed him into the room and stood behind the chair he was sitting in. I know it's a cliché, but I finally understood the meaning of the saying 'so close yet so far away'.

He sat in the darkness and I stood behind him feeling numb.

It was only after he had sat for a long time that he finally leaned over and switched on a lamp. He sat for a few more minutes before he picked up the phone.

Marc has no siblings and not many close friends but Liam was one of the few he did have. They had been friends since they were at school together and Liam had been best man at our wedding.

I watched Marc punch Liam's number into the keypad. His eyes moved around the room as he waited for his call to be answered.

'Liam.' Marc sat forward in the armchair and with his elbow on his knee and rested his head in the heel of his hand. 'It's Ellen …' His mouth was opening and closing but no words came out. 'She's dead,' he said.

I heard the knock on the door and without thinking went to answer it. I'd walked a few steps before I gave myself a metaphorical slap across the face for being so stupid.

'Liam's here,' I said.

Maybe Marc hadn't heard the knock or maybe he'd chosen to ignore it, but either way he didn't move from his chair. I looked to George for help. He touched the handle and the door opened. Liam had a surprised look on his face and as he came in he looked behind the door as if to question how it had opened. He closed it gently but firmly behind him.

He moved towards the only room with a light on.

Marc?' he said. 'It's me, are you in …?'

Liam didn't even try to hide the shock on his face as he looked at Marc, who was sitting in the chair and staring straight ahead.

'Jesus, Marc. What's happened?'

Marc didn't move a muscle, not even to blink as far as I could see.

At first Liam looked like he was going to say something, but didn't. Instead, he moved nervously to the end of the sofa and sat down.

Liam leaned forward, resting his elbows on his knees. He ran his fingers through his hair and joined his hands and let them fall and hang in the space between his knees. He ran his tongue over his lips. All the while he looked at his friend who just stared into the space ahead.

Without thinking, I moved away to give them privacy and I joined George in the corner of the room. It seemed like he'd already had my idea. I held my breath as we watched the men.

There was a long period of silence where the only sound was the clock ticking. Or was that my heart beating?

Liam looked uncomfortable. I'd heard the conversation he'd had with Marc and knew it had ended as soon as Marc had said 'She's dead.' Either Liam had hung up and raced here at that point or Marc had shut down and not said any more. I wasn't sure which. Either way, Liam was in the dark about the exact nature of the problem. He started to probe that darkness a bit.

'I don't understand,' he said cautiously. 'What did you mean ...?'

Liam didn't finish because Marc shifted his head. He was facing Liam now, allowing Liam to see properly for the first time the full horror of what he was going through.

'She's dead, Liam.' He swallowed hard and took a deep breath. I could see his lip trembling as he spoke. 'Ellen's dead.'

Liam's head moved to the side and he shook it ever so

49

slightly. His mouth tried to form a word but then he changed his mind and looked for another. Eventually he settled on, 'What happened?'

Marc didn't reply immediately and Liam didn't press him. He watched Marc's suffering from a few feet away although by the look on Liam's face I'd say the distance felt much greater. Liam obviously didn't know what to do.

They sat in silence, Liam leaning forward and Marc sitting back. They sat like that for a long time before Marc spoke.

'She'd picked Naomi up from school.' Marc's voice, though barely above a whisper echoed through the silence. He looked at Liam before turning away. When he turned back, his eyes were angry. 'He was drunk, Liam.' Marc struggled with the words. 'The police said the bastard was drunk.'

Liam's eyes widened. His mouth moved into the position to make a 'W' sound but never got any further.

Marc took a deep breath and let it out slowly. 'She never stood a chance,' he said. His eyes were drawn to the photograph that sat beside the telephone. It showed us on our wedding day, happy and smiling. 'She never stood a chance. They said he came out of nowhere and she never ...'

I didn't know if he was planning on saying 'stood a chance' or 'knew a thing' but either would have been true.

'Bloody hell.' Liam's words were almost lost as he ran his hand over his mouth. 'Mate, I am so sorry.'

I felt like an outsider, as if I was watching two actors playing out a scene, but instead of sitting in the audience I was on the stage with them.

'I identified her.' There was a pathetic note to Marc's voice. He looked up from his clasped hands. 'They said they could arrange for me to spend time with the body but

50

I said no.' He blew out a breath. 'I couldn't do it,' he said slowly. 'I couldn't look at her, not laid on a cold slab like a piece of meat. I didn't want to see my wife like that.'

Liam nodded his head.

I could feel myself shaking and once again George steadied me. 'Maybe we should go,' he whispered in my ear but I shook my head. It was uncomfortable but it felt like I had to be there. To tell you the truth, I'd been a bit upset that Marc hadn't wanted to spend some time with me … with my body. It made me feel like, I don't know, like he didn't care. I knew in my heart that wasn't the case but I needed to see how he was feeling. I could see he was barely holding things together.

When Liam stood up and moved slowly towards us I could see how distraught he was too. There were no tears, and I wouldn't have expected there to be, but shock was painted over his face. Though he had started out as Marc's friend, over the years we had become friends too. He stood inches from me as he collected two glasses and a half full bottle of whisky from the table in the corner before moving slowly back to his seat and pouring two fingers of the liquid into each glass. He put the bottle on the floor by his feet and handed one of the glasses to Marc.

'Go on,' Liam coaxed.

The men sat in silence again. I watched the minute hand on the clock move from ten to fifteen before either of them spoke.

'I love her so much,' Marc said.

'I love you too,' I whispered through fingers that were covering my mouth.

'What am I going to do?' Marc asked. 'What am I going to do?'

Liam didn't even try to answer. He took a mouthful of whisky and swallowed it before asking, 'What about

Naomi?'

'What?' Marc looked confused.

'You said Ellen had picked Naomi up from school,' Liam said. 'Was she in the car?'

'Yes.'

'Oh God.' Liam said the words slowly and hesitated before asking, 'Is she alright?'

The first hint of brightness forced its way into Marc's voice. 'She's fine, or at least that's what the doctor tells me. She's got to stay in hospital for observation. The only thing is,' he took a deep breath. 'She hasn't asked where Ellen is. In fact, she hasn't spoken a word. The doctor says it's normal and that it'll pass but what am I going to do then?' He started to get agitated. 'What am I going to do when she asks where Mummy is? How can I tell her Mummy is dead?' He closed his eyes and I could see from the clenching in his jaw that he was inches from falling apart.

After a minute he opened his eyes and looked around the room. He shook his head as he did so. 'I don't believe this,' he said. 'How can this be happening? It's a normal day. How can this be happening?' He drained his glass and held it out for a refill. 'It was a normal day until the police were parked outside the house when I got home from work.' He was lost in a dream as he recalled the events. 'I could tell from their faces that something terrible had happened.' He started to shake his head again. 'But not this...'

'Do you want to stay with us?' Liam asked as he loosened the top on the bottle again.

Marc shook his head.

'Not even for tonight? You shouldn't be on your own.'

Marc shook his head again.

'Are you sure you're going to be OK?' Liam asked tentatively.

Once more, Marc shook his head. 'I don't know if I am or if I'll ever be again,' he said. 'But I want to stay here.' He put his refilled glass on the floor beside him. He looked right at me when he said, 'I can smell her perfume. The one I bought her last Christmas, the one she always wore.' He took in a deep breath. 'If I close my eyes, it's as if she's still here, right in this room.'

It felt so odd to be in the bedroom with Marc, the bedroom I had shared with him for eight years. A room so familiar, yet one I barely recognised. Everything looked different. Everything *was* different.

My eyes were drawn to the table, where the book I'd been reading sat beside a ceramic dog Naomi had given me last Mother's Day. The piece of scrap paper I'd been using as a bookmark showed the page I'd been on when I closed the book the night before. I realised I would never know if Miranda lived long enough to tell Gareth that she loved him. My new circumstances made her fictitious situation all the more significant and I hoped that the author had allowed Miranda the strength to fight her disease until Gareth made it home from Mozambique. I realised the importance of saying things before it was too late. I chastised Miranda for not telling him sooner. Too late could happen any time.

At least Marc knew I loved him and I was grateful for that.

I looked at him as he lay on the bed, our bed, a bed I had shared with him just last night. His hands were behind his head and he was staring at the ceiling.

'Ellen,' he whispered.

The sound of Marc saying my name gave me more pain than a dead person should be able to feel.

I sat on the bed a few feet from him head. 'Marc.' My

words were also said in a whisper. 'I'm here.'

'Ellen,' he said, 'what am I going to do about Naomi?'
I felt completely helpless.

He put the heels of his hands over his eyes

'What the hell am I going to do? What would you do?'
I backed away as he turned his head on the pillow and
looked at me. 'You'd tell her, wouldn't you? You'd be
brave and face it head on. I know you would.' He was still
looking at me. 'How can I do that?'

Did he know I was there? I didn't think he could see
me because I didn't sense it in the way that I had when
Naomi had looked at me but I definitely got the feeling he
was talking to me.

'Is he talking to me?' I asked George, who was stood
by the window looking out at the dark street.

He turned his head towards me.

'He is, but not in the way he did before.' I didn't
understand and it must have shown on my face. 'He's not
talking to you as a person sitting opposite him, one that
can give him a straight answer, anyway. He …'

I stopped George mid-sentence because I didn't
understand.

'Can I talk to him?'

George smiled and his face softened in the half light of
the street lamp. 'You'll always be able to talk to him.' He
turned to look out of the window again. 'But whether he'll
take any notice is another question,' he said to the glass.

I crouched down beside the bed. 'You have to tell her,'
I urged him. 'Naomi needs to know.'

'I can't tell her,' he said, moving his head back to its
original position and looking at the ceiling again. 'I can't.
You would, I know that you would. But you're so much
stronger than me, Ellen. I can't tell Naomi you're gone.'

I appreciated what George had said but it felt like Marc
and I were having a conversation. My hand went out to

him but I stopped just short of stroking his hair. 'You're right, I would. It would be so hard but I would tell her. I would have to, because she would wonder where her daddy was.' This time I did touch his hair and I hoped that he could feel it. 'You have to summon up all the courage you can and you need to tell her. Once you've done that the worst part's over. All you need to do …'

The telephone interrupted me. The shrillness of its ring made us both jump. Marc moved slowly and picked it up on the third ring.

'Hello.' Marc's voice was croaky. 'Oh hello, Mum.'

Marc's mum had been practically housebound for the last two years. Like me, her life had changed in an instant. One minute she was fine and then a brain haemorrhage later and she was paralysed from the chest down. All that worked now were her arms and her head. One day, she had been a fit, healthy woman who walked for miles and did yoga three times a week and the next she was confined to a wheelchair. There was a time they'd thought she'd never get out of bed again. She'd once told me she wished she was dead and I'd agreed with her that I'd want to be dead too if I was in her position. Now I would give anything to be alive.

'Thanks,' Marc continued, and I listened to the rest of the one-way conversation. 'Yes … yes, she was very lucky … Yes thank God. She's fine … I promise she's fine … I've just seen her.' There was a longer pause. 'No … not yet … I know, I will … I just don't know how.' He struggled to control his breathing. 'Look, Mum, I've got to go. I'll come round and see you tomorrow … No, not yet … I'm seeing someone tomorrow … It'll probably be next week sometime, but it won't be a burial, Ellen wanted to be cremated.'

Cremated!

Oh God, they were going to burn me.

My breathing quickened and I felt panic start to wash over me. I toppled from my crouching position and landed on my backside. I felt George's hands under my armpits as he lifted me up.

Had I really said I wanted to be cremated? I knew I had, but now that it came to it, it was a bit of a shock to hear the words spoken. I didn't much like the sound of them.

The first time I'd said it, we'd been watching a film where a girl had woken up in her coffin and could hear the soil being thrown on top of her. I'd told Marc that I didn't want that happening to me and I wanted to be cremated.

Marc had laughed and asked me if I knew what embalming was. I'd had to admit that I didn't and he assured me that after I'd been embalmed I wouldn't be waking up in a coffin. Even so, I'd stuck to my guns and said that I wanted to be cremated. Marc's aunt had been cremated last year and after the service I'd said that I thought it was wonderful that her daughters could take her ashes away and put them in a spot that was special to her. I remembered meaning that it was what I wanted when the time came. I just hadn't expected it to come so soon.

I tried to get a grip of myself. He was only doing what I'd said I wanted.

Even so, I felt sick and closed my eyes tightly, half hoping that when I opened them again I would have woken up from this nightmare. Sadly, nothing had changed.

I'd been so preoccupied with thoughts of cremation that I hadn't noticed Marc move, so I was surprised when I saw him sitting on the edge of the bed with his back to me.

His breaths were long and heavy. His head was lowered and resting in his hands. He pushed his fingers through his hair and gave it a tug before finally letting go.

It was just what I had seen Phil do earlier that day. He brought his hands down onto his knees with a slap and used them to push himself up. He walked the three steps to the wall and turned around. He looked ten years older than the man I had kissed goodbye that morning. Or was it yesterday morning? Did it make any difference?

Slowly, he lifted his arms towards the ceiling before wrapping them around his head so his elbows were near his eyes and his hands were joined at the top of his neck. He leaned against the wall and slowly slid down it until he was crouched on his haunches. He lowered his head into his chest and rolled onto the floor. He lay there in silence for a long time.

The clock had moved fifty-three minutes before he uncurled himself and crawled towards the bed. For all that time I watched him helplessly from the corner of the room.

Marc didn't bother getting undressed, he just climbed into bed. That made me as sad. He lay for a few minutes before I could tell from the sound of his breath that he had fallen asleep.

'He's exhausted,' George said.

'I know,' I replied.

'Come on,' George said, taking me by the elbow. The next thing I knew we were in the back garden.

The swing that Naomi was quickly growing out of stood on the lawn to our left and a couple of wooden garden seats sat on the paved area to our right. My mother liked to call it our patio but I always thought it was a bit grand for half a dozen paving slabs. I noticed the washing was still on the line, now soaking after the earlier downpour.

I loved that garden.

'Nice garden,' George said.

'Thanks.' I smiled at the compliment. 'It was a tangle of weeds when we bought the house but we sweated blood and tears to turn it into something beautiful.' I looked around, my eyes picking up every detail. 'We were always planting this or fiddling with that. And you see those,' I pointed to the ornamental finials sitting on top of the fence, 'they went up just a fortnight ago.' My tone of voice changed from pleasant to bitter. 'Eight years,' I said. 'It took us eight years to finish this garden and I only get two weeks to enjoy it. How can that be right?'

'No-one said it was right,' George said. 'It's just the way it is.'

I moved to one of the chairs and sat down.

The first signs of daybreak showed in the sky and birds broke into chorus.

The sun was going to rise and the birds were going to sing. Life was going on.

CHAPTER EIGHT

I stood on the outskirts of my life and watched. No, not my life, their lives. The one I wasn't part of anymore. Just as I'd realised it would when I'd sat in the garden listening to the birdsong and watching the sun rise, life was going on.

I watched Marc crying in his mother's arms.

Sadie's arms were about the only thing that still worked for her but they were strong and she held her son tightly. He knelt by her wheelchair as she stroked his hair and whispered in his ear.

'What am I going to do?' he asked her. 'What am I going to do?'

I couldn't hear Sadie's response or if she even made one. Her face was buried deep into her son's neck.

They sat like that for a long time.

Sadie was the strongest woman that I had ever known and always would be. That strength may have all but left her body but in her mind it was a different kettle of fish. She wasn't crying; there'd be time for that later. Maybe she'd cry when she was on her own. Right now though, her son needed her to be strong.

'I wish there was something more I could do,' Sadie said. 'I'm useless to you in this body.'

'No, you've helped.' Marc squeezed her arm and sniffed hard. 'More than you can imagine.' He wiped his eyes with the cuff of his shirt and looked away as the tears started again. 'I needed my mum and you were there.'

'I just wish that there was more I could do.'

He looked at Sadie again. 'What am I going to do when Naomi needs her mum?'

'Don't worry, love, her mum will never be far away from her,' Sadie said as she wiped Marc's tears away with her fingertips. 'Ellen might not be able to put her arms around Naomi any more but she'll always be there.' She brushed a stray hair away from his eyes. 'Darling,' she whispered, 'my mother died when I was eleven and I didn't know what I was going to do. I was the only girl in a house with four brothers.' She cupped his chin. 'But my mother had to go away just like Ellen did. They didn't have a choice, you see. It wasn't that they wanted to die, but just because my mum died didn't mean that she stopped loving me or that I stopped loving her. I've felt my mother at my side a thousand times, and I feel her every day here.' She touched her chest. 'I can feel her right now and I get great comfort and strength from that.'

I wondered if Sadie was telling the truth.

I knew she was telling the truth about her mother dying when she was a girl, but had Sadie really felt her mother with her? Or was she saying it to make her grieving son feel better?

'I thought I could smell her perfume last night,' Marc said quietly. Sadie almost spoke but changed her mind at the last second. Marc pushed himself up from his knees and sat on the edge of a nearby chair, a movement he completed without letting go of his mother's hands. He took a couple of deep breaths and swallowed hard. 'I was sitting in the living room after I got back from the hospital,' he said, 'and for all the world it felt like she was standing beside me.' The look on his face was a mixture of sorrow and desperation. He looked at Sadie. 'I could still smell her, Mum. And in the bedroom it was there again.' A half smile found its way to his lips. 'I know it's stupid but I was talking to her.'

'Why's that stupid?' Sadie asked. 'I talk to your dad all the time.'

Marc's dad had died the year Naomi had been born. He'd lived long enough to see his only grandchild being christened before succumbing to the illness he'd fought for two years. He'd told us he was dying a happy man.

'But she's dead.'

'And so's your dad but it doesn't stop me talking to him. Sometimes I think he's answering me. I'll ask him a question and suddenly the answer just pops into my head.' She let go of his hands for the first time. 'Go and make a cup of tea, love,' she said. Marc went to the kitchen and did as he was told.

The tea had been made, brewed, and partially drunk before Sadie said, 'You will get through this.'

Would he?

Did I want him to?

Of course I did … didn't I?

Marc and my parents sat in a triangle, each of them on a separate piece of furniture. They didn't look at each other and no-one spoke. Dad moved his mug of coffee in a circular motion, watching its contents swirl around. Marc was also looking at the contents of his mug, cradled in his hands. My mother sat in her chair with her arms folded across her chest and her head lolling forward.

She started to shake her head and threw her hands up to her face. She said something that nobody heard. Both of the men looked at her and Dad said her name gently.

Marc looked at the coffee again.

Marc had come to my parent's house after seeing the

funeral director but had not told them I would be cremated the following Tuesday morning.

Eventually my mother took a deep breath and asked. 'Have you seen Naomi today?'

'No.' He sounded apologetic. 'I had some stuff I had to sort out this morning. I'll go to the hospital this afternoon.' After a pause he added, 'You can come if you like. I expect Naomi would be pleased to see you.'

My dad seemed about to say something but Mum got there first. 'I don't think I can do that … not yet.' Her voice faltered.

'It might do you good, Peg,' Dad suggested.

My mother turned away and put her hand to her mouth. After a few seconds she turned back. 'I carried that girl,' she said through the tears. 'I carried that girl inside me and after seventeen hours in labour I brought her into this world and I fed her from my breast until she was ten months old. She was my child, my only child, and now she's gone.' Mum paused to wipe her eyes with a tissue that had been stuffed into the sleeve of her cardigan. 'I'm sorry, Marc, I don't think I can see Naomi at the moment because seeing her would remind me of what's happened to Ellen. I can't really face that yet.'

'I wish that was a luxury I could afford.' Marc said, I think without realising, because he looked at my mother and added. 'I'm sorry, Peg,' he said. 'I didn't mean that. I just can't handle this. I don't know what to do. I haven't even told Naomi.'

The silence that followed lasted minutes rather than seconds.

'You know under the circumstances it's what Ellen would have wanted.' My father's voice was flat and expressionless. 'If one of them had to die she would have wanted it to be her.'

'Every time,' Marc agreed. 'Every time, she would

have wanted it to be her.'

'I wish I'd had the chance.' My mother's voice was weak and shaky. 'Why wasn't it me?' she wailed. 'Why isn't it me that's dead? I've had my life but Ellen ...'

Marc put down the empty mug and readied himself.

'I saw an undertaker this morning,' he announced.

'What did he say?' Dad asked.

'He's booked the crematorium for half ten on Tuesday.'

'Crematorium!' The word filled the room. My mother sounded horrified.

'There'll be a service at St Aidan's at ten o'clock.' If Marc's words were intended to placate my mother they failed.

'Ellen's not going to be cremated.' Mum looked towards Dad for help. 'Brian, tell him. Ellen can't be cremated.'

'It's up to him, love.' Dad said softly.

'No,' Marc corrected. 'It's up to Ellen.' He looked directly at my mother. 'It's what she wanted.'

'She didn't,' Mum said.

'She said she did.' Marc said the words slowly.

'I don't believe it, she wouldn't.'

I moved into the centre of their triangle. 'I did, Mum,' I tried to tell her.

'I won't allow it,' Mum said as she started to rock back and forth in her seat. 'I'm sorry but I can't allow it. We can't allow it.' Poor Dad didn't get a chance to say anything. 'There's never been a cremation in this family.' She was shaking her head. 'If it's a matter of money ...'

'It's nothing to do with money.' Marc cut her off mid-sentence. 'It's what Ellen wanted.'

Mum stopped rocking and leaned forward. 'Look, Marc. I know you were her husband and I know you loved her but we were her parents and I think we know a bit

63

about what she wanted. And apart from that, surely what we want has to be considered.' She paused to take a deep breath. 'And we want her buried.'

'Ellen wanted to be cremated,' Marc insisted.

'How do you know that?' I was surprised by my mother's reaction and couldn't understand why she was getting so upset. 'She was my daughter and I think I would know what she wanted and I know that she would want to be buried. She was brought up to be buried.'

Brought up to be buried? How can anyone be brought up to be buried?

I went over to Marc's side. I sat on my haunches and tried to give him strength. 'Don't let them bury me, Marc. Don't you dare let them,' I told him.

Marc shifted forward in his seat. 'I'm sorry you feel this way but it's not going to change anything.'

'I will fight you over this, Marc,' she said.

I couldn't believe my ears. 'What are you talking about?' I asked.

Marc asked a similar question. 'Fight me for what?'

'You will not burn my daughter,' she announced.

'But it's what I want,' I told her. Why couldn't she hear me?

'Look.' Marc's voice was calm and quiet. 'I'm sorry if this is upsetting for you, but trust me it can't be any worse for you than it is for me. Ellen is gone and there are only two things I can do for her now. One is that I can raise our daughter the best I can, and the other is to see that her body is dealt with in the way she wanted it to be. I intend to do both. That means a cremation and that's the end of it.'

'No,' Mum sobbed, 'we won't allow it.'

'But if it's what she wanted ...' Dad tried to calm her.

She threw him a black look. 'What she wanted! How do we know what she wanted? We've only got his word for it.' She transferred the look to her son-in-law.

Marc said nothing but his look was as black as hers.

'Peg,' Dad tried again, 'they'll have talked about it. Of course Marc knows what she wanted.'

'But what about when you want to visit her?' Mum asked. 'You need a gravestone to have somewhere to go.'

'She didn't want a gravestone.' Marc said.

'Rubbish.' Mum almost laughed. 'Of course she wanted a gravestone.'

'Why?'

Mum looked to my dad for inspiration but none was forthcoming. Her voice broke as she spoke. 'Because it's somewhere for us to go when we need to talk to her,' she said sadly.

I moved from Marc to my mother. 'You can talk to me now.' I stood less than six inches away.

'Margaret.' I could tell that Marc had reached that point where he didn't want to argue anymore. 'Brian. Ellen wanted to be cremated.' Mum opened her mouth to speak but Marc stopped her. 'I repeat,' he emphasised, 'Ellen wanted to be cremated and that's a fact. She was terrified of being buried and waking up in the coffin. And she used to say that she didn't want anyone building a supermarket on top of her in fifty years' time.'

'She wouldn't be so stupid,' my mother scoffed.

'So I'm stupid?' I stood in front of her with my hands on my hips. I heard George chuckling but I was undeterred. 'It's no stupider than being brought up to be buried.'

'You've got to respect her wishes, Peg,' Dad said. He could understand. He wouldn't have called me stupid.

'But what about a grave?' Mum's argument was weakening. 'Where will I go?'

I was still annoyed by the 'stupid' comment. 'You hardly talked to me when I was alive, why do you want to now that I'm dead?' I challenged.

Being dead was very liberating.

Dad moved closer to Mum and reached out to touch her hand.

'Talk to her here,' Dad said. 'Remember her here. Remember her when she was little and she used to help you with the dusting. Or when she first got interested in boys and you had to comfort her through heartache.'

My mother admitted defeat and sank deep into her chair. Her head fell to the side and she stared straight ahead.

Dad and Marc looked at each other with a hint of embarrassment.

'I'm sorry, Brian,' Marc said, 'but I swear it's what Ellen wanted.' He stood up slowly. 'I'd best get to the hospital,' he said. Dad nodded and pushed himself out of his own chair and they moved to leave the room.

'Why St Aidan's?'

They stopped and turned to my mother, who still sat in her chair.

'Sorry?'

Mum turned to him. 'Why have a service at St Aidan's? Ellen didn't go to church.'

'You do.'

Marc's answer surprised me but my mother's reaction surprised me more.

'You shouldn't have bothered,' she said. 'I'm done with all that.'

Dad and Marc looked at each other again.

'Give Naomi a hug from me.' Dad gave Marc his cue to leave.

'I will.'

'I'm just trying to do what's best,' Marc said as Dad opened the door.

Dad nodded and patted Marc sympathetically on the

back as he left.

He closed the door and turned back to look at where his wife still staring at a wall.

Marc went to the hospital.

We went with him.

I stood close by as Marc sat on the edge of Naomi's bed. She was still a little pale and looked tired but forced a smile onto her face.

'Have you got a hug for me?' Marc asked.

Naomi's climbed onto his lap and into his arms in silence. He rested his cheek on the top of her head and held her close.

I could see the fear in his eyes.

'Come on,' I whispered. 'Do it now, get it out of the way.'

He pulled her closer and she nestled herself against his chest, playing with one of the buttons on his shirt.

'You ...' His voice croaked. He coughed and started again. 'You must be wondering about what happened when you were in the car,' he said. She stopped playing with the button and shifted in his arms until she could look into his eyes.

I took a step back.

'Yesterday,' he said, as if he were choosing his words carefully, 'something happened to Mummy.' Each word was dragged out of the last. 'Do you remember what happened in the car?' he asked and Naomi nodded her head. Even from a distance I could see the horror in her eyes. I willed Marc to move on swiftly and thankfully he did. 'Well, Mummy got hurt very badly,' he said, 'and she had to go away. She didn't want to leave us but she didn't have a choice.' He said the words quickly. Maybe that made them easier to say. I doubted it. He swallowed hard.

'She's had to go far away to a place called Heaven where she doesn't hurt anymore. And because she's in Heaven we won't be able to see her every day like we used to.' He stopped talking and I noticed there were tears in his eyes again. As he talked he stared ahead like he was focusing on a single spot. Maybe that was helping him keep his emotions under control. Even from my distance I could see the muscles in his face twitching. He kept his eyes on his whatever it was he had focused on as he rested his lips on the top of Naomi's head. He closed his eyes and tightened his grip around his daughter. He sat like that for what seemed like a long time.

I could see the fear and confusion on Naomi's face and I willed Marc to get a grip of himself. Marc must have sensed it too. He opened his eyes and blew out a breath.

'Mummy's had to go away and that might make you sad,' he said, 'because I know it makes me sad.' He took another second to compose himself. 'But just because we can't see her doesn't mean Mummy can't see us. I know in that faraway she can still see us. And I know she'll care about us and love us, just like we'll care about her and love her.'

Naomi shifted her gaze and looked at me. Her eyebrows knitted together and she opened her mouth as if she was going to say something.

Then something in her eyes changed.

With a heavy sigh she turned to her father. The tears he had kept out of his voice were flowing down his face and off the end of his chin. Naomi moved so she was kneeling in front of him. She put her tiny arms around his neck and pulled him close. Marc allowed himself to be cradled. I have never been more proud of my daughter.

I motioned to George with my head and moved away. I felt like an intruder.

CHAPTER NINE

Marc held Naomi's hand as they walked out of the hospital. Dr Moran was there to ruffle my daughter's hair before they left. After the doctor walked back inside, Marc scooped Naomi into his arms and carried her to the car.

We walked behind them and I could feel Naomi's eyes on me all the time. At one point she almost smiled at me.

Marc pointed the key towards the car and pressed the button to unlock it while they were a distance away. He opened the back door and lowered Naomi into the seat, being careful that she didn't hit her head on the way down. He was always gentle with her but he was even more so now. Or at least that's how it seemed. It occurred to me that there was a good chance he would become over-protective of her and who could blame him? I didn't. If I were him, I'd never want to let her out of my sight.

Marc fastened the seat belt around her and took extra care to make sure she was secure. He checked it once and then again. I could see the effort it took for him not to check a third time.

He closed the door and gave it a push before walking to the driver's side. He stood with the open door in his hand and looked at the hospital. God knows what was going through his mind.

He slowly climbed into the car and started the engine.

Something told me this wasn't a good time to hitch a lift so we watched them drive away. We were waiting for them at the end of their journey.

Naomi walked slowly down the path towards our house. Marc was a couple of steps ahead of her. He transferred her bag from one hand to the other so he could dig deep into his pocket for the keys. Naomi lifted her head and watched. Eventually Marc found what he was looking for in the pocket of his jacket. He opened the door and held it open.

At first Naomi, didn't move. She just stood in front of the doorway, staring ahead.

I moved towards them as Marc crouched beside her. I could see that he was talking to her but wasn't close enough to hear what he was saying. I guessed he was trying to coax her to go in. When he stood up he stooped so his arm was around his child's shoulders and they moved together. I went with them.

Naomi entered the house reluctantly and once inside I noticed that she was looking around. It was as if she was searching for something and I realised that it was probably me.

It was only after she had checked every room including the bathroom that she went back to the kitchen where Marc was waiting for her. He had poured her a glass of orange juice and left it on the table. Naomi went straight to the table and sat down. She put both of her hands around the glass and held them there.

Marc poured boiling water into a cup of instant coffee. He placed the kettle carefully back on its stand and turned around slowly.

'Sit with her,' I said. 'Just sit with her.' To my surprise, he did.

'Talk to her.'

But he didn't; he just looked at her.

I stood where I had a thousand times before between the two people I loved most in the world.

'Naomi.' I leaned my hands on the back of what used to be my chair and looked at her. 'Ask your daddy what you want to know.'

She looked at him.

Marc watched our daughter through tired eyes. She was staring at the drink she had not touched.

'What do you think you're doing?' George asked. He was watching from the doorway to the living room. I waved away his objections and crouched down beside Naomi. She didn't look up. Maybe she couldn't see me after all

I looked at Marc and willed him to speak.

I had to will him three times

'Do you want to talk about what happened to Mummy?' he asked

She remained silent.

'I'm glad you're home,' he said awkwardly. 'Are you glad you're home?'

She gave the merest shrug of tiny shoulders.

He left it at that for a minute or so before proceeding cautiously.

'I understand that you don't want to talk about what's happened,' he said gently, 'and that's all right. But do you know what?' He reached out and tapped her hand. 'Look at me,' he said, motioning with his fingers that she should lift her head. 'Do you know what?' he repeated. 'Even though you haven't told me, I know what you're scared of.'

She looked quizzical. Marc reached over and took Naomi's hands in his. 'Mummy had to go away and I think that you must be scared that I'm going to go away as well.'

That never occurred to me. 'Why didn't I think of that?' I looked at George. He shrugged and I turned back quickly to find Marc and Naomi exactly where they had been.

'It's alright to be scared, Naomi,' he told her. 'I'm scared too. Do you know what I'm scared of?' Naomi shook her eyes rather than her head. 'I'm scared,' Marc said slowly, 'that you could have had to go away too. I don't know what I would have done if you'd both gone.'

Naomi's words were little more than a whisper. 'Why did she have to go away?'

I saw the look of surprise in Marc's eyes as Naomi spoke. I forgave him the hint of a smile that had formed on his lips for the first time in two days.

'She had no choice,' he said.

'Why?' Naomi challenged him. 'Who made her go away?'

Marc searched his mind for an answer she would understand. 'I'm not sure, God, I suppose.'

'I hate God.'

CHAPTER TEN

'It's not fair,' I said as George and I walked through park in the afternoon sun.

'And what would that be?'

'This.' I held my hands out to indicate my body.

George stopped his gentle stroll and looked at the grass beneath his feet. After a few seconds he looked up. 'No, it's not,' he admitted, 'but there's nothing you can do about it.' He resumed his stroll and I followed him.

'I need to know why it happened.'

'Why?'

'What do you mean why?' My voice was raised and I looked around, hoping the joggers and dog walkers had not heard me. Once again, the realisation hit me like a brick in the face. 'What am I worried about?' I shouted. 'They can't hear me.' I looked around as I screamed. 'They can't hear me because I'm dead.'

George stopped mid-step, turning slowly on his heel. His eyes looked at me from a lowered head. 'They may not be able to hear you,' his voice was calm, 'but I can. And as I'm only three feet away from you,' he raised his voice, 'there really is no need to shout.'

'What's wrong with you?' I asked.

'You nearly burst my eardrum.'

'You're not being nice to me anymore.'

'Am I not?'

'No.'

'Yeah, well, you were having a bad time before.'

'And I'm not now?'

'Now it's just life.'

I felt my lip start to tremble and tears run down my cheek. George put his arms around me. I sobbed against his chest as people walked past us.

'Come on,' he said. 'Stop that. Crying's not going to change anything.'

'I don't want to be dead,' I whispered. 'Why do I have to be dead?' I got comfort from feeling George's hand stroke my hair. I was glad he was there. 'Why did it have to happen?'

When my sobs had subsided, George gently pushed me away. He looked directly into my face, wiping away my tears with his thumbs.

'You will find the answer.' He put an arm around my shoulder and started to walk, taking me with him. 'I promise. You will know why.'

'When?'

'Always a question,' he said, trying to smile. 'You'll get your answer when the time is right.'

'But when will that be?' I asked with fresh tears falling down my face.

I was calm after my outburst. I didn't know why I was dead but George had convinced me there was a reason, and that I would discover it one of these days. I just hoped it would be worth it.

We were still in the park but it was getting darker and there were only few people around. Not that people made a difference to us. We had stopped at the top of the hill and watched the streets below.

'Why did you die?' I asked.

'What difference does it make?'

'It's just a question.'

George took slow, deep breaths and looked over my shoulder. His throat bulged as he swallowed and he wet his lips with the tip of his tongue. He took a step and indicated that I should do the same.

'The last thing that went through my head was that I thought I would have liked to be a dad.' He sounded very sad. 'Turned out that would never have happened. Apparently I fired blanks,' George glanced at me briefly. 'I would never have given Marianne a kid'

'Was Marianne your wife?'

'Yeah,' I thought he might be crying. 'We'd been married less than a year when I died.' He stopped walking and looked at me.

'I don't understand.'

George used the fingers of his right hand to rub the stubble on his cheek. 'I had to die for Peter Gutteridge to be born,' George said quietly. 'Marianne's second husband was a bloke called Alfie Gutteridge. Nice bloke.' He smiled. 'We went to school together.' He looked more relaxed now and stood with his hands in his pockets. He glanced at me every now and then but spent most of the time looking at the floor. 'Alfie's mum worked two jobs and took in ironing so she could afford the uniform when Alfie got into the grammar school.' George kicked an imaginary stone away with his foot. 'He ended up selling insurance. Anyway, after he married Marianne they had a kid, a little lad, Peter.' He kicked another imaginary stone. 'Peter became a doctor.' George paused between each sentence. 'He spent some time in Africa and when he was there he saved the life of a little girl. He was the only doctor for miles. Without him, the little girl would have died.'

I didn't hide my confusion very well. 'So you died so

Marianne's son could save the life of a little girl on the other side of the world.'

'Peter's saved a lot of lives.' 'Me dying has saved a lot of lives,' he said philosophically

Later that day, George took me to a hospital, but it wasn't the one I had become accustomed to over the past few days.

'Where are we?' I asked.

'Liverpool,' George said.

'Why?' I asked.

He pointed to the large building we stood in front of. 'Because I wanted you to see something in here.'

'It's a hospital.'

'Come on.' George led the way through doors that opened to let two nurses out. George looked after them admiringly.

He still had an eye for a pretty girl.

I wondered how long it would take me to become as relaxed as George was.

Once inside the lobby, George consulted a list displayed on the wall. He located the department he was looking for. 'Come on,' he said again and I followed without question.

That was, until we got to where he was taking me.

'What is this?' I asked, looking around at the hospital equipment that surrounded us. Some of it was beeping, some ticking, and it all looked very serious.

Three of the beds had people occupying them and every one of them was hooked up to something.

There were two nurses attending the patient furthest from us. 'Why have you brought me here, George?' I asked, following him to a corner.

He stopped at the bottom of one of the occupied beds.

I looked at the man sleeping in it.

'Who's that?' I asked.

'Ben Andrews.'

'Who's he?'

George turned to me. 'He's got your liver.'

Suddenly, another nurse burst into the room and went to the bed in the corner, where the nurses were still attending the patient. I gave them scant attention.

'What do you mean he's got my liver? How can he have my liver?'

'He needed one.' George looked at the bed and then at me. 'You donated one. Luckily for him, you were a good match.'

I walked slowly around the bed. 'So my liver's in there right now?'

'Yeah.'

'Working and everything?'

'Looks that way.' George sounded amused.

'Why?' I looked up from the bed to look at George.

'What do you mean?'

'I mean why did he need my liver?'

George was being evasive. 'His own didn't work so well.'

'Why?' I said the word slowly.

'Does it matter?' George could not maintain eye contact.

After thinking over, I decided it didn't. My liver wasn't much use to me anymore so someone may as well see the benefit. 'He'd better look after it,' I said, 'because if I find out I died so some bloody alcoholic could ruin my liver as well as his own I won't be amused.' I had been waving my arms around and turned on my heel. As I did, I noticed a man had joined the nurses by the bed. He was wearing jeans and a T-shirt and looked out of place. He stood back from the nurses and looked like he was

77

waiting.

When he looked at me and asked, 'Everything alright?' I knew what he was waiting for.

He didn't have to wait long. Within a minute or two there was a flash of light and the man who had been lying in the bed stood beside the man in jeans. He didn't look confused in the least, which surprised me. He turned to the man wearing jeans and shook hands with him. They looked like two old friends. Was that how George and I were supposed to meet?

The newcomer looked at the body in the bed and shook his head slowly. As he turned around the back of his hospital gown opened to reveal the pale skin of his bare backside.

It made me glad that I had been dressed when I died and hoped someone would get the bloke some clothes quickly. He might be dead but I'm sure he didn't want to walk around like that for all eternity.

The nurses were still working on the body in the bed when the two men disappeared.

I looked at Ben again and as I did, his eyes fluttered open. He looked at me and a hint of a smile curled his mouth.

'Hello, Ben,' I whispered.

His mouth moved as if he was trying to speak, but no words came out.

I touched his hand where it lay under the sheet.

The nurses had given up trying to revive the body so one of them came over to check on Ben. She checked his pulse as she looked at the watch attached to her lapel. She wrote something on the chart that hung on the bottom of the bed and moved onto the next bed.

'See you, Ben,' I said. I looked at George, who gave a slight nod and started to move towards the door.

As George passed the bottom of the bed he had a piece

of advice for Ben. 'Don't bugger it up this time,' he said, taking me by the arm and leading me away.

'Where did the rest go?' I asked as we left the building.

'Here and there. Your heart's gone to a bloke from Rochdale; one of your kidneys went to a teenager from Rotherham and the other to a woman in Birmingham.'

'Spread about a bit, aren't they?'

'There's shortage of donated organs and they have to go where they're needed.'

'But why so soon? I've only been dead a few days.'

'Can't hang around where these things are concerned.'

'It's not fair,' I said. 'Just the other day, those things were inside me,' My voice became faster and louder. 'They were working inside *me*. How can they be working in other people now?' I ranted. 'How can they belong to them now? They're my organs.'

George stopped walking but I didn't and I'd taken a couple of steps before I realised. I turned and looked at him.

'You can't use them anymore.'

There was something in George's voice I couldn't work out, something I hadn't heard before.

'You all right?' I asked.

'Yeah.' He took a cigarette from his pocket and popped it into his mouth. I could sense there was something wrong. 'It's a great thing you did.' I didn't understand. I hadn't done anything. 'You donating your organs has saved at least four lives.'

'Well, like you said, they were no good to me.'

I walked a few steps before the thought hit me and in one movement, I stopped and spun to face George. My movement surprised him and it showed on his face.

'What's wrong?'

I asked the question slowly. 'Is it one of them?' I

asked.

'Is what one of them?'

'The reason I died.'

Confusion replaced the surprise on his face.

'I'm not with you.'

'Did I die so one of those people could have my organs?'

'No.' He screwed up his face as he spoke.

'Are you sure?'

'Positive.'

I narrowed my eyes as I said, 'If you say so.'

'This isn't a puppy farm,' he said as he came up beside me. 'We don't grow organs to order, you know.'

'Good.'

CHAPTER ELEVEN

'No,' I said firmly, hoping Marc could hear me. Maybe he did, because he put the dress back in the wardrobe where it had hung unworn since the day I'd bought it.

'Why?' George asked. 'I liked that one.'

'What?' I screwed my nose up in disbelief.

'I did,' he shrugged. 'I think purple can look very ...' he struggled to find the right word, '... fetching in the right light,' he said it with a smile.

I shook my head. 'It's not purple, its aubergine and I must have been asleep when I bought it.'

Marc lifted every garment out of the wardrobe and studied it before putting it back. Eventually he came across one that he studied longer than the rest. He nodded ever so slightly and threw it onto the bed. He shut the door to my wardrobe and left the room, closing the door behind him.

The eyes of all three women showed tears.

'Who are they?' George asked.

'That's Molly,' I said, pointing to the eldest. 'The one in the red top is Allison and the other one is Gail.'

'Are these the women you worked with?'

'Yes.'

'No men?'

'No.'

He nodded and I wondered what difference it made.

'So,' he nodded his head as he looked around, 'a librarian?' He started to finger the books on the rows to his right.

'Not really.'

'But this is a library.'

'I know, but it's Molly who's the librarian. The rest of us are volunteer helpers.'

'Oh.' He was still nodding. 'How often did you work here?'

'Wednesday afternoons,' I told him. 'The good thing is that it's only open during term time so I did it while Naomi was at school. It's just as much a social thing as anything else. I get ...' I corrected myself, '*got* a lot of pleasure out of it.'

George had wandered over to the desk where the women sat. 'Did you get to use one of those stamp things with the date on it?' He made the motion with his hand.

'Sometimes,' I said. I think I may have smiled.

We watched the women. There were a few people in the library but they were all busy looking for books so my former colleagues stood together by the desk. They each had a mug in their hands and drank as they talked.

'It's tragic,' Molly said, wiping something from her eye.

'I can't believe it,' Allison said. 'She was here last week telling us how she was going to have lunch with that friend of hers on the Thursday. How can she be getting cremated tomorrow?'

'That poor man,' Gail said. 'I don't know what he's going to do without her. And Naomi, I mean, how old is she? Five? Six?'

'She'll be seven this year,' Allison said. 'She's in the same class as our Michael.'

'Poor little mite.'

'It just shows you,' Molly said as she straightened a pile of papers that sat on the desk in front of her. 'You can't take anything for granted. Any one of us could be dead before tea time.'

'You never know,' Gail agreed.

'Why?' Allison asked. 'That's what I'd like to know.'

You and me both.

After a mouthful of coffee, she continued. 'You know, you see these bad buggers roaming the streets picking on kids, mugging old women, and they're as right as rain. Nothing happens to them. Then you've got Ellen who's the sweetest person you could hope to meet and this happens to her.'

'It makes you wonder,' Molly said, 'if Him upstairs has got a bloody clue.'

'My mum always says that everything happens for a reason,' Gail told them. 'But I think she'd struggle to find reasons behind this.'

They all stared silently into their mugs for a moment.

'Is it right that he died as well?' Gail asked, putting her empty mug under the counter. 'You know the bloke that hit her.'

'That's what it said in the paper,' Molly said, as she put her mug on her desk and took a book from the old man that had approached the counter. 'Best thing that could have happened to him,' she said as she stamped the date onto the flap of paper with the library's name printed on it. George seemed unduly interested in the stamp for some reason and he watched Molly carefully.

The old man started to shuffle away but stopped after a few steps. He turned and leaned heavily on the counter. He spoke slowly in a throaty voice. 'Is that the accident on Silver Street you're talking about? The one where the lass was killed?'

'Yes,' Molly told him, 'she was a friend of ours.'

'I'm sorry to hear that,' the old man wheezed.

'They said that the bloke who did it was three times over the limit,' Gail said, leaning towards him.

'Is that right?' the old man asked.

'Yes,' Gail said. 'Him dying was probably the best thing that could have happened. I mean, what would have happened to him if he'd lived? A slap on the hand, a couple of points on his licence?'

'So you think he deserved to die?' The old man struggled to catch his breath.

Gail's face flushed. She probably hadn't realised what she was saying. She wasn't usually so outspoken.

'I'm just saying,' she blustered, 'that he deserved more, that's all.'

The man nodded slowly, almost pushed himself away from the counter, and shuffled off.

'Who was that?' Allison asked.

'Don't know,' Molly said. 'He comes in now and again and gets a couple of books for his wife.' She picked up the ticket he had exchanged the book for. 'Harold Webber,' she said.

Webber? I looked at George. He was nodding his head before I'd even asked.

'Harold Webber,' he said. 'Phil's dad. He'll be dead within the fortnight.'

CHAPTER TWELVE

I stared at the coffin in the middle of the room.

Nervously, I walked towards it, almost stopping as I caught sight of the body that lay inside.

I lay inside.

'They did a good job,' George commented.

I nodded. I had to admit, I did look pretty. In fact, the make-up job was much better than I'd ever managed. I looked at the clothes that I was wearing. I approved of the lavender skirt that Marc had decided on. It had been a favourite of mine because the length hid my chunky calves. I wouldn't have put the blouse with it but in the grand scheme of things, what did it matter?

The door to our left opened and the man who had dressed me earlier walked in. My parents followed.

My father had to support my mother the entire way, and by the time they reached the coffin, his support was the only thing that was stopping her from hitting the floor.

She gave a whimper as she finally saw me. Her hand covered her mouth and she shook. I could only stare at her. I had never seen this woman before.

She pushed against Dad's arm and forced herself to stand by my coffin and look inside it. Her hand went out to me. It shook as she stroked my cheek softly and I instinctively put my hand to my face.

'Night, night, darling,' she said, the way she had a

million times before. 'Sleep tight.'

She turned away briefly. 'This is wrong,' she whispered. 'It should be me in there.' My dad looked uncomfortable. 'It should be me in there.' My mother's words were louder the second time.

'Come on, Peg.' Dad took hold of her elbow with one hand and put the other arm around her shoulder.

She shrugged his arm and hand away and stood frozen, staring into my coffin. Although my dad was only inches from her he may as well have been miles away. I had never seen anyone look so alone.

'You don't understand.' She shifted her gaze and locked eyes with my dad. 'It should have been me. She wasn't supposed to be there.' Mum's eyes went back to the coffin.

My hand went to my mouth but could not prevent a noise from escaping.

'Naomi was supposed to stay with us on Thursday night.' Dad appeared confused and Mum started to pace the floor. 'Ellen asked me if I'd pick Naomi up from school and let her stay over. I said I was feeling a bit under the weather and wasn't up to having her overnight. That's why they called on their way home.' Her voice was louder than it should have been considering where she was. 'Ellen thought I was ill. I wasn't ill. I was just feeling sorry for myself. I was put out that Ellen was going to have lunch and an afternoon's shopping with her friend.'

She put the palms of both hands against the wall and let them take the weight of her body. After a few seconds she pushed herself up. As she walked back to the coffin she sobbed. 'Now because of me ...' there was a pause as she forced herself to say the words, '... my baby's dead.' After one loud primal scream she yelled, 'It should have been me.' With that she fell to her knees and rocked as she sobbed. Dad looked at her and rubbed his hand back and forth over his mouth.

I stared at my dad, who after a few seconds slowly lowered himself to his haunches beside his wife.

I didn't try to hide the anger from my face as I turned to George. He had anticipated my reaction and took hold of my shoulders.

'I don't believe her,' I screamed.

I think George said, 'She's wrong,' but I'm not sure because I wasn't listening.

'How could she do that to me?' I asked as I struggled to escape George's grasp.

'She didn't do it to you,' George said, forcing me to look at him.

'Just because I wanted to see Megan.' I managed to free myself. I felt him try to grab me again but I had moved too far away. I stood over my parents. 'I don't care if you didn't like Megan, she's my friend.' My tempo picked up as I continued. 'Did I stop you from seeing Beryl even though her moustache terrified me? Did I ever say I wouldn't go with you when you wanted to see whatever that woman was called who stunk of lavender and lived on Custard Creams? Did I, Mum? Did I?' I knew I was ranting. 'No, Mum, I didn't. I went with you every time you asked and I was polite to them when they came to your house.' I glanced briefly at George, who seemed perplexed. I turned back to my mother. 'They were your friends and I accepted them. Why couldn't you accept Megan?'

I stared at her and felt spent.

'I'm so sorry, Brian.' Mum looked at Dad. 'If I'd known what was going to happen I would've said yes.' She started to sob again. 'I didn't know.'

'It's not your fault, love,' Dad soothed.

'It is,' she whimpered through sobs.

'No, it's not.' Dad rested the side of his face on the top of her head.

'Isn't it?' I asked. If I'm being honest, I was annoyed that Dad wasn't angrier.

'Course it's not her fault.' The words were George's and came from over my shoulder. 'It's not,' he said quietly. 'It wouldn't have made any difference.' He spoke slowly and I felt myself calming down, which annoyed me but seemed beyond my control. 'Whatever your mother did last Thursday would not have altered what happened. She would never have been there.' I looked at my mother, who had retrieved a tissue from her bag and was wiping her eyes. 'Think about it. She would never have been driving along Silver Street; she would have had no need to. She and Naomi would have been at her house by the time the accident happened.' I reluctantly conceded that he was right. He took hold of my shoulders again but this time he rubbed them gently. 'You would have been on Silver Street. You would have been going home.' I let him pull me forward and I rested my head on his chest. 'It was always going to be you.'

George and I were alone with my body. I stood at my feet looking at myself.

'This is weird,' I said with massive understatement.

George had been sitting on a chair by the wall but I felt him by my shoulder. 'Yeah.'

I looked at him before I took the seat next to the one George had been sitting on.

'I've never been in one of these before,' I said, looking around. The décor had a calming effect and there was a stillness you could almost touch. 'Were you in one?' I asked.

'One of these? No. Well, yes.' I must have looked

confused. 'Obviously I was at the undertakers. I mean, I was buried in a coffin and everything, but I wasn't in one of these.' He gestured to where I lay. 'Not like this. I spent the night before my funeral laid out in the parlour at my mum's. The lid was off all night and she kept coming to look at me. I think she was hoping that she'd look in and I wouldn't be there. Like the whole thing had been a bad dream or something.'

I knew how she felt.

His eyes were distant and he was smiling. He tapped my arm and rubbed his nose. 'The bloke came round to put the lid on,' he said, 'and just after he'd finished my Uncle Charlie rested his mug of tea and an ashtray on top of it.' He laughed out loud.' My mum came in and flicked him across the back of his head with a wet tea towel and told him if he'd left a mark on it she'd unscrew the lid and throw him in the coffin with me.'

We laughed together.

Marc and Naomi came later. I had wondered about Marc's decision to let her see me in my coffin but Naomi had been adamant. Maybe she needed to see me.

As they walked towards the centre of the room, I noticed that Naomi was holding a daffodil in her hands.

They stopped a few feet from the coffin.

Naomi climbed up onto the stool the undertakers had left by my head. She struggled to hold onto the daffodil and stand up but she managed it. Even on the stool, Naomi's waist was still below the level of the box and she had to raise her arm to get it over the coffin's edge. She laid the daffodil where my hands were joined.

'I brought you a flower, Mummy,' she said quietly.

I stood in the corner of the room with George, tears falling effortlessly down my cheeks.

Marc stood at the other side of the coffin. He was looking at the side of my face that had been hidden when he identified me. I hadn't seen my face properly and George told me that it was probably a good thing.

Marc gently stroked my hair and I was amazed that I could feel it. How could that be? There was no mistaking his touch as Marc brushed the side of my face with his fingertips. As I watched him lower his head to mine I tingled with anticipation of what was coming next. I had never felt as alive as I did when he kissed me. It felt like I had been struck by lightning and I half expected to sit up and spit out the piece of apple that had kept me asleep for a hundred years. My lips still tingled after he had stood up. I noticed that he was touching his own and wondered if he could feel it too.

He took in a deep breath which he let out in stages.

'I miss Mummy.' Naomi's words seemed louder than they were.

'So do I,' Marc agreed.

He took the four steps over to his daughter and lifted her into his arms. She latched onto him and they cried together. I cried on my own. George held me but he did not cry.

Eventually, Marc and Naomi left. They had only been gone for a few minutes when a man came in carrying what I quickly realised was the lid to my coffin. I staggered backwards.

'Come on,' George said. 'You don't need to see this.'

I couldn't help but take one last look backwards before the door closed behind me. The man was screwing down the lid.

CHAPTER THIRTEEN

'I'm not sure this is a good idea,' Sylvia said. 'It's most unusual.'

'Yeah,' George agreed, puffing extra hard on his cigarette. 'And I've told her but she wouldn't listen.'

'I don't mind.' Phil appeared from behind Sylvia and once again I was face to face with the man who had killed me.

'Why would you?' George's tone of voice was more aggressive than I thought necessary and the look I threw him told him so. 'Look, I'm sorry,' he said to me. 'But I don't understand.'

I wasn't sure if I understood either. All I knew was that I wanted, needed, to talk to Phil.

I took a deep breath and turned to Phil. 'They're cremating me tomorrow,' I told him. His head dropped to his chest. 'I just watched my mother say goodbye to me.' I tried and failed to swallow a sob. 'She thinks it's her fault.' I wiped my runny nose with the back of my hand. There was more vehemence in my voice with every word I spoke. 'My father had to practically carry her.' I took a step towards him and Sylvia made to intervene but George stopped her. 'My daughter brought me a daffodil,' I said. 'I'm going to be burnt with that daffodil in my hands. My husband kissed me for the last time.' Tears were now streaming down my face and I shouted, 'I watched a man screw the lid down on my coffin.' That was when the tears took control. I held my hands to my mouth and sobbed.

Through those tears I could just about see Phil, who still stood with his head down. Slowly, he raised it and looked at me. We stared at each other for a few seconds. He mumbled something.

'What?' I asked, pushing the tears away with the heel of my hand.

Phil coughed and twisted his neck as if he was getting rid of a crick. 'Sharon had an abortion today.' He pronounced every word clearly.

I looked at George and the way he bobbed his head told me he already knew. I wondered why he hadn't told me. I turned back to Phil, who had the thumb and forefinger of his right hand pressed into his eyes.

'Why?' I asked.

'What do you mean why?' he said, glaring at me. It was the first time I had ever heard aggression in Phil's voice. He was crying and little drops of saliva formed around his mouth. He took a minute or two to calm himself. 'I guess she didn't want my kid,' he said simply.

'I'm sorry,' I said.

'So am I.' He sighed deeply and looked at the ceiling. 'Now I'm responsible for three deaths instead of two.'

'You didn't kill your baby,' I said, forgetting my anger.

'Might as well have.' The eyes that looked at me were filled with anger. 'Do you know?' He started to walk and I walked with him though Phil was talking more to himself than me, and I wondered if he realised that I was following him. 'She didn't hesitate at all, not for a second. It was as if she couldn't wait to get my kid out of her. Like it was going to poison her or something. Am I really that evil?' He looked at me for an answer. I shook my head. 'How can you say that?' He started to rant again. 'How can you say I'm not evil? I killed you. Didn't you just tell me, you watched a man screw the lid on your coffin?' I nodded. 'I'm responsible for that.' He took one step away before slowly turning around. He looked weary. 'But why did she have to kill my kid?'

'He doesn't know about his dad, does he?' I asked George when we were alone.

'Wouldn't have thought so. Sylvia won't tell him until the last minute.'

'He's going to blame himself for that death, isn't he?'

'He should.'

George quickened his step and walked ahead of me.

'What will have happened to Phil's baby?'

'What do you mean?'

I felt a lump forming in my throat and moistened my lips with the tip of my tongue. 'What happened to Phil's baby when Sharon ... lost it?'

George looked at me with sadness. He started to say something but seemed to think better of it and stopped himself. He looked away for a second and cleared his throat. 'She went to the nursery.'

'It was a girl?'

'Is a girl,' he corrected.

CHAPTER FOURTEEN

George and I sat on the wall outside the house I had shared with Marc and Naomi. The sun was shining and our mood was light, which was strange considering the circumstances.

I was looking at my feet where they dangled two feet off the ground when I heard a familiar voice ask, 'You all right, love?'

'Yeah, fine, thanks,' I said like I had hundreds of times before. Of course we'd both been alive then and lived next door to each other.

'Thought I'd pop along and check on you. Funerals are never easy, especially when they're your own.' Both she and George burst into fits of laughter and I even managed a smile. Mary had been my next-door neighbour for a year and I had missed her since her passing.

She gestured with her hand and George shuffled along to make room for her. She jumped up onto the wall as easily as a child would have done. She must have seen the look of amazement in my eyes. 'No arthritis on this side,' she explained. 'I may look like the old woman I was when I died but I'll tell you, I don't feel like it.' I nodded as if I understood. 'So how's George looking after you?'

'Oh, OK,' I said, looking towards him. 'Is there anyone you don't know?' I asked.

'A few,' he conceded.

'Anyway, Ellen,' Mary continued as she rested her hand on my forearm. 'Today'll be a funny day for you, won't it, George?' He agreed. 'Just try not to think about it too much,' she advised.

'I'll try.'

'Do you remember mine?' she asked. 'You were carrying Naomi and you had a devil of a job finding something black to wear.' She tightened her grip on my arm. 'You were really kind to Bert that day and I was very grateful.'

'Where is he?' I looked around for her now-deceased husband.

'He's sorry, but he said he couldn't come.' Mary patted my arm again. Apparently you take your habits with you into the afterlife. 'But he sends his love. He said he'd catch up with you soon.'

Our attention was grabbed by the black car that had turned into the street.

'The curtains'll be twitching now,' Mary said and as I turned I saw that she was right.

A second car turned the corner. Outwardly they were identical except that the second had seats in it.

The first car carried my coffin.

'They're shiny, aren't they?' I said before I realised how ridiculous it sounded.

Thankfully, I don't think anyone heard.

The cars moved slowly and came to a halt right in front of us. A sombre man dressed in black got out. He walked right past us and we watched him all the way. There was no need for him to knock because my father waited for him in the open doorway. We watched as my dad exchanged a glance with the undertaker and then lowered his head and looked inside the house. He moved aside to let my mother pass. She was dressed from head to toe in black and I noticed with some interest that the black hat she wore had a feather in it.

'Bet she bought that special,' Mary said with a giggle before adding, 'Oops, sorry, I was forgetting myself.'

I waved away her apology and smiled. My mother had often been the butt of our jokes in that previous life. It felt like old times.

My eyes were on my husband as he followed my mother out.

'Oh, he is handsome,' Mary said and I agreed with her. He was wearing a charcoal suit, a white shirt, and the only black tie he owned.

'He bought that tie for yours,' I whispered to Mary.

Just behind Marc, practically hidden, was Naomi.

The night before, George and I had watched Marc open the door to my mother.

It was late and Naomi had been in bed a long time.

We had watched Marc pour himself a whisky and sit in his favourite chair only for him to stare into space and leave the drink untouched. After his visit to the Chapel of Rest I had been worried about Marc and wanted to check that he was OK. The way he was behaving did nothing to make me feel better.

The knock on the door had startled him. I had followed him to the door, wondering who would be calling so late. I was as surprised as he was to see my mother.

My mother had bought Naomi a dress that was black apart from the tiniest ribbon of white at the collar and the cuffs.

'I know you won't have had time to get her anything,' my mum had said.

Marc had looked at the dress and to my mother. 'Thanks but I hope you kept the receipt.'

'Why?' My mother had clutched the dress close to her

chest.

'Naomi has a dress.'

'A suitable dress?'

His voice had remained firm. 'Naomi has chosen what she wants to wear.'

Mum didn't press the point. She just put the dress back in the bag and swallowed hard.

'I was just trying to …' She sniffed and held her lips tightly together.

'I know,' Marc said, gesturing towards a seat but Mum shook her head and remained standing.

'No, I'll not stop,' she said and moved towards the door.

Marc opened the door and leaned against it. 'I know you were only trying to help,' he said, 'and I am grateful, honestly I am. But Naomi chose what she wants to wear. She's going to have a hard enough time getting through tomorrow as it is and if wearing whatever it is she's chosen helps her through it then I'm all for it.'

Mum nodded her head. 'Of course,' she said. 'We've all got to get through it the best way we can.'

Marc watched Mum walk to the car where Dad was waiting. Dad waved goodbye as they drove away and Marc closed the door.

He rested his head against it for a long time.

Now, as Naomi came into view I smiled and I approved of her choice. She was wearing her favourite yellow dress and matched it up with a white lace cardigan.

We had bought the cardigan on our last shopping trip together. Was the really just the weekend before last?

My father made up the rear of the group as they made their way up the garden path. My mother was already in the car and didn't notice that Naomi had stopped walking.

She was holding Marc's hand so he stopped walking too. I found myself looking into my daughter's hazel eyes. She smiled at me and I smiled back. She took a couple of steps towards the car and turned to look at me again before nodding and following her daddy into the car. She climbed onto his knee and watched me, first through the side window and then the back one as the car pulled away to follow the hearse.

I jumped down from the wall and stood wide-eyed, looking after the cars with my hand over my mouth. When they disappeared around the corner I turned to Mary.

'Did you see that? She saw me.'

'Yes, she did.'

I grabbed hold of her hand and squeezed it. 'She did, didn't she?'

'She did, love, and her clinging onto Marc like that was her way of telling you she's going to look after him for you.'

'Do you think?'

'Definitely.'

George agreed.

It seemed the most natural thing in the world to be holding onto George's arm as we followed the mourners into the church. My husband, daughter, and parents had been joined by a flock of relatives, most of whom I hadn't seen since my wedding day, a handful of friends from my school days, and a host of mums from Naomi's school. My colleagues from the library huddled together at the back. Megan and what I presumed was her new husband were in front of them.

My grandfather stood at the front of the church, his eyes fixed firmly on my coffin. He was shaking as he sobbed.

As the congregation took their seats, George manoeuvred me to the back of the church. The three pews nearest the back were filled with people I didn't recognise.

'Who are all these people?' I whispered. 'Is that Mrs Charlton? It is, isn't it? And that's Mrs Mowbray sat beside her.' I waved at the two women who had been responsible for everything I had learned in my first two years at school. They waved back.

I examined each face in turn, trying to find another familiar one. There were none, or so I thought, until I saw her. I clasped my hand over my mouth to stop the squeal from escaping and looked at the face I knew so well and had missed so much. I ran to her and threw my arms around her neck. She enveloped me in her arms and once again I was a little girl.

'There you are, love.' I heard her sweet voice and felt her soft hands stroke my hair. 'It's all right, don't be upset. Gran's here.'

'I can't believe you're here,' I said looking into the face I hadn't seen in over twenty years.

'I wish I weren't.' She pushed my hair away from my eyes.

'Yeah, you and me both,' I agreed. 'But it's lovely to see you.'

She asked those next to her if they would shuffle along to make room for us. It was a bit of a squeeze but it was good to be close to her again.

'Morning, George,' my grandmother said.

'Betty.'

'How do you know my gran?' I asked.

'That'd be telling,' George said with a smile. He held a finger to his lips and nodded to the front of the church.

I strained to hear the priest's words.

'Take comfort,' he said, 'from knowing that Ellen now dwells in a better place. She is with the Eternal Father in a place without pain … a place without hatred.' He paused and looked at those assembled before him. 'Tragic though her loss is, rejoice for her that she is with the Lord.' I noticed that Marc was squirming in his seat. 'Ellen was a good and loyal wife to Marc and a loving mother to their daughter Naomi …'

I moved my head close to my gran's. 'I've never met this man before,' I whispered.

'… Weep not for Ellen but for yourselves. Ellen has no need for your tears.'

'Don't I?' I asked through the corner of my mouth.

'There are worse places,' Gran said in that way that grans do.

Maybe she was right; this wasn't such a bad place when you compared it to the likes of the Calcutta slums or a Dickensian workhouse, but I'd rather be alive. So go on, I almost shouted, cry if you want.

My mother was crying a lot. Her shoulders shook and her head was buried in her hands. My dad has his arm around her trying to give what comfort he could. Marc's eyes never seemed to leave the coffin but I couldn't say if he was actually looking at it or not. His eyes had been vacant when he'd passed us in the churchyard and I don't know if he was seeing anything. Naomi, my darling child, was she oblivious to what was happening? She appeared to be playing with the hem of her dress.

The saddest figure of all was my grandfather. Tears poured from his eyes and fell off the edge of his face and onto his chest. He made no attempt to hide them. He didn't sob the way his daughter did, his tears seemed effortless. I found it painful to watch him but too difficult to drag my eyes away. I turned to my grandmother and saw she was watching the man that death had separated her from so long ago. She felt my eyes and turned to me. I noticed the merest hint of a smile on her face.

'He'll be free soon,' she said.

'What do you mean?'

She squeezed my hand. 'He tries to hide it,' she explained,' but he's in a lot of pain. The drugs don't work as well as they used to.'

'Why doesn't he get stronger ones?'

She laughed 'Because he's proud.' She looked at her husband with gentle eyes. 'Your granddad doesn't want to admit that the disease has got the better of him.' She looked at me and sniffed away a hint of a tear. 'You've got to realise that when we were younger, cancer was a dirty word ... and a death sentence.'

'But it's not now,' I told her. 'They can do all sorts of things that they couldn't then.'

'He's tired, love.' We both watched as he struggled to stand. 'He's ready.'

'When?'

'Soon.' We stood up along with the rest of the congregation. 'Soon.'

It's an odd feeling watching your loved ones touch a coffin in a final farewell knowing you are the one lying inside it. It was family members only at the cremation and each one took a turn to touch me one last time. My dad's sister Claire stroked the coffin and her husband Paul patted it. My cousin Philip made a fist and thumped it gently. My mother couldn't bring herself to touch the box. She stood in front of it with her eyes wide open and her hands over her mouth. My dad kissed his fingertips and laid them where my head was.

Marc and Naomi were the last to approach the coffin.

Naomi raised her arms and Marc lifted her up. In her hand was another daffodil. I hadn't noticed it because its colour was a perfect match for her dress. She took the flower, my favourite, and laid it where my hands would be resting on my stomach, a partner for the one that she had laid inside the coffin the night before. Marc lowered her to the ground. Slowly, he nodded his head, then he adjusted the daffodil's position slightly to the left. He stepped back and gathered his daughter into his arms again. She wrapped her arms around his neck and held him tightly. Our eyes locked and I know Naomi saw me.

Everyone watched as the coffin moved slowly through the velvet curtains, and the ordeal was over.

I'd thought that there would be music, so the silence surprised me.

CHAPTER FIFTEEN

I didn't go to the wake. That would have been too weird. Besides, I wanted to spend some time with my gran. I had missed her so much.

'I don't have a lot of time,' she warned me as we left the crematorium.

'Why?'

'Got to get back.'

'Where?'

'Upstairs,' she laughed. 'Well, that's what we call it but there aren't really any stairs to climb.'

'I don't understand.'

'Has George not explained this to you?' I shook my head. She looked at him. 'I know this is your first time, George, but I thought they trained you before they let you loose on folk.'

George shrugged and gave a grin.

Gran looked at me, 'This isn't where I live,' she said, taking hold of me hands.

'Where do you live?'

'Like I said, I live upstairs.'

'Then where is it?'

'I don't know exactly,' she admitted.

George came up behind her and put his arm around her shoulders. She tried to smile at him.

'Sorry, Ellen, your gran's right. I should've explained

this to you earlier but there's just so much to remember. Anyway, here goes. I'm a Greeter.' He held the hand that wasn't around my gran towards himself.

'A what?'

'A Greeter.'

'Like in a supermarket?'

'Yeah. But we existed before they did.'

'So you "Greetered" me?'

'Yeah, I am your Greeter.'

'Just mine?'

'For now, you're my first.'

'But not your last?'

He smiled. 'That depends on how well I do with you.'

I was struggling to understand. 'So this is a job for you?'

'You could call it that.'

I was puzzled. 'And what exactly is it that you do?'

'In a nutshell, it's like this. Do you remember the light?' I nodded. How could I forget it? 'Well, when you die ...' I winced at his word. 'Sorry,' he said, 'but it's a technical term. When you die you come through the light to here, to where we are now. You stay here until all of your issues have been addressed.'

'What issues?'

He shrugged. 'I don't know. They're your issues. You know, unfinished business, something you need to take care of before you can move on.'

'Move on to where?'

'Beyond the light.' He used his arm in a rolling, forward motion. 'Where your gran lives.'

'But she's here.' I reached out and touched her.

'Yes.' He brought his hands together in front of his chest. 'But only for today.'

'Which is why I said we don't have much time.' She was still holding my hands and she squeezed them. Then she shook them to make sure she had my full attention. 'I have to go back soon,' she said. 'I just came because ...' She couldn't finish the sentence and I fell into her arms. It felt good to be back in a familiar place.

'I've missed you, Gran,' I cried as I held onto her.

'I know, darling,' she soothed. 'But I've watched you every single day. I was there when you married Marc and I was with you when Naomi was born and ...' She held me at arm's length. 'Listen carefully, darling. I was there with you last year.'

What was she talking about?

Then it dawned on me. My hand clasped over my mouth.

'He lives with me,' she said softly.

'He?'

She nodded. 'When they brought him from the nursery he didn't have a name. I had to give him one so I called him Matthew.'

'After Granddad?'

'You don't mind, do you? I didn't know what else to do. I did think of calling him Marc but I thought you'd have a Marc later on, I didn't know ...' She didn't need to tell me she hadn't known. How could any of us have known a drunken knobhead would cut me off in my prime?

'Where is he?' I turned my head frantically.

'He's not here,' she said, squeezing my hands.

'Why? Why didn't you bring him?' I asked.

'It wouldn't have been right,' she said and I knew that was true.

'When will I be able to see him?' Now it was my turn to squeeze her hands.

'When the time is right.' She freed one of her hands from mine and stroked my face. She looked deep into my eyes. 'Darling,' she said, 'I don't have much time.'

'Why do you have to go?' I asked

'Because I can't stay here,' she said. 'This is not where I belong.'

'But I don't want you to go.' I felt five years old.

'I know, darling.' Gran was talking to that five-year-old. 'And I don't want to go but I have to. You won't be on your own, though.' She tried to laugh. 'You'll have George.'

Even I laughed.

George was talking to a woman. She was about my age and I didn't have a clue who she was or why she was at my funeral but that didn't matter.

Gran and I sat on the bench on the grassed area opposite the house where my wake was taking place.

'She'll never get over this,' Gran said in a voice filled with sadness. 'You were all she had.' She paused for a second or two like she was thinking of what to say. 'There were times when I wanted to slap her. Many times.' She paused and looked straight ahead. 'Oh, I know after you were born there was no chance of any more.' She turned her head slowly and fixed her eyes on me. 'But that didn't matter, she had you. Still your mother was spiteful.'

I must have looked surprised.

'Oh yes, she was. When Lizzie was having her trouble your mother used to parade you around like a trophy.'

I hadn't noticed that Gran was crying until she wiped her tears with a lace handkerchief.

'I always knew she would be paid back for that spitefulness.' She stared silently at her hands. She was twisting the handkerchief, rolling her finger around the fabric again and again until it became a single rope. 'What goes around comes around, isn't that what they say?' I nodded. It was my mother's mantra. 'There's never been a truer word said.' She flicked the handkerchief open and wiped more tears away. 'She'll never get over this,' she repeated. 'It'll finish her off.'

'No, it won't.' I said confidently.

'You mark my words, Ellen,' she said. 'I know my daughter. She'll never be the same.'

There was another pause.

'She blames herself,' I said.

'Why?' Gran finally shifted on the seat so she was looking into my face.

'She said it should have been her.' I shifted so I was face on with the grandmother I'd missed so much. 'I'd asked if she would pick Naomi up from school and let her stay overnight. I was meeting my friend Megan and we were going to have lunch in town and do some shopping. Megan's just got married and Marc and I were going to go out with her and her husband for a drink. But Mum said that she wasn't very well and couldn't do it so I picked Naomi up from school and called in to see her on the way home.'

My grandmother was nodding but said nothing.

'When she and Dad came to the Chapel of Rest last night, she kept going on about how it should have been her in the coffin. Apparently, she wasn't ill at all, she just said that because she was hacked off that I was meeting Megan.'

Gran's eyes looked bigger than ever. 'You know that's not right, don't you?' she said.

I nodded my head slowly. 'I do,' I said. 'George told me. But I don't understand.' I put my hands over my face and took a deep breath. 'I know it wouldn't have made a difference and I would still be dead, but I am so angry with her.' My gran said nothing. She just watched me and nodded her head. That was giving me a green light to rant, which I took without hesitation. 'What right had she to say who I should and shouldn't meet? It's not up to her who I'm friends with. And then …' and then there's that cremation business. She wanted me to be buried because there's never been a cremation in the family. What's that all about? And she wants a gravestone so that she's got somewhere she can go to talk to me. Why?' I looked at my gran through wide eyes. 'She was never interested in my opinion, she never listened to me. So why does she want somewhere she can come and talk to me now I'm dead? It's all show. She wants a dirty great headstone she can lay flowers at every week so everyone will know what a wonderful mother she was.'

'Was she really so bad?' Gran's question stopped my tirade in a heartbeat.

'No,' I had to admit. 'But I don't understand why she behaved that way. Why was it always about what the neighbours thought?'

Gran smiled. 'That's just the way she is, love.' She took my hand again. 'Your mother loves you so much.' I knew that was right.

'And I love her, honestly I do. But sometimes she doesn't make it very easy.'

'You don't need to tell me,' she said with a chuckle.

'And then there's Phil.'

'Who's Phil?'

'The bloke who killed me.' I was amazed by the matter of fact way that I could say that. 'I've seen him a couple of times and I'm angry with him. I am really angry with him. I sometimes think that I could kill him but he's already dead. But so am I and it's his fault and I hate him for doing it.' I took in a deep breath and blew it out through loose lips. 'Now I've started to feel sorry for him.' I looked to where George still sat with the woman I didn't know. 'I know that really annoys George because he can't understand it, but I can't help it. I just feel sorry for him.'

She smiled at me. 'That's because you're a good person,' she said. 'You've always thought of others before yourself and that'll never change. Your personality doesn't alter just because you're dead.' She smiled and gave a sigh. 'All I can tell you is that what you're going through is normal. One minute you're up, the next you're down and you don't know if you're coming or going.'

'Was it like that for you?'

She nodded. 'You'll get through it.'

'What are these issues that George keeps going on about?' I asked. 'What were your issues?'

She smiled at me in a way that said they were hers and they were staying that way. She made a move to get up from the bench and I knew she was getting ready to leave.

I helped her to her feet.

'Don't fight the way you feel,' she said. 'Go with it. It's part of the process.'

'What process?'

'The one that'll take you beyond the light.'

CHAPTER SIXTEEN

Gran had gone and I was alone with George.

We were sitting on the wall again.

'Who was that woman?' I asked

'Which woman?' He sounded like a man who had been caught doing something he shouldn't have been.

I laughed. 'The one with the red hair and the gingham dress you were talking to after my funeral.' I couldn't believe how easily the last two words had tripped off my lips.

'Apparently she was a friend of your mum's. They used to work together. She reckons she used to change your nappies.'

'I've never seen her before.'

'You wouldn't remember her. She died when you were one. There was a fire in the office block she worked in and their office was on the fifth floor. Nobody got out.'

'What was she called?'

'Maggie.'

I'd never heard Mum mention her, which made me wonder if my friends wouldn't talk about me either.

'I don't understand,' I said

'What?' George didn't look up from his feet.

'This.' I waved my arms around. 'I was at my own funeral this morning, for God's sake. I spent the afternoon with my grandmother who died when I was a little girl. But now she's had to leave to go back to wherever she came from because she doesn't live here any more. And I can't go with her because I have to stay and resolve my issues. I don't understand any of it.'

I looked at George. He had lifted his head and looked at me. Although it was dark, I could see the sadness in his eyes.

'I've not done a very good job, have I?' he said, looking away again. 'Maybe they were right. I'm not cut out for this.'

'No, you have, George.' I reached out and took his arm. 'You have done a great job. It's just me ... I don't understand anything.'

'What's to understand?' he asked. 'You're ...'

'Dead, I know. Thanks for reminding me.'

He let his head drop back and puffed out his cheeks, letting the breath out slowly. 'Sorry,' he said. He forced a smile and I felt sorry for him.

'It's not you.' I tried to smile back. 'I never was the top of the class. My science teacher used to have a hell of a job explaining things to me.'

I heard him laugh. 'What do you want to know?'

'Where's my gran?'

'Here,' he said and I was about to protest before he added, 'but in a different dimension.'

'What do you mean a different dimension?'

'Don't know,' he said, 'but that's how it was explained to me.' George took out a cigarette, and inhaled deeply. 'Look, I'm no scientist, so I don't understand how these things work either. All I know is that when you first come here you are met by someone.' He pointed to himself. 'That person is sent to help you.'

'Why didn't Gran greet me?'

'She's not a Greeter.'

But she knows me.'

'What difference does that make?'

'I thought you'd be met by someone who knew you.'

'Why would you think that?' He laughed as he pinched the end of his cigarette.

I wasn't sure why I had thought that… Hollywood, I guess.

'Anyway, the new arrival,' he pointed to me, 'has to stay here while they prepare to make the final journey.'

'To where?'

'The other place. During their – *your* time here you'll have the opportunity to resolve any outstanding issues.'

'What are these issues you keep going on about?'

George scratched his forehead and then the line along his head where his hair parted. 'You were taken suddenly,' he said. 'You didn't get the chance to say goodbye or finish things the way you should have. We all have outstanding issues. When yours are resolved that will be the time to move on and go to where your gran is.'

'And my son?'

'And your son.' He looked away.

'When were you going to tell me about him?'

'I wasn't. Your gran said that she should be the one to tell you.'

'My gran? When did she say that?'

'She came looking for me before you arrived. She had your son and she asked if she could be the one to tell you.'

'She had my son with her.' I stood up and started to walk. Stopping, I turned and found George's face inches from my own. He backed off. 'Why didn't she bring him with her?'

George shrugged and fell into step beside me. 'I'm sure she had her reasons.'

I grabbed hold of George's arm. 'What did he look like?' I asked.

'He looked like a baby.' My eyes implored him to tell me more. 'Blond hair,' he said, 'rosy cheeks.'

I felt torn between my two children.

I wanted to be with Naomi. I was convinced that she could sense my presence and I was desperate for her to know I hadn't abandoned her.

But then there was Matthew, the child I'd never even held.

'What will my issues be?' I asked.

'Can't say for sure,' George said as he looked at the ground. 'They're your issues.'

I felt like he was holding out on me.

'Can't you give me a clue?'

He looked up from the floor. 'Think about the bench,' he said.

'Why?'

The bench? What did he …?

'Of course,' I whispered as the penny dropped. 'Things I should have said and done.'

CHAPTER SEVENTEEN

Marc stood in front of my open wardrobe and looked inside. I stood at one shoulder and George at his other.

'Do it,' I whispered. 'It has to be done.'

With dismay, I watched him close the doors and leave the room.

'Where's he going?' I asked. 'It needs doing.'

'Does it need doing now?' George moved closer to me.

I looked into his eyes but couldn't hold the gaze. 'It needs doing.' I repeated.

'He's not ready.'

It was a couple of weeks after my funeral when Naomi went back to school. She held Marc's hand tightly as they walked together through the gates. I could see that Marc was talking to her all the time but I couldn't hear what he was saying. As they walked through the crowd everyone had a word for them.

'Good to see you back,' said one of the mothers gathered in the yard.

'If there's anything we can do,' another said to Marc.

Marc nodded his thanks and kept walking.

'These people never knew me,' I told George. 'That

one there,' I pointed to the one that had spoken first, 'has twins in Year 6. She couldn't pick me out of a police line-up.'

George laughed. 'Have you been in many police line-ups?'

'No, have you?'

'That'd be telling.'

My eyes searched out Marc and Naomi and I was pleased to see he was taking her straight inside. Part of me realised that this made her different from her classmates, who were still outside underneath grey clouds.

I ran to catch up with them.

'You all right, Naomi?' asked a blonde girl with pigtails.

'Yes, thank you,' Naomi answered, without looking up.

It broke my heart to see Naomi this way. My bright, lively, noisy daughter. Her beautiful body had been stolen by an invading mouse.

'It'll take time,' George said.

'How long?' I asked.

He shrugged and shook his head. 'Don't know.'

I watched her in silence for a few minutes.

'Will she be the same as she was?'

'No.'

I was horrified. 'What?'

'She'll never be quite the same.' I could feel George's arm brushing my shoulder. 'But eventually she'll adapt. Children are resilient.'

I wept inside for the child as lost as I was.

●◗ ●

We stood in the middle of the yard at playtime with children rushing around. But for us, there was only one child that interested us. She was easy to spot. She was the one standing alone close to the door. She was the child that watched but didn't join in.

Slowly, I moved through the crowd to my child. Her eyes moved to take in what was happening around her.

I stood beside her and looked down onto the top of her head. I noticed that her parting was crooked. I gave a half laugh at how unimportant that sort of thing was. I crouched until I was on a level with her.

I had to lean against the rough brick wall to steady myself. I could feel myself shaking and my breathing was short and shallow. There was so much I wanted to say but I didn't know where to start. I didn't even know if she would be able to hear me. George had told me that seeing a dead person was one thing, hearing was something totally different. The two things didn't automatically go together.

All I knew was that I had to try.

I opened my mouth and the words came slowly. 'Naomi,' I said. 'I'm sorry. I didn't want to leave you but I had no choice. And I haven't really left, because I'm still here. I can still see you every day like I always did. I can still love you.' I felt tears forming. 'I love you, Naomi. I love you now and I'll love you forever. And I know you will always love me. Just because we live in different places won't stop me from being your mummy.'

It felt good to talk to my daughter even if it was one-sided. I had no way of knowing if it was helping her but I knew it was helping me. I paused to sniff back the tears and gather my racing thoughts. 'I need you to do something for me, Naomi,' I told her. 'I need you to be a big girl for me. I need you to look after Daddy for me.'

Naomi's head moved and I followed her gaze. She was looking at a group of girls who were talking to each other. I recognised one of them as Amanda, who had been to our house for tea a few times. Amanda was one of Naomi's best friends, or at least she had been a few weeks ago.

'Why don't you go and talk to Amanda?' I suggested, but Naomi didn't move. 'It's all right, darling. It's all right for you to want to play with your friends.'

But it was too late and, at the sound of the bell, children formed lines in front of the door. Naomi started to make her way to the back of the line along with her classmates. Not quite at the back of the line was a ginger boy and he took a step back to make room for Naomi. Naomi seemed surprised and she eyed him suspiciously. Cautiously, she moved into the space and I saw her mouth the word 'Thanks.'

I too thanked the boy.

'She couldn't hear me, could she?' I said sadly as the door to the school closed behind the last of the children.

George moved his head from side to side in a non-committal motion.

'But I thought ... She could see me ...' I said as we walked out of the school gate.

He didn't say that he'd warned me this might happen. Instead, he asked. 'Did you never ignore your mother when you were mad at her?'

Dad had gone back to work the day after my funeral. 'No point hanging around,' he'd said. 'Moping won't bring her back.'

If it could have brought me back my mother would have resurrected me all by herself. She didn't have a job to take her mind off her loss nor did she have any close friends to comfort her. My mother just had her thoughts.

George grudgingly told me it had been over a month since my funeral and I hadn't seen my mother in almost that long. I couldn't believe what I was seeing now.

She sat on the edge of the sofa with a china cup and

saucer balancing on her knee. Periodically, she lifted the cup to her mouth and took a sip.

I sat on the arm of the chair to the right of my mother. George sat on the seat of the same chair. We watched in silence. She looked straight ahead and continued to lift the cup to her mouth long after it was empty.

'Were you close?' George asked.

I turned to him. 'She's my mother.'

George smiled in that way that I was becoming accustomed to. 'That's not what I asked.'

'I'm an only child,' I said.

'Were there never any other children?'

'No,' I looked at my mother as I spoke. 'She had a difficult pregnancy. After I was born the doctors advised that she shouldn't put herself through it again.'

'Had she wanted more?'

I shrugged my shoulders. 'Don't know. I think she would have liked a son but accepted it wasn't to be. She said it was God's decision. I think she thought herself lucky to have any children at all.'

'Which parent were you closer to?'

'Dad,' I said without hesitation.

'Often the way.'

'But I loved her,' I said defiantly. 'I do love her.'

'But …?'

I turned from my mother to George briefly before turning back. 'She had a hard time accepting that I was grown up,' I said. 'There are still days when she treats me like a five-year-old. "Have you done this, Ellen? Why have you done that, Ellen?"' I spoke without taking my eyes off her. 'She doesn't come to my house often but when she does I can feel the scrutiny. She's looking for specks of dirt on the carpet or a shelf I haven't dusted. If I make her a cup of tea she'll hint that it should have been brewed longer. The last time they came to my house for a meal she commented on everything I had made. Too much pepper in the soup, not enough salt in the potatoes ...' I looked at my hands. There was a lump in my throat as I realised I had been talking in the present tense. That was behind me now. 'It all seems so pointless now.'

George didn't let me dwell. 'Do you think she resented the relationship you had with your father?'

'Yes.' Once again there was no hesitation.

I could have spoken about my relationship with my mother for hours but, fortunately for George, the sound of a knock at the door grabbed my attention. My mother looked at her wrist for a watch that wasn't there. She put the long-empty cup on the table and moved to answer the knock.

'How old is she?' George asked.

'Not as old as you'd think,' I replied, shocked by how slowly she moved.

We heard the front door open.

'Just thought I'd pop in to see how you are.' It was a woman's voice.

'How'd you expect?' my mother asked sourly.

The door closed with a firmness I doubted was necessary.

'It'll take time, Peg,' the woman said as she followed my mother into the room.

'It's my aunt Lizzie,' I told George. 'Mum's sister.'

George nodded and I realised there had been no need for an introduction.

'Want a cup of tea?'

I was pleased to see that despite everything, my mother had not lost her manners. Her sister nodded and Mum went towards the kitchen, taking her used crockery with her.

Once Mum had gone, Aunt Lizzie looked around the

122

room. I did the same and we took in its disarray together. Lizzie lifted some magazines from the seat of the chair near where my mother had been sitting. She brushed the seat and sat down. I'd never seen my aunt look so nervous and I watched her fidget in her seat.

'Do you need a hand?' she called into the kitchen.

There was no response and she remained seated.

'Are they close?' George leaned over and whispered to my ear.

'Not really,' I whispered back.

Eventually, Mum came back carrying a tray, which she set down on the coffee table. She handed a cup and saucer to her sister and offered a plate of biscuits which were declined.

The women sat in silence.

'Have you been out yet?' Lizzie asked.

'I went to the funeral.' The frown on Mum's face was set like concrete.

'I meant since then.' Lizzie's was softer.

'Haven't needed to.'

There was silence again.

'Brian's gone back to work?' Aunt Lizzie was working hard at starting a conversation.

'Yes.' Mum was staring into her cup. 'He said he might as well.' She paused. 'He behaves like normal. He goes to work, he comes home. It's as if everything is the way it was before.'

My aunt was staring at the floor. 'I'm sorry, Peg,' Lizzie said, putting her cup and saucer down, 'but you can't go on like this. You've got to pull yourself together.' My mother didn't respond. She didn't shift her gaze or open her mouth. 'You're not doing yourself any good staying in the house brooding all day.' Lizzie leaned forward as she spoke.

'Lost many children, have you?'

I was horrified, but Lizzie was controlled.

'You know I have.'

They locked eyes for what seemed like minutes.

'A miscarriage isn't the same.' It seemed like Mum was spitting the words.

'It was my child, Peg.' The calmness in my aunt's voice couldn't hide her anger. 'They were my children ... all five of them.'

'But you never knew them.' I was appalled by my mother. I knew she was grieving but I could find no excuse for the words she was saying.

'So what you never know you never miss, Peg?' My aunt struggled to hold onto her composure.

'That's not what I meant.' Mum put her cup down, her hand shaking. 'She was all I had ... and now she's gone.'

I noticed the compassion in my aunt's eyes as she looked at her sister. 'You've still got your memories.'

'I don't want my memories.' We were all surprised to hear my mother scream. 'I want *her* ... I want my baby back.' She put her hand to her mouth to stifle a sob.

They didn't speak or look at each other for a long time. Eventually, it was my mother who spoke.

'How could you do it, Lizzie?'

'Do what?'

'Keep trying again and again.'

'I wanted a child.'

'But how could you put yourself through it knowing what had happened before?'

'I wanted a child,' she repeated.

Silence again.

'You come to terms with it,' Lizzie said, her voice quiet and slow. 'You realise that things don't always turn out the way you want them to. You have to move on.' She looked at my mother. 'Life has to go on, Peg.'

'Why?'

'Because you're alive.'

'Ellen's not.' The sobs that racked my mother's body were painful to watch. She shook with each one.

'Mum, don't cry,' I said, my hand outstretched to her.

'She needs to.' I felt George's arm around my shoulder and I leaned into him. I was glad he was there.

Aunt Lizzie knelt in front of my mother. Their hands were joined together, knuckles white with the force of their grasp.

'I miss her so much,' Mum sobbed.

'I know you do, Peg.' Lizzie smoothed her sister's hair. 'But you'll see her again one day.'

My mother stopped crying and stared at her sister with a look that scared me. 'Don't say that,' she said.

'Say what?'

'That I'll see her again.' She was breathing heavily. 'If I thought that by being dead I'd see her again I'd go in that kitchen and slit my throat with the bread knife.'

'Don't you dare say that.' Lizzie seemed shocked by Mum's outburst.

'I mean it, Lizzie.' She pulled her hands free. 'Ellen always said that once you were gone you were gone and she was right.'

'You're wrong.'

'I'm not. She's gone.'

'But only from this world.'

Mum pushed herself away from her sister. 'What other world is there?'

'This one, Mum.' I moved towards her. 'There's this one.' But of course, she could not hear me.

'I get great comfort from knowing that my babies are in a better place,' Lizzie said as she pushed herself to her feet.

'Well, I get no comfort from knowing my baby is dead.'

My aunt looked at her sister with sad eyes.

'How's Naomi?' she asked.

Mum shrugged. 'All right, I think. Marc was talking about taking her back to school this week.'

'That's good.'

'Why?'

'It'll do her good to get back into a routine.'

'Will it?'

'Yes.' Lizzie was losing patience.

Mum fell into the chastised younger sister mode.

'Will it help her to forget her mummy?'

'Of course it won't,' Lizzie dismissed. She tried to reach out to her sister again but Mum pulled away. 'Naomi's never going to forget Ellen, Marc won't let her.'

'Won't he?'

I looked at George. He shook his head but I noticed his shoulders shrugged at the same time.

'No, he won't. He loved Ellen very much and she loved him,' Aunt Lizzie insisted. I realised I was nodding. 'There is no way he'll let that child forget her mother.'

'But will he remember her mother?'

'Every time he looks at his daughter.'

126

CHAPTER EIGHTEEN

Marc managed to clear my wardrobe at the second attempt. I watched him take each item from its hanger and fold it before placing it into the black bag sitting on the bed. Each one was put carefully on top of the last one. Marc worked methodically and silently.

He had taken the day off work and set to his task as soon as he got back from taking Naomi to school.

He worked his way from left to right, emptying each hanger in turn.

Occasionally he would hold a garment for a moment longer than necessary, as if what he was holding had some significance. I didn't look at what he was holding because I couldn't tear my eyes away from his face.

Eventually, all the hangers were empty and Marc closed the doors, pushing them into place with a finality that cut me like a knife.

He fastened the top of the bag into a double knot before gently lifting it to the floor.

He ripped another bag from the roll and opened it wide at the neck. He snapped it like a windsock. He moved to the set of drawers beside the window and opened the top one. My underwear lay just as it had on the morning I died.

Marc had his back to me. He started to shake, slightly at first but then more vigorously. I realised he was crying

127

and I felt his pain as if it were my own. He reached into the drawer and took out a handful contents. He lifted them to his face and held them there as he sobbed. He took a deep breath before stuffing them into the black bag he held in his other hand. There was no care in the way he stuffed the contents of the drawer into the bag. He bundled them in and sobbed all the time.

'I'm sorry, Ellen,' he said through sobs as he quickly tied a single knot and threw the second bag to where he had placed the first one so carefully.

Marc slowly closed the drawer he had just emptied. He lowered his head as his hand rested on the handle of my secret drawer, the place I'd kept all of those special little things that were precious to me.

Slowly, Marc pulled and my secrets were revealed.

He pulled the drawer out completely and carried it to the bed as if his legs were no longer able to support his weight.

The first thing Marc took was the plastic wristband Naomi had worn for the two days she was in hospital after she was born. Her name, her date of birth, and her weight were all recorded in faded ink. Marc twisted it in his fingers and put it back. The next thing he took out was a beige vellum envelope. He opened it and pulled out one of our wedding invitations. When he opened the card a pressed flower fell out. It was all that remained of the bouquet of freesias and lilies I had carried as I walked down the aisle. Marc read the details of that day.

'Mr and Mrs Brian Price have the pleasure of inviting you to join them in celebrating the wedding of their only daughter Ellen to Marc Philip Reed at St Oswald's Church, Cavendish Street on 2nd October at 3pm. RSVP'

I didn't need to see the words to know them. They would be with me forever.

He put the card and flower back into the envelope and

returned it to the drawer.

He did a similar thing with everything else in my drawer. He took it out and looked at it before putting it back. When everything had been examined he carried the drawer back to where he had taken it from and slid it back along the rollers.

Once it was closed he patted it and turned to the bags on the floor. He lifted one in each hand and carried them out of the room. A couple of minutes later we heard the front door open and we heard Marc start the car and pull away.

I stood in the room I had once shared with the man I loved and, for the first time, I truly felt like I was dead.

●◆●

I sat on the swing and gently moved it to and fro. George was balanced in the middle of the see-saw. Dusk was falling and children had long since deserted the playground.

'Will he forget me?' I asked.

'Wouldn't have thought so.' He shuffled to get a better position. 'But he'll move on.'

'Move on?'

'Yeah, you know, get on with his life.'

'Will he?'

'Course he will.'

'When?'

'When he's ready.' I could feel George watching me. 'Life has to go on,' he said gently.

'I know,' I whispered.

I started to work the swing and it moved higher and higher. I felt the cold night air flow through my hair.

I still loved Marc, and I wanted him to be happy. But the thought of him with another woman ... I closed my eyes and forced the image away.

It was a long time before the swing came to a stop, and that meant a lot of time to think. George was still balanced on the see-saw with his head down. He looked up as I stopped.

'Can I ask you something, George?'

'Yes.'

'What …?' I couldn't ask because I didn't know what it was I wanted answering.

'He'll always love you.'

'Will he?' I rested my head against the chain I was holding.

'Yeah.' George jumped down and straightened the collar of his jacket. 'If he loved you when you died he'll love you forever.'

'How can you know that?' I asked as he walked towards me.

'It's a proven fact … like Pythagoras.'

'Then how can he move on?'

George settled himself onto the swing by my side. He used his feet to sway gently.

'He has to … for his own sanity, he has to.' He watched his feet for a moment then, stopping the movement of the swing, he concentrated on me. 'Marc is a young man with a long life ahead of him. Like anybody else he has needs.'

'Needs?' I wasn't sure I wanted to think about that.

I could just about make out George's smile in the fading light.

'Marc might need a hobby,' George suggested. 'Look,' he said, swinging to me and taking hold of my hand. 'Marianne was married within a year of my death.' He moved his head to the left until it almost touched his shoulder. 'She needed a man in her life.' He looked up to the sky as if he was looking towards another place. 'Marianne wasn't the type of woman who could live without a man.' George smiled and so did I.

'How did you feel?' I asked

'How could I feel?' He failed to hide the sadness from his voice. 'I was dead and she wasn't. She had a life to lead and there were things she needed to help her do that. If I'm being honest, it hurt. Of course it did. How could she get over me so quickly? My mum went mad when she found out Marianne was seeing another bloke. "How can you do it?" she said, "with my son still warm in his grave." I suppose that's how I felt too.'

I opened my mouth to ask one of the many questions I had but George hadn't finished. 'But Marianne couldn't cope on her own ... She needed a man to support her ... She needed a man to love her.' He closed his eyes. 'I still loved her but I couldn't hold her in the night when she was scared. The love of a dead man was no good to her.' He started to inch his swing forward and back and I sensed he was coming to the end of his speech. 'She may not have loved me last,' he said moving the swing further with each motion, 'but she loved me longer.'

'Is she still alive?' I asked after a few seconds.

'She's like us,' he said over his shoulder.

'And her second husband?'

'He's here too ... and her third and her fourth.' My eyes and mouth were open wide but George just laughed. 'I told you she wasn't the kind of woman who could live without a man.'

'But who is she with now?' I asked.

'All of us.'

'What?'

George laughed as he worked the swing. 'Things are different here.'

He was right. I knew he was right. But dealing with it was hard. I knew that Marc had to move on; like George said, Marc was a young man. It was just the thought of him with another woman in his arms or worse, his bed.

I felt George's swing slowing by my side and after scraping his feet along the ground several times it stopped.

He looked at me and smiled. 'No-one ever said being dead was easy,' he said.

I smiled too.

CHAPTER NINETEEN

Marc emptied the contents of the saucepan onto the plate. He gave it a shake to spread everything evenly before setting it down in front of our daughter.

'Eat up,' he encouraged. 'They're your favourite.'

This was the third time this week I'd seen Marc give Naomi Spaghetti Hoops.

'I'm not hungry,' she said.

'You must be hungry,' he said, pushing the plate towards her. 'You're always hungry.'

'I'm not today.'

'Why not?'

She shrugged her little shoulders.

'That's not an answer.'

She shrugged them again.

'Naomi.' Marc had allowed the merest hint of anger to form in his voice.

'I don't like them.' Naomi pushed the plate away and spoke with her chin on her chest.

'They're your favourite,' he said again but something pitiful had replaced the anger.

'Not any more,' Naomi said defiantly.

'Why?' Marc asked.

Naomi caught four or five hoops on one of the prongs of her fork. She lifted and angled it so the hoops fell off.

She carefully placed her fork on the edge of her plate. 'Because you don't make them like Mummy did.' And with that, she jumped from her chair and ran from the room.

I started to run after her but a noise from Marc stopped me.

I turned and watched as Marc slid down the wall until he was on the floor with his back resting against the cupboard. I half expected to see him adopt the foetal position, but he remained upright. He stared at the floor in front of his feet, the only movement an occasional twitch of his cheek. After a minute the rate of his breathing increased and he started to shake. After another minute his body racked with sobs and tears flowed down his cheeks.

'Had to come,' George's voice came from close to my ear.

'I've never seen him like this,' I said from behind hands that were now inches from my mouth.

'He's never had to grieve the loss of a wife before.'

'But it's been weeks since I died.'

'He's been bottling this up for weeks.'

I dropped to my knees in front of Marc.

'Why did you leave me, Ellen?' he asked, unknowingly looking straight into my eyes.

'It wasn't my fault.' I said.

'Why?' he asked again

'I don't know.'

'I miss you so much,' he whispered. 'I need you. I can't do this by myself.'

Eventually the sobs stopped but not the tears. They flowed down his cheeks and off the end of his chin.

'I don't know what to do,' he said. I winced as I watched him move his head forward and bang it on the cupboard door. 'I don't know how to do a plait in her hair. I don't know how to iron the pleats in her school skirt and

I can't make Spaghetti Hoops taste the way that you did. They come out of a tin, for God's sake.'

He allowed his head to rest on the cupboard door and closed his eyes.

The hands on the wall clock moved slowly. Marc sat on the kitchen floor for thirty minutes without moving or making a sound.

All I could do was watch.

Day became night and the only light came from the security lamp outside the back door, which cast an eerie glow over the kitchen. Naomi opened the door and stood in silence. Marc didn't seem to notice her silhouetted in the doorway. She moved towards her father. And even in the half-light I could see she had been crying.

She stood beside Marc's outstretched legs and looked at him. At last he opened his eyes. The pain that they shared was visible. He held out his arms and she joined him on the floor. She sat on his thighs and rested her head on his chest.

'I miss her,' she said.

'I know, sweetheart,' Marc whispered. 'I miss her too.'

'Why did she go?'

'I don't know.' He kissed the top of her head. 'But I know she didn't want to go. She didn't want to leave us.'

'I'm sorry I didn't eat the sketti hoops, Daddy.'

'That's all right.' He brushed a stray hair from her face. 'But it's spaghetti.'

'Sketti.'

'Spag ... hetti.' He separated the word out.

'Mummy let me call it sketti.'

I saw Marc's chest rise and fall as he controlled his breathing. He forced a smile onto his face. 'Sketti it is, then.' He rested the side of his face on her head and the tears in his eyes glistened in the darkness.

'Where's Mummy now?' Naomi drew circles on the table as she asked.

George and I watched Marc as he examined the plate he was washing in minute detail. He placed it carefully back in the frothy water, plucked a tea towel from where it sat on the bench, and dried his hands. He turned slowly and walked the three steps to the table.

He pulled out a chair and sat opposite Naomi. We watched him rest his elbows on the table and temple his hands in front of his face.

Even though I knew it was impossible, I swear I could feel my heart pounding in my chest. I was anxious to know how Marc was going to answer her. We had discussed how we would answer things like 'where do babies come from?' but not 'where's Mummy now she's dead?'

As was his way, Marc was considering his answer carefully.

'She's in here,' he said, tapping his chest.

'Good answer,' George muttered.

'How can she be in your chest?'

'Not my chest, darling.' Marc smiled as he spoke. 'In my heart. And not just in my heart, in your heart too.'

'How can she live in my heart?'

'As long as you remember her, she's alive in there.'

Naomi nodded her head in a very grown-up way and then announced. 'She lives here too.'

'I knew she'd seen me.' I whispered in George's direction, clapping my hands together in excitement.

'I saw her,' she elaborated.

'Told you,' I shouted, punching George just below the shoulder. He rubbed the spot and pulled a face.

In my excitement I hadn't noticed that Naomi had left

her seat and the room.

Once more, Marc's elbows were on the table and his head was buried deep into his hands

'I did see her, Jessie.' Naomi sat on her bed and cradled her doll in her arms. She stroked the doll's blonde curls with her fingers. 'I did see her,' she insisted. 'I'm not lying.'

It had been hours since Marc had turned off the lights and retired to our bedroom. I wondered if he was asleep. George and I sat in the living room, the one Marc and I had finished decorating just a few weeks before the accident. I admired the décor I had helped to choose.

'Why, George?'

'Why what?'

'Why me?'

'Why not you?'

There was no answer. I pursed my lips and thought for a moment.

'I didn't want to die.'

'Yeah, I know. Most people don't.'

'You don't seem to mind.'

He pondered for a moment, resting his head on the sofa. 'I've got used to it,' he said, 'but that doesn't mean I enjoy it. Anyway, the world is different place now from when I was alive. I don't know how I'd have fit.'

'How long have you been here, George?'

'You mean dead?'

'I suppose so.'

'Don't know. A long time.' He lifted his head and looked around. 'Nice room,' he said, seamlessly changing the subject.

'Thanks.' I smiled with pride. 'I picked the colour.'

'Oh.' He looked around. 'What do we call that colour?'

'Pistachio.'

'OK,' he said, nodding his head slowly.

'It's a nut,' I explained.

'Really?'

'What? You don't know pistachios?'

'Never heard of them.'

'George,' I pushed him playfully. 'You've been here longer than I thought.'

'Clearly.'

Dawn was almost upon us and we were still sat in the pistachio room. There was nowhere else to go and besides, this was my home. I sat on the end of my sofa with my legs curled under me. George and I had been silent for most of the night. I was going over the evening's events again and again.

'I knew Naomi had seen me.' I broke the silence.

'At last,' he sighed. 'I thought you'd never mention it.' He shuffled in his seat until he was facing me. I twisted and we sat facing each other.

'What does it mean?'

'What does what mean?'

'Do you ever answer a question with anything other than a question?'

'Rarely, but in this case I couldn't if I wanted to. I don't know what you mean.'

'What does it mean that Naomi saw me?'

'It means just that.'

'What?'

'That she saw you.'

'But why did she?'

138

George coughed. 'You want the honest answer?'

'Of course,' I said eager for the revelation.

'I don't know,' he said.

'What?'

'I don't know.'

'You must.'

'Why must I?'

'Because you must.'

He scratched his head.

'But I don't,' he said slowly. 'I don't know why it happens, just that sometimes it does. It's an intermittent thing. It doesn't happen for everyone and, like I told you, seeing and hearing are two different things. Even though she's seen you doesn't mean she'll ever be able to hear you.' He paused a second. 'And I should warn you it won't last forever.'

'Why not?'

'Because you won't be here forever.'

'Where will I be?'

George sighed heavily like a teacher losing patience with a child that doesn't listen. 'The other dimension.'

'Where Gran lives?'

'Yes.'

'Why does Matthew live there?'

George looked puzzled – or was he just bored? 'Your son has no issues to be resolved.'

I nodded. How could he have any issues when he had never been born? He hadn't had to wait in this holding place. George and I reverted back to the silence we had shared for most of the night.

I rested my head on the back of the sofa and looked at the ceiling while George surveyed the entire room.

'Did you really choose this colour?' he asked.

'Yes,' I said indignantly. 'Why?'

'Is this how you imagined it would look?'

I did as George was doing. By the time my eyes were resting on the third pistachio-coloured wall I could see what George meant and I laughed out loud.

'What are you laughing at, Mummy?'

CHAPTER TWENTY

Naomi stood in the doorway with one small hand holding onto the door handle, the other one clutching the teddy bear that dangled by her side. The light behind her formed a halo around her body.

'Naomi,' I finally managed to say.

'I told Daddy I'd seen you.' She had moved from the doorway to stand in front of me. Her eyes flitted over me. 'I was right.'

'Oh ...' I didn't know what to say. I turned to George for inspiration but there was none forthcoming.

'Who's he?' Naomi asked. It hadn't occurred to me that she could see both of us.

'He ...' I finally had the chance to speak to my child and no words would form.

'I'm George.' He waved the fingers of his right hand.

'Hello, George, I'm Naomi. I'm very pleased to meet you.'

I felt great pride in Naomi's politeness.

'I've heard a lot about you,' he said. 'I'm pleased that we finally get a chance to talk.'

'Are you Mummy's friend?' she asked in a very manner of fact sort of way.

'Well, I don't know if ...'

'Yes,' I interrupted. 'George is my friend.'

Naomi climbed up onto the sofa and sat in between us.

'What were you laughing about?' she asked.

'We were laughing,' I said the words slowly, trying to remember, 'about the wallpaper.'

She looked around and at each of us in turn. Her girly giggles were music to my ears.

'It looks like mushy peas,' Naomi said through her laughter.

'It looks like frogs,' George joined in.

'Hey,' I said defensively.' I picked that colour.' I smiled at the two happy faces then admitted, 'You're right it's awful. I can't imagine why Daddy put it on the walls.'

Naomi suddenly became more serious. 'Daddy said you lived in Heaven now,' she said.

'I know, sweetheart, I heard him.'

'Do you?'

'Do I what?'

'Live in Heaven.'

I looked at George and found he was looking at the floor. 'No, I don't.'

'Were you bad?'

'I don't understand, darling,' I said. 'What do you mean?'

'I mean, were you bad and that's why you don't live in Heaven?'

The idea surprised me. 'I don't know,' I looked at George again and this time he was looking at me. 'Was I bad, George?'

His body shook as he chuckled. 'No, you weren't bad.'

'So why isn't Mummy in Heaven?'

He scratched his head. 'That's a very grown-up question for a young lady.' He shuffled forward in his seat until his head was close to hers. 'It's just that your mummy needs to do some things before she goes to Heaven.'

'Like what?'

'Just things,' he smiled and tilted his head to one side.

'Oh.' Naomi accepted the answer with a nod.

The sound of buzzing made the three of us look towards the ceiling. The alarm clock was louder these days, probably because Marc had trouble rousing himself in the morning.

'Daddy's up,' Naomi said excitedly. 'I'll go and get him.' She started to climb from the perch on which she sat.

I put my hand out. 'No, darling.'

'Why?' she asked, furrowing her brow.

I didn't have to answer because Marc, realising his daughter wasn't where she should have been, had come to look for her. He appeared at the still-open doorway, tying the belt of his robe and running his hand through his hair.

'What are you doing up?' he asked in a sleepy voice.

She twisted her face to look at him and I noticed the ever so slight nod of her head towards where I sat.

'Come on, let's make breakfast.' He was already making his way to the kitchen.

She turned back to me. 'Daddy can't see you, can he, Mummy?'

'How come, Naomi can see me but Marc can't?' I asked the words slowly.

George shrugged slightly, which he did a lot. 'I don't know,' he said. He did that a lot too.

CHAPTER TWENTY-ONE

'Where've you been?'

It had been almost a week since Naomi had found George and me in the living room.

'Here and there.'

'I thought you'd be here when I got home from school,' she said.

'I'm sorry, darling,' I said softly. 'I wanted to be.'

'Then why weren't you?' She was sitting on the window seat that Marc had built for her last summer. She looked through the window onto the garden. I squirmed on the edge of the bed.

'I had to be somewhere else.'

'Where?'

I know had I still been alive I would have scolded Naomi for speaking to me so rudely. The reality of my situation stopped me from doing so.

* * *

'It's so hard,' I said, gazing above at the night sky. Thousands of stars glittered through the dark blanket.

'Yes,' George agreed, 'it's almost impossible.'

'What should I do?'

'Well, the way I do it is to lie on my back, start at the left, and work my way over to the right.'

'What?' I looked at him and found he had his head

thrown up. He moved it from side to side before lowering it. 'Causes a stiff neck otherwise.'

'What are you talking about? Have you replaced the nicotine in that cigarette with something stronger?'

'You said it was hard, I agreed and was just giving you the benefit of my experience.'

'Experience at what, exactly?'

George looked puzzled. 'Counting stars.'

'Why would I want to count stars? It's impossible.'

'Almost impossible. You need a clear night and a lot of patience.'

I gave a laugh.

'When I said it was hard I was talking about Naomi.'

'But you were looking at the stars.'

'Because she's not here.' I said as if I was talking to a half-wit.

George put his cigarette to his mouth and inhaled. 'I think it might be easier to count the stars.'

He started to walk down the deserted street and I followed closely. It didn't matter which world I was in, I was still afraid of being alone at night.

'She's never spoken to me the way she did earlier.' I was slightly out of breath as I tried to keep up with him.

'So why did you let her?'

'What else could I do?'

'What would you have done before?' He gave me a sideways glance.

'I'd have sent her to her room to think about what she'd said. Why, what would you have done?'

'Doesn't matter. It's not up to me, she's not my daughter.'

'Well, I couldn't send her to her room, could I?' I sounded defensive without realising it.

'No, you couldn't,' he said slowly. 'Not as she was already in her room.' He tried to make a joke but I wasn't

146

in the mood. His mood changed too. 'But you could have done something else.'

'Like what?' I asked sharply.

'She still needs discipline.'

'How exactly would I do that?'

George stopped walking and turned so suddenly that I almost bumped into him. 'You're the parent. You know what would affect her.'

'But I don't,' I said.

'Alright,' George said, in that patient way your grandfather did when he was trying to explain what half a crown was. 'What used to work won't work now. You can't tell Naomi to go to her room because you can't make her. You have to think of the one thing that will make her stop and think.'

'But I don't know what that is.'

'Yes, you do.' The left half of his mouth curled in a strange half smile. I shook my head. 'Tell her you won't come to see her ever again.'

'I couldn't do that.' He held up the little finger on his right hand and moved it in small circles. 'What's that supposed to mean?'

'This, Ellen,' he exaggerated the circles, 'is what Naomi is doing.'

'No, she's not,' I was indignant.

'She knows your weak spot,'

'What weak spot?'

'All children know their parents' weak spots.'

'But I'm dead.'

'And yet she can still hurt you.' He walked away and I had to run to catch up.

We walked in silence.

I hadn't liked the way Naomi had spoken to me and, yes, she had hurt my feelings. I didn't want that behaviour to become a habit for her. But how could I punish a child

147

who had suffered so much already?

It was the first time I'd seen where Marc worked.
Obviously I'd seen the building, but Marc's office was on
the second floor and not visible from where I parked the
car on the rare occasions I had picked him up.

Marc's office was open plan and he shared it with
three other people.

I could see Marc at the desk in the back corner of the
room. His eyes were fixed on the computer screen in front
of him and I could hear fingers tapping a keyboard.
Stephen, who had started working for the company on the
same day Marc had, sat at the desk to the front of Marc
and seemed to be occupied in a similar manner. The desk
to Marc's right was empty but two women stood by the
other, looking out of the window.

George looked around the room like a policeman
looking for a clue.

'What does he do?' George asked.

'Don't know,' I admitted. 'Something with computers
and numbers.'

'Do you know these people?'

'I know Stephen. We sat with him and his wife at the
Christmas party last year. One of those girls is Diane and
the other one is Rosie. I've heard Marc mention them but
I've never met them.'

'What? They don't like Christmas parties?'

I laughed. 'According to Marc they hadn't fancied
spending an evening with their middle-aged colleagues
and their middle-aged spouses.'

'But you're not middle-aged?'

'It's all relative, I suppose.'

As the two women moved to their desks I noticed that
neither of them could be over twenty-five. The brunette

148

looked the older of the two. She sat sideways to her desk and pretended to be looking through a stack of papers but I saw she was really giving all of her attention to my husband.

'Shouldn't she be working?'

I wondered if I sounded as catty as I felt.

'Who?' George was admiring the younger woman and had to force his eyes away from her.

'Her.'

'She is,' he said.

'No, she's not,' I scoffed. 'She might think it looks like she's reading something but she's looking at Marc.' The sound of jealousy in my voice surprised me but if George noticed he didn't mention it.

I moved my eyes from her to Marc, who seemed oblivious to the scrutiny he was under. Maybe he did feel her eyes on him because he looked in her direction. She looked away quickly and I detected a hint of a smile on her lips as she shared a look with the blonde.

Stephen swivelled his chair and looked towards the brunette's desk. 'Any chance of that report?' he asked.

'Keep you hair on, Stevie.' She laughed at her own joke.

Stephen looked bored in a 'haven't heard that said to a bald bloke before' sort of way. 'I need it by lunch time, Rosie.'

So she was Rosie.

George and I sat on Naomi's bed and waited for her to come home from school. I had thought about what George had said and he was right. I might be dead, but I was still Naomi's mother.

We didn't have to wait long before we heard the sound of voices. The closing of the front door was quickly followed by Naomi's footsteps climbing the stairs.

I shuffled nervously and waited for my daughter to come in. She did, but not before I heard her shout, 'Can I have some sketti?' to Nancy, who would be going into the kitchen to prepare Naomi some food. Nancy was the sixteen-year-old daughter of our next-door neighbour. Marc had hired her to pick Naomi up from school and look after her until he got home. She had apparently worked out that the secret to making Spaghetti Hoops taste the way Naomi liked them was to add a handful of grated cheese.

Naomi came in swinging her school bag. Her surprise at seeing us was obvious and she dropped her bag on the floor. The look was replaced by a smile and she ran the short distance between us.

'Mummy, where've you been?' she asked. 'I thought you weren't coming back.'

I glanced at George and he threw me the faintest of smiles.

'You didn't seem too pleased to see me last time we were here.' She looked puzzled. 'You sat looking out of the window,' I reminded her.

She lowered her head and looked at her hands. 'I didn't.'

'Yes, you did, Naomi,' I said quietly. 'And I think you know that you did.'

'I'm sorry,' she whispered.

'You hurt me very much,' I told her.

'But you hurt me too,' she said quietly.

'How?' I asked.

She paused and I could tell that she was thinking of what to say.

'You went away,' she whispered.

'I didn't.' Now it was my time for denial.

'You did, Mummy,' she insisted. 'You went away and

150

then you came back and I thought you'd come back for ever.' Her eyes were huge as they looked into mine. 'Then you went away again.'

I could feel tears forming behind my eyes. 'I didn't want to go away, Naomi.' I said defensively.

'But you did.'

'I know I did but it wasn't my fault.'

Naomi screwed up her nose in the way that she always did when she was thinking.

'Why didn't you take me with you?' she asked.

'I couldn't,' I said lamely.

There was more silence.

'It was horrible.' Naomi's voice was barely audible. She held her head down as if it were too heavy for her neck.

'What was?' I coaxed.

She lifted her head slowly until our eyes were joined once more. 'The car came straight at us,' she said slowly. 'It didn't stop like it was supposed to. He was driving too fast.' Her words came slowly and her eyes looked at a point somewhere over my shoulder. 'Then he hit us.' The tempo of her speech increased. 'I pulled my legs up because I thought that he was going to hit them ... but he didn't, he just hit you.' Her eyes were moist as they looked into mine. 'He hit you, Mummy. You were bleeding. I shouted at you. I shouted "wake up" but you didn't.'

I didn't know if the tears I was wiping away were real or not but I wiped them anyway.

'And then I heard you shouting my name,' Naomi continued, her words slower now. 'I didn't understand because you were asleep and you were bleeding but I could hear you shouting.' Her eyes flitted from me to George and back again. 'And then I saw you standing with him.' It sounded like she was accusing George of stealing me.

'George came to look after me,' I explained.

'And I knew you were dead,' she said.

'That's why you couldn't go with your mummy,' George intervened. 'It wasn't your time.'

'Why was it Mummy's time?'

'I don't know. We don't make those decisions.'

'Who does?'

'There's a man in Heaven who makes those decisions.'

'Do you mean God?' she asked eagerly.

George laughed. 'Yeah, I think that's what they call him.'

'Then I hate Him.'

George stopped laughing.

CHAPTER TWENTY-TWO

I'd half expected to see my mum in the kitchen making my dad's tea. In all the years they'd been married, they had always eaten within five minutes of my dad getting home from work. I checked the clock and saw that dad was due home in less than half an hour and yet the kitchen was empty.

We found my mother in the living room. I barely recognised her. She looked much worse than the last time I had seen her.

One of the things about Mum that used to make me laugh was that she always wore make-up. She had always got up early to 'put her face on'. I had rarely seen her in her natural state before. She looked like an old woman, years older than she actually was.

Her clothes were equally shocking. I would never have imagined that my mother even owned a pair of jogging trousers.

'My God, what's wrong?' I realised how stupid the question was before I had finished asking it.

My mother was one of the old breed. In the house, my mother wore a pink polyester housecoat over a floral dress and fluffy mules on her feet. It didn't matter if she was only going to clean the toilet, she always wore those clothes and a full face of make-up. So who was this woman before me wearing a pair of grey jogging trousers with a baggy T-shirt hanging loose over the top of them?

And she was watching television. My mother never watched television during the day. Even when I was a child, the television was never switched on before six o'clock when she and Dad would watch the news. I was the only kid in my class who didn't watch *Blue Peter* and didn't understand the fuss when Shep died.

It was hard to tell if Mum was actually watching the programme or if she was just staring at the box. On the screen was one of those American shows where a mother introduces the child from hell who goes backstage to return through a mist a totally changed person.

'What does it matter what she wears, you stupid cow?' my mother suddenly shouted. Apparently, she was watching it. 'So what if she's the size of a house and dresses like a tart? What does it matter?' she screamed. 'At least she's alive.' Tears were rolling down her cheeks and she used the heel of her hand to scrub them away. She had leaned forward to spit the words but then she flopped back in her seat as if all of her energy was used.

'What's wrong with her?' I asked, viewing from a safe distance. George said nothing as I circled my mother slowly, taking her in from all angles.

'Mum,' I said cautiously. 'Mum.'

'You silly cow.'

I was shocked by her outburst. I couldn't take my eyes from her even though what I saw distressed me.

'Shouldn't you be making Dad's tea?' I suggested, even though I knew she probably wouldn't hear the words.

I was braver now and moved closer. 'What's wrong with her, George?' I asked, my face only inches from hers.

'She's your mother.' His voice came from over my shoulder. I knew he was nearby and was looking at her

154

too.

'What's that supposed to mean?' I asked her.

'It means that she's your mother, not mine, so you know her and I don't. But if I had to take a guess I'd say she still hasn't come to terms with your loss.'

'But it's been months.' I hesitated momentarily. 'Hasn't it?'

'It's been a while,' he conceded.

'But she's such a strong person,' I told him. 'Nothing ever fazes her.'

'She's never had to deal with anything like this before.' His voice was close and I could feel his breath on my cheek.

'I should've come earlier,' I said. I leaned backwards to stretch my back. 'I've been so worried about Naomi and Marc that I didn't think to see her again.'

'You can't blame yourself for putting them first,' George consoled.

'Look at her, George.' He said nothing. 'I should have known.'

'Known what?'

'That she was like this.'

'How could you?' He crouched on his haunches beside my mother.

'Because she's my mother.'

'And you've been dead before?'

I looked at him. He stood up and took my hands in his.

'It was ten years before my mother could go into the room I'd slept in when I was a lad and I hadn't lived at home for six years before I died. It's not natural for a mother to bury her child.' He looked towards my mum. 'She brought you into the world; she never expected to see you out of it. If you'd been ill she might've been able to prepare herself, but the way you and me went, one minute we were there and the next we were gone. I'd had

155

a cheese and pickle sandwich in the afternoon and that night I was dead. How does a mother prepare herself for that?' He looked at my mother with compassion. 'How could she prepare for that?'

I too looked at my mother. 'Did your mother ever get over it?' I croaked.

He shook his head. 'Not really.' He let my hands fall and walked away. 'She said it was the happiest day of her life when she died.'

'What?' I could see there were tears in his eyes.

George couldn't maintain eye contact. He looked away as he wiped his nose on the back of his hand. 'She was nearly ninety when she came over, but when I saw her she looked nearer sixty. She had a smile on her face and looked better than I'd seen her in years. She wept in my arms. My dad was with me but it was me she was pleased to see.'

I looked at my mother again. 'Will she be like that?' She had stopped wiping the tears away, allowing them to fall freely.

Again, George's only response was a shrug of the shoulders.

'Oh God, Mum,' I whispered.

The front door opened and closed a few seconds later.

'It's me, Peg.' My dad sounded weary. When he came into the living room I could see his face was as weary as his voice. He stood in front of his wife.

I moved towards him. 'Look at her, Dad,' I said.

We were both looking at her but she was completely alone. Her eyes were fixed on the television screen, where the original mother and daughter had been replaced by a new pair.

'Have you eaten, Peg?' Dad asked.

It was as if she hadn't realised he was there.

'What?' she said, looking up from the screen and

finally acknowledging his presence.

'Have you eaten?' Dad sounded so tired.

'Look at this, Brian,' she said, throwing her hand towards the television and ignoring Dad's question. 'They're complaining because their daughters are fat or dress like tarts ...'

'Peg.'

'Like it makes any difference.' She paused as a sob caught in her throat. 'Don't they realise ...'

Dad turned away. 'You need to eat.'

'Why?' she snapped.

I was inches away from my dad and could see the pain painted all over his face.

'I'll make you something,' he said.

I stood behind my dad and watched his clumsy efforts to prepare a meal. The kitchen had always been his wife's domain and was alien to him. I had never seen my dad prepare food before, not even toast, and it clearly didn't come naturally to him. Food debris was scattered over the work top, which was something my mother would never have allowed. He seemed to be using every pot, pan, plate, and bowl available.

'Dad, your pan's boiled dry.' I tried to warn him but he carried on, totally oblivious to the burning smell. 'Dad,' I said. Still, the pan burned. 'Dad!' I shouted.

At last, he sensed that something was wrong and lifted the lid of the saucepan that sat on the front burner. He dropped the lid onto the floor as steam rose and burnt his forearm.

'Bugger,' he exclaimed as he jumped back. He grabbed hold of the pan by its handle but dropped that too as it burnt his hand. 'Shit.'

I had never heard him use even the mildest of swear

words yet here he was cursing twice in a minute. Was this what my death had brought him to?

'You OK, Dad?' I stood beside him at the sink as he held his hand under the running water. He lowered his head until his chin rested on his chest.

'Peg,' he said through gentle sobs.

'You've got to help her, Dad.'

'What am I going to do?'

'You have to get her help.'

'How?'

'How what?'

'How am I supposed to help her when she won't let me near her?'

I was surprised when he turned his head ever so slightly towards me. I looked at George to gauge his reaction. He gave a shrug.

'She needs a doctor,' I said.

'She won't see a doctor.'

'You have to make her.'

He looked at his hand where it still rested under the running tap. 'I've told her a thousand times she needs to see a doctor but when does she ever listen to me?'

'You have to make her listen to you.'

'I've never met a woman as stubborn as her.'

'What about the priest?' It seemed the most natural conversation in the world, but was it a proper conversation? Probably not, but it felt like one.

'She's given up the church so I can't even call the priest.' Dad's voice was weary.

'All right,' I said. 'If she won't see a doctor or a priest what about Aunt Lizzie?'

'Even Lizzie's stopped coming round. Probably sick of getting her head bitten off.'

'Make Aunt Lizzie come and talk to her. Tell Aunt Lizzie you need her help. She'll help if you ask her to.'

He turned the tap off and dried his hand on a tea towel that hung over the back of a chair. 'I might give Lizzie a ring tomorrow and tell her I need her help.'

'No, Dad,' I urged, 'not tomorrow, tonight. Why don't you ring Aunt Lizzie tonight?'

A few seconds later he looked at his watch, and to the telephone on the wall.

'Go on,' I said. 'Ring her now.'

To my amazement, he did. He leaned against the fridge and waited for the connection to be made.

'Oh, hello, Paul ... yes, I'm all right,' he said without conviction. 'Well, she's not so good. In fact, that's why I'm ringing. I was hoping to have a word with Lizzie ... It doesn't matter then, I'll call back later ... Oh, only if you're sure.'

Dad looked at the devastation that was the kitchen. From that he turned and looked through the open doorway, presumably at my mother. Then he turned his whole body and stood with his back to his wife.

'He looks so tired,' I whispered to George.

'Oh, hello, Lizzie,' Dad said, forcing himself upright. 'I'm really sorry to interrupt your tea ... Well, it's like I was saying to Paul, she's not too good. She's just sitting in front of the telly ... No, I couldn't tell you the last time she went out. If it wasn't for the neighbours we'd starve. In fact, I couldn't tell you the last time she got dressed. All she wears is a pair of bloody tracksuit bottoms and a T-shirt, day after day. I don't think they've ever been washed.' He ran his hand over his head. 'I don't know what to do, Lizzie. She won't see a doctor, she won't see the priest ... I was wondering if you could talk some sense into her?' He sounded embarrassed. 'I know you did, Lizzie, and I don't blame you for not coming round but I think the time for treading on eggshells has passed ... We've got to stop worrying about her feelings and concentrate on her sanity. I don't know what Ellen would think if she could see her ... Would you? Oh, thanks, Lizzie ... I can't tell you how grateful I am ... All right, love, I'll see you then.'

As he replaced the receiver I noticed that his face had lost some of its weariness. He looked again at the kitchen's mess and shook his head.

'Bugger it,' he said.

He walked over to the cooker and made sure that the burners were off before leaving the room.

We followed him through the doorway. Dad had never been what you'd call a decisive man, preferring to leave that sort of thing to his wife. I was seeing him in a different light.

'Think we'll have fish and chips tonight,' he said, reaching for the coat he had thrown over his chair. As he put it on he said, 'Lizzie and Paul are coming round tomorrow night.'

'Why?'

He was buttoning his coat when he said, 'Paul and me are going for a pint and you and Lizzie are going to have a natter.'

'What have we got to natter about?'

'You used to have plenty.'

'She hasn't been to see me in weeks,' Mum sneered.

'Have you been to see her?'

I would have expected her to have some reply even if it was only something like 'How dare you talk to me like that?'

Dad felt in his pocket, presumably checking that his wallet was there. 'Do you want haddock or cod?' he asked.

She looked at him as if she hadn't understood. 'Whatever you're having,' she answered.

'Haddock, then.'

'She hates haddock,' I told George out of the corner of my mouth.

'You could put the kettle on while I'm gone,' Dad said over his shoulder. 'Peg, kettle,' he reminded her before he left the house.

Mum sat for a few minutes before heaving herself out of the chair in stages. Slowly, she made her way to the kitchen with what was more of a shuffle than a walk. To get to where she was going she had to pass inches from me and I moved backwards into George. She stood in the doorway to the kitchen. I stood at her shoulder and looked at the kitchen with her. Armageddon came to mind. There were pots and pans everywhere.

Mum made as if to back away. She half turned and without knowing it, her face was almost touching mine.

'Go on,' I whispered. 'Put the kettle on.'

My eager eyes locked her weary ones briefly before she turned back and walked into the chaos.

She moved to the end of the bench to a spot that had escaped Dad's devastation and plucked the kettle from its stand. She took five steps to the right, which brought her to the sink and turned on the cold tap. It seemed a struggle for her to turn the tap off and she pulled the kettle away to avoid overfilling it. She made the journey back, this time taking six steps. She placed the kettle onto its stand and retraced her steps. This time it took seven.

She placed her hands on its edge and stared into the sink. George and I were now either side of her and we saw what she saw: nothing. She stared into the empty sink for a couple of minutes. Eventually, she reached over and took the plug from where it rested on its chain and pushed it firmly into the hole. She picked up the bottle of washing up liquid, turned it upside down, and squeezed. The top was still on the bottle but the pressure forced it off and a huge spurt of green liquid dropped out. Mum turned on the tap and as the water hit the detergent, masses of bubbles started to form. But Mum was oblivious to this as she was concentrating on the saucepans that sat on top of the stove. Like she had with the sink, she was giving the saucepans far too much attention. All the time she was looking at them, water was pouring out of the taps. Bubbles were almost at the top of the sink, then they were at the top, then they were over the top and running down the front of the cupboard door. By the time Mum had turned back to the sink with a saucepan in her hand there was water and bubbles flowing onto the floor.

She moved without urgency to turn the tap off. She stood with her bare feet covered in soapy water and laughed.

'What're you laughing at, Mum?' I asked. Of course, she didn't have an answer.

Then, as suddenly as it had started, the laughter stopped and there was silence. George and I looked at each other.

What happened next started as a moan, a low sound somewhere deep inside my mother that gained both sound and ferocity until it came out of her mouth as a scream. She made the noise again and once more before stopping. Then the crying started. Like the noise, the crying started quietly and evolved until she was sobbing and her body was shaking. Oddly, no tears fell from her eyes.

'Why?' Mum asked. She lifted her right hand and thumped it into the water, sending suds flying. Some landed on her hair and her face but she seemed not to notice. 'Why?' she asked again.

'Why what?' I moved my hand to wipe away the suds from her face.

'Why did it have to be you?' she shouted.

I felt myself start to shake.

'Why couldn't it have been me? Why not me? I would

have gone if you could have stayed. Why did He have to take you? Why did the bastard have to take you?'

I watched in horror as she leaned forward, resting her stomach on the sink's edge. Water and suds lapped against her, wetting her clothes.

She was stood like that when Dad came back.

'So, Peg,' he called as he made his way through to the kitchen. 'Is the tea re ...?' The sight stopped him in his tracks. 'Oh, Peg,' he said gently as her set the paper-wrapped parcel on the table. Then he moved towards her, stopping to pull the plug from the sink. 'Come here,' he said. He held her at arm's length. He tried but failed to smile. He put his hands on her shoulders as if to pull her to him but she pushed him away.

'Why? Why did it have to be her?'

'I don't know, love,' Dad said tenderly.

'It's not fair.' Mum said through the sobs that were now accompanied by tears.

Dad did pull her to him this time and put his arms around her. 'No, it's not fair.' He squeezed a little tighter and she sobbed a little harder.

'Can we go?' I asked George. 'I can't watch this.'

have gone if you could have stayed. Why did he have to
bring you? Why did the bastard have to take you?'

I watched in horror as she leaned forward, resting her
hand on the sink's edge. Water and suds lapped
against her, wetting her clothes.

She was stood like that when Dad came back.

'So, Peg,' he called as he made his way through to the
kitchen, 'what's the score?' The slight stoop of his
shoulders . . . 'Our Peg,' he said, getting nearer her for the umpteenth
time, a panic on his table. Then he moved towards her,
stopping to pull the plug from the sink. 'Come here,' he
said. He held her at arm's length. He tried but failed to
smile. He put his hands on her shoulders as if to pull her
to him but she pushed him away.

'Why? Why did it have to be her?'

'I don't know, Peg,' Dad said sadly.

'It's not fair,' Mum said through the sobs that were
now accompanied by tears.

And did he pull her to him, like, then, and put his arms
around her. 'No, it's no, fair.' He squeezed a little tighter,
and she sobbed a little harder.

'Can I stay?' I asked Grant. 'I can't watch this.'

CHAPTER TWENTY-THREE

We had sat in silence for a long time. What we had witnessed at my parents' house had left me feeling ... what? What was it? I wasn't sure. I didn't know what it was but I knew I didn't like it.

'That was horrible.' I said.

George didn't reply but when I looked at him I saw he was looking at me. George had lovely eyes.

'Was it like that for you?'

'Seeing my mum a wreck? Yeah, course it was. How could it be any other way? You know, there's this woman who's always been there for you, and the one time she really needs you there's nothing you can do. I couldn't stand watching her most of time.' Those eyes were looking at me again. 'I wanted her to get over it. I was dead and it didn't matter how much she cried, I was still going to be dead. I couldn't understand why she couldn't get over it.' I could feel his sadness as he spoke.

'Gran says she'll never get over it,' I told him. 'She said that Mum will blame herself forever.'

'Why?'

'What, apart from the fact she threw a wobbly at me seeing Megan?' He looked embarrassed as he nodded. I took a deep breath. 'She'll think she's being punished.'

'For Lizzie?'

'Yeah.'

'Your mum was wrong, you know,' he said brushing a stray hair away. 'The pain was just as real for Lizzie when ...' he stopped himself. 'But you'll know that.'

I nodded. I had grieved for my lost baby for months and thought about him every day. I wondered how my aunt had coped with thinking of her lost babies every day.

'Did she really parade you like a trophy?'

'Apparently. I talked to Aunt Lizzie a lot when I lost my ...' I stopped myself from saying the word baby. My baby had a name now. '... Matthew. We shared a lot of secrets.' I contemplated my feet a moment. 'She was very hurt but wouldn't give Mum the satisfaction of knowing how much.' After a long silence I added, 'She would have made a fantastic mother.'

'Will she be able to get through to your mum?'

I shrugged. 'Hope so.'

We sat in silence for what felt like a long time.

'What was that with my dad?' I asked eventually.

'What do you mean?'

I half shrugged and moved my head to one side, not really sure. 'It felt like we were having a conversation.'

'Yeah,' George agreed.

I expected him to say more.

'Could he hear me?' I asked. 'No, he couldn't. But I was getting through to him, wasn't I?' I said eagerly.

'It looked like it,' George agreed.

'So why can't I get through to Mum?' I asked.

Once more, Mum was wearing those clothes and sitting in the same chair.

There was a knock at the door and I heard my dad shout, 'Coming,' from somewhere, swiftly followed by the sound of steps on the stairs. The front door opened and

166

Aunt Lizzie came into the room, followed by Uncle Paul.

My aunt couldn't hide her shock at the sight of her sister though Mum didn't seem to notice. Dad couldn't hide his sadness. Aunt Lizzie quickly regained her composure and a smile split her face.

'Well, go on,' she said to the men, 'shoo!' She waved them away. 'Off you go. You're wasting valuable drinking time.' She turned to her sister, 'And we're wasting valuable gossiping time.' I saw pity in her eyes.

I had thought that my mum was oblivious to the scene that was being played out in front of her, but the flicker of her eyes towards my aunt showed me she was not.

'Alright,' said Uncle Paul. 'We can take a hint. Come on, Brian.'

My dad was torn. I knew him and I knew what he was feeling. Yesterday, this would have seemed like such a good idea but now he was fearful of what would happen in his absence. He was about to say something to my mother but Aunt Lizzie's eyes caught him.

'See you girls later,' Uncle Paul said, pulling on Dad's arm.

'Bye, love,' Aunt Lizzie said. I saw her mouth 'Don't worry,' to my dad.

She watched them close the door before turning her attention to my mother.

'What do you want?' Mum asked.

'What do you mean?'

'What I said.'

'To talk,' Aunt Lizzie sat on the end seat of the sofa.

'Why?'

After a pause, Aunt Lizzie asked, 'Shall I put the kettle on?'

'If you like,' Mum said.

Lizzie had started to get out of her seat but sat down again. 'No, I don't like,' she said. 'It's your house and your kitchen, you make the tea.' She leaned forward to pick up the remote control and pointed it towards the television. She flicked through three or four channels before hitting the standby button, making the picture disappear into a spot in the centre of the screen. The room was silent.

The two women locked eyes and even I could feel the tension. I wasn't sure which of them would back down first. They could both be incredibly stubborn. I was pleased for my mother's sake that it was her who did. This was one battle my aunt could not afford to lose, for her sister's sake.

My mother huffed as she forced herself out of the chair and made her way to the kitchen. After she was gone, Aunt Lizzie took a deep breath and puffed out her cheeks. This would not be easy for her.

'You all right?' George asked.

I nodded.

I looked at Aunt Lizzie and willed her to be strong. The sisters had always had a volatile relationship. They had never been close, not even when they were children but apart from Naomi, they were the only blood relation either of them had.

I was surprised to see my mother return with a mug in each hand. The surprise was also evident on my aunt's face. My mother usually treated guests to a tray set with cups, saucers, and the tea pot. She'd had to buy the mugs a couple of years before when they were having some work done on the house and she didn't want the builders breaking the china. I doubted they had been used since. I hoped for Lizzie's sake that Mum had washed them. Mum put the mugs onto the coffee table and sat back down in the chair.

There was a long silence.

'Get on with it.'

'Get on with what?' Aunt Lizzie asked, picking up her mug.

'What you came for.'

'And what's that?' She took a gulp of tea and tried to hide her disgust at its taste.

'God knows.'

'Would he?' Aunt Lizzie replaced the mug on the table and pushed it away. She sat back in her chair. 'I hear you haven't been to church lately.'

'You can talk.'

'Hey.' Aunt Lizzie held her hands up. 'I make no bones about the fact I lapsed a long time ago.' She paused before continuing, 'But you always got such comfort from the church.'

My mother took a mouthful of her own tea before dismissing that comment. 'That was before.'

Aunt Lizzie leaned towards her sister only to have her advances swept aside. 'Come on, Peg,' she pleaded.

'What?' my mother snapped.

'Talk to me.'

'About what?'

'Anything,' Aunt Lizzie pressed, 'just say what you feel.'

'What's to say?'

'Everything. Anything. Tell me how you feel.'

'How do you think I feel?'

Aunt Lizzie took a deep breath. 'I think you feel like your life is over,' she said.

'It is.'

'No.' Aunt Lizzie reached out and touched her sister's arm. 'Your life is not over.'

'Might as well be.'

'Peg, listen to me.' I detected a change in her tone. She progressed cautiously. 'Ellen is the one who died.'

'And you think I don't know?' my mother sneered.

Aunt Lizzie sighed before repeating, 'Ellen is the one who died, not you. You're still alive and you have so much to live for.'

'I've lost my child.'

'I know you have. I know you have and it's a terrible thing but you have so much to be grateful for.' She did not pause or give my mother a chance to interrupt. 'You had a beautiful daughter, Peg,' she said slowly. 'A beautiful daughter you loved and who loved you back. Can you imagine what I would have given to have had what you had?' She looked deep into my mother's eyes through tears that had formed in her own. 'I would have given anything to have had that just for one minute.'

My mother closed her eyes for what seemed like a long time and when she opened them again there was compassion in them. 'I know,' she whispered.

'Just one minute,' my aunt repeated. 'I would have given anything for one minute. I would have happily died if I could have held them.'

The sisters eyed each other in tearful silence. Part of me rejoiced because it seemed that Lizzie had finally made a connection with my mother but the rest of me grieved for the losses.

My mother was the first to turn away and without realising it, she was looking straight at me.

'Why?' she asked.

'I don't know.'

'Why her?' She turned away and back to her sister.

'I don't know,' Aunt Lizzie said again.

I took a step towards her but felt weak. 'It's not like that.' My words sounded as weak as I felt.

Mum took as deep breath. 'I'll never forgive Him for this. That's why I haven't been to church apart from her funeral, and that wasn't even a proper mass. I'd never seen that priest before in my life. Don't care to see him again, either. All that "rejoice that she is in better place" rubbish. Hippy nonsense. I'm hardly likely to rejoice and thank Him for taking my only daughter away from me.'

Aunt Lizzie proceeded cautiously. 'You always got such comfort from the church, Peg. Didn't you say when I was having my troubles that I should talk to a priest?'

'And did you?'

'You know I didn't.'

The conversation paused and Mum breathed deeply.

'They'd say it was God's will and that I shouldn't question it,' she said. 'But I have to question it because I don't understand it. How can a loving god do this to me? Why would He?'

'You never questioned God's will before.'

'I should have,' she said. 'I should have done what you did years ago.'

Aunt Lizzie held out her hand to my mother, who hesitated before taking it. Then, as if they were performing a dance, they seemed to pull each other from their chairs and knelt on the floor, their knees inches apart. They continued to hold hands as they sat staring at each other.

'You can get through this,' Aunt Lizzie said.

'I can't.'

'Yes, you can.'

'How?'

My aunt inched herself forward. 'Listen, Peg,' she said. 'You've got to pull yourself together.' Mum started to shake her head. She paused a moment. 'You'll never get over it, don't expect to because you won't. But you have to move on. Because you've got the rest of your life to lead.'

The only sound was the ticking of the clock above the fireplace.

'The last time I saw my baby she was lying in a

coffin,' Mum said in a broken voice. 'I didn't see her at the hospital. I wanted to … I did. But I couldn't do it. I couldn't bear the thought of seeing her on a mortuary slab.' She didn't see Aunt Lizzie's nod. 'She was so badly …' Mum gave into the sobs that had been bubbling under the surface. She bent over, clutched her arms to her stomach, and rocked in time with the sobs.

My aunt put her arms around Mum's shoulders, whispered gently into Mum's ear, and stroked the top of her head. As Mum continued to rock, my aunt settled into the same rhythm.

I fell into the rhythm without realising it until I felt George's arm around my shoulder.

'Come on,' he said. 'You don't need to see this.'

Nor did I want to, and I allowed him to turn me away. But when I heard Mum speak I turned back.

'I would have told her I'm sorry,' Mum said in a voice that broke intermittently. 'If I'd had the chance I would have told her I was sorry for all the things I'd done.'

Mum had straightened herself and sat back on her heels. Aunt Lizzie did the same.

'I need to say sorry to you,' she said hoarsely. 'I'm sorry for not understanding your losses.' My aunt lowered her eyes. 'I'm sorry for rubbing your nose in it by always going on about Ellen this and Ellen that. It was wrong of me.'

'It's water under the bridge.'

'What goes around comes around, isn't that what our old mum always said? She wasn't wrong; I'm paying for it now.' Saliva was escaping from the corner of Mum's mouth and she wiped it viciously.

'You can't think that.'

'Course I do,' Mum said in a loud voice. 'This is His way of punishing me. But I'll tell you something.' The sobs suddenly stopped. 'I'll tell you something, Lizzie.

I'm finished with Him.'

I looked at my mother and leaned into George. 'Can we go?' I asked.

And we left.

CHAPTER TWENTY-FOUR

We walked the dark streets in silence. I was thinking about my mother.

'What would she apologise to you for?' George finally broke the silence.

'Don't know.'

We walked a little further.

'She's just so ...' I struggled to find the word. 'Different.'

'Didn't you realise that she would be?'

'I suppose I did. I mean, I knew that my death would affect her but I don't recognise her as my mother anymore.' I stopped walking. 'If you'd asked me before I died how she would react, I would have said she'd turn to God. I would have said she'd never be away from the church praying for my soul. I would have said that she'd be at church every day but she's not been once. I don't understand it.'

'It's very common.'

'Yeah but my mother always said that everything happens for a reason and even though we can't always see those reasons, God can and He will always do what's best for us.' I looked George square in the face. 'I would never in a million years have said that she would turn away from the church or reject God. I thought He would be the one thing that would get her through this.'

'Like I said,' he shrugged, 'it's very common.'

'Really?'

'Yeah,' he said, 'but don't worry, He's used to it. He won't hold it against her.'

'Won't He?'

'No, He doesn't bear grudges.' George started to walk again. 'He knows it's because we can't understand death.'

'Yes, we do.' I objected on behalf of mankind.

He shook his head. 'No, we accept that it's going to happen but we don't understand why.'

I stopped walking again. 'And what is it that He thinks we don't understand?' I asked.

George stopped and looked at me. 'That all death is natural.' He started to move on.

'Hang on a minute,' I said as I grabbed hold of the arm of his jacket. 'I was side-swiped by a drunk driver. How can that be natural?' I could hear the anger in my voice.

He put his hand on mine and gently removed it from his arm. 'The way you died wasn't natural but it was natural that you would die. From the second you were born you were always going to die.'

I walked away with my head down. I'd taken about a dozen steps before I waited for George to catch up with me. 'Was it His decision?' I asked quietly.

'That you should die?'

'Yes.'

He considered for a moment before saying with a nod of his head, 'Ultimately.'

'But why?' I asked. 'What was the point?'

'Do you think your death was pointless?'

'Of course it was,' I said with disbelief.

'You'd be wrong.'

'Would I?'

'Daddy took me to see Granny Alice yesterday,' Naomi said nonchalantly.

'Did he? How was she?'

'Not very well. One of her legs has gone puffy and purple.' Naomi looked me in the eye. 'Have you been to see her?'

'No.' I was embarrassed. It had never occurred to me to visit my mother-in-law and I hadn't seen her since the day after I had died and Marc had gone to see her. 'I saw Granny Peg the other day, though.' I tried to sound enthusiastic.

'Did you?' She sounded excited and her face lit up.

I exchanged a brief glance with George and his head nodded just a fraction.

'Does Daddy take you to see Granny Peg?' I asked nervously.

I was sorry to see the light leave her face. 'Not for a long time. The last time he took me she was acting funny.'

'What do you mean?'

Naomi searched her limited vocabulary for the words she wanted. 'Just funny. She looked at me funny and cried a lot.'

'What did you do?'

'Nothing. I didn't know what to do.'

'Of course you didn't, darling.' I gave myself a mental slap across the face for asking a child such a stupid question. Naomi looked crestfallen.

'What's wrong with her, Mummy?' she asked. 'Daddy won't take me to see her anymore.'

'Why not?'

'He says she's not very well and he doesn't want me to get upset.'

'Were you upset when you saw her before?'

'A bit,' she admitted sadly. 'I don't know why I made her cry.' As Naomi looked at me, her large eyes wore a film of tears.

I squirmed on the bed where I sat beside her. 'It's not your fault that she cries,' I told her.

'But it must be,' she said in a way that reminded me how young she was.

'No, darling,' I soothed. 'It's not. Granny Peg cried because she's sad I died.'

'I'm sad too but I don't cry all the time.'

I was going to speak but George held up his hand.

'Naomi,' he said. He leaned close to my daughter. 'Your mummy was Granny Peg's little girl.' Naomi's eyes went the full length of my body. 'I know she doesn't look like a little girl to you but she was Granny Peg's little girl. Just like you'll be your mummy's little girl even when you're all grown up. Your gran is very, very sad that her little girl has died.'

'So why does she cry when she sees me?'

'Because you remind her very much of what she has lost. I think that you must look a lot like your mummy used to when she was a little girl. So when Granny Peg sees you she remembers the little girl she used to have.'

'But you go to see her sometimes, don't you?'

'Yes,' I told her. 'But Granny Peg can't see me.'

'You'd have made a great dad,' I told George.

George shrugged and walked in silence.

178

CHAPTER TWENTY-FIVE

I liked watching Marc work. This was the only part of his life I hadn't shared with him.

Although he wasn't alone, Marc was the only one doing any work in the office. He was looking through a pile of papers stacked on his desk. Stephen wasn't there but Rosie was sitting on the edge of the desk that Diane sat behind.

Their heads were together and they were whispering. I walked over to them. I wanted to know what they were talking about. Something told me it was Marc.

'Yeah, but he's got a kid, hasn't he?' Diane said

'So?'

'Well, its baggage.'

'And?'

George nudged me. 'Can that girl use a sentence with more than one word in it?'

I laughed but didn't say anything because I didn't want to miss any of the conversation.

'And what about his wife?'

'She's dead.'

George and I looked at each other. 'Apparently she can,' he said.

They were both looking at Marc but he seemed unaware. I looked at him too. He was looking better. He had regained some of the weight he had lost and his face had lost the grey pallor.

Watching him was wonderful. Watching him made me feel alive again, which was great for a while but then I would remember and it was like dying all over again.

Movement to the left of me made me take my eyes away from Marc. Rosie moved slightly on the edge of the desk to expose more thigh.

'Look at that.' I turned to George and realised I had no need to point Rosie out. His eyes were fixed firmly on her.

The girls were continuing their whispered conversation.

'How old is he?' Diane asked.

'Too old for her,' I found myself shouting as Rosie shook her head.

'Thirtyish,' she suggested.

'Thirty-five,' I corrected.

'Really?' George said.

'Yes,' I answered with pride. 'Doesn't look it.' I turned my attention back to Rosie. 'And just how old are you?'

'If he's thirty that only makes him eight years older than me. That's OK.'

'Yeah, but you work with him.' Diane said.

'So?'

'I think you're playing with fire.' Diane rolled her chair to the right and hit the keyboard of her computer. It appeared that Diane was bored with the conversation and was going to do some work.

'Too right she is.'

My face was inches from Rosie's as I gave her the warning.

'Why does it bother you so much?' George asked.

'Why does what bother me?'

'That girl.' He pointed his thumb over his shoulder towards the office building we had just left.

'Which girl?' I knew exactly what he was talking about but I was not happy acknowledging it.

'I don't know what she's called. The one that's set her cap at Marc.'

'Rosie.' I made the word sound dirty.

We'd walked about a hundred yards before he repeated, 'Why does it bother you?'

'Why do you think?'

He took a step backwards. 'Tell me.'

'I know it's stupid.'

'It's not stupid.'

I appreciated George's tone. It wasn't patronising and I knew he understood.

'She was talking about my husband.' I stopped and leaned against the wall of a building we were passing. George leant facing me.

'It's not stupid,' he repeated.

'Then why do I feel stupid?'

He shrugged.

I turned so that it was my back and head that were against the wall. 'He'll find someone else, won't he?'

'Probably.' George still rested on his shoulder and I could feel him looking at me. 'But I don't see it being the girl upstairs.'

'Really?' I felt cheered by the thought. 'It'll be somebody else though, won't it?' I said, my cheeriness gone.

George moved his head down and up.

'I can't bear it.'

'Yes, you can.' He pushed himself off the wall and shrugged his jacket back into position. 'Otherwise you and I are going to be here a long time.' He started to move off.

'What do you mean?' I asked. I grabbed his arm and forced him to turn around. 'George?'

He sighed as he looked over my shoulder to where we'd come from. He pursed his lips and the tip of his tongue poked out. He jerked his head in the direction of Marc's office as he said, 'Does that look finished to you?'

As I watched George walk away, I understood.

Hours later and I couldn't get the thought of Marc with another woman out of my mind.

George and I were in my parents' house but it was late, well past their bedtime, and the house was quiet. It was also dark and I was happy for that. I was lying on the sofa looking at the ceiling. George was sitting in the chair my dad usually occupied.

I knew I was being unreasonable. I was dead and Marc was alive. They were the facts and I accepted them. But I still loved Marc. Being dead didn't make the feelings I'd had when I was alive any less potent. I loved him as much now as I'd ever done.

'It's so hard,' I whispered.

'Did you think it would be easy?' He

'I didn't think about it at all,' I said, turning onto my side. 'Why would I?'

George didn't answer. I could just about make him out in the darkness and I knew he was looking at me.

'What did you mean earlier?' I asked, lifting myself up onto my elbow.

'What about?'

'About us being here a long time.'

'I think you know.'

He was right.

'I want him to be happy,' I said without conviction.

'Really.' I sat upright. 'I do.'
George looked sceptical. 'If you say so.'

CHAPTER TWENTY-SIX

I was surprised by the sight of my mother entering the living room. My first thought was that we had been there longer than I realised and it was already morning. A quick glance at the window showed me that wasn't the case. It was still the middle of the night.

Mum walked through the room in darkness and went into the kitchen. As she put the light on, a faint beam of light shone into the living room. That beam fell over the clock on the wall. I could just about make out the time – three o'clock. I could also make out that Mum was wearing the dressing gown I had given her last Christmas.

Mum turned the light off and moved carefully to a chair, carrying a mug of hot liquid. As my eyes adjusted to the light I could follow her progress by the gentle waft of steam that rose from her cup.

She sat down and took a sip from the mug.

She took a deep breath. I saw her resting her head against the back of the chair.

'Ellen, I'm sorry.' Her words echoed in the silence.

'It's all right,' I said instinctively, without knowing what it was she was apologising for.

'I've let you down so badly,' she said quietly. 'I wasn't the mother you deserved.'

'It doesn't matter, Mum.'

'I expect you'd say it doesn't matter,' she said with a

smile on her face. 'That's because you were such a sweet person. You never held grudges. Live and let live, that's what you used to say. But it does matter. To me, anyway.'

She lifted the cup to her mouth and took two huge gulps. I winced because the liquid must have been scolding hot. She didn't seem to notice.

'Too late for that now. Can't go back and send you to ballet class, can I? Can't take you shopping for your first bra.'

I was still embarrassed by the memory of being the only girl in PE class wearing a vest instead of a bra. She emptied her mug and put it on the table.

'It's too late for that now. I promise you, wherever you are, I won't let you down any more.' She pushed herself up and balanced on the edge of the chair. Her words were just a whisper in the darkness. 'I just hope I've not left it too late.'

She got to her feet and walked out of the room. She closed the door softly behind her.

Naomi eyed my mother warily for a second before running up to her. Naomi threw her arms around my mother's thighs and squeezed. The left side of Naomi's face, her eyes closed tightly, was buried in the pleats of my mother's skirt.

Naomi's reaction caught my mother off guard. She looked at the creature that had attached itself to her legs. Her surprise was followed by something else when the faintest smile appeared on her face as she put her hand on the top of my daughter's head. She held her hand there for a few seconds and stroked the hair gently. Just as gently, she was whispering her granddaughter's name.

I wiped away tears I thought I could feel on my cheeks. Aunt Lizzie wiped away tears of her own but my mother let hers fall untamed.

Marc, who had let the women into the house, watched from the doorway. His eyes were on his daughter.

Naomi was mumbling.

'What's that?' Aunt Lizzie asked as she bent down to Naomi's level.

Naomi said it again but still no-one could hear.

'Can you say it a bit louder, sweetheart?' Aunt Lizzie laughed. 'Your auntie's going a bit deaf in her old age.'

Naomi adjusted her face so her mouth was clear of the pleats. She was laughing too. 'You're not old, Auntie Liz,' she said. She moved her head back so she could see my mother's face. 'I said I missed you, Granny Peg.'

My mother could only smile.

'Why didn't you come to see me?' Still words eluded my mother. Naomi turned her attention to my aunt. 'Why didn't Granny Peg come to see me?'

My aunt chose her words carefully. 'Granny Peg's not been well.'

Simple usually works best.

Naomi looked up to my mother. 'Have you been poorly?' My mother's smile could not hide her embarrassment. 'Are you still poorly?' Naomi persisted.

Marc moved from his position in the doorway. 'I'll put the kettle on,' he said as he disappeared towards the kitchen.

Naomi finally relinquished her hold on my mother's thighs and the three of them moved to the sofa. The women sat at either end and Naomi perched herself between them. She pushed herself to the back of the sofa and looked from her grandmother to her great-aunt and back again.

No-one spoke, not even Naomi. No words, just glances, nervous ones from the adults and curious ones from my child.

Marc came back with the drinks and still no-one had spoken. He looked at his mother-in-law, then at her sister, and finally his daughter. He wrinkled his nose at her and smiled. If my heart had still been working, the look he gave her would have stopped it.

'Right,' he tried to sound breezy, 'if you'll excuse me I've got some work to do. I'll leave the three of you to catch up.'

Naomi laughed as she watched him leave the room but still no-one spoke.

'Oh, for goodness sake,' I said impatiently as I walked to the centre of the room. I directed my words at my mother. 'I thought you wanted to talk to her,' I said. 'She's right beside you, talk to her. Or at least give her a cuddle.'

'Hello,' Naomi said.

'Hello, darling,' I said instinctively before returning my attention to my mother. I was about to speak when I realised what had happened. I looked at George and he looked as nervous as I felt.

Both my mother and her sister were looking at Naomi, who in turn was looking at me.

'Who are you saying hello to, darling?' Aunt Lizzie asked.

'Where's George?' Naomi was looking straight at me. My eyes gave away his location and she turned to look at him. 'Hello, George,' she called as she waved her hand.

Aunt Lizzie and my mother looked where Naomi was looking.

George waved back to Naomi and mouthed the word 'hello'.

The two women looked at each other. Both wore a look of confusion.

'Why are you hiding in the corner, George?' Naomi asked. George looked embarrassed as everyone looked in his direction.

'I'm not hiding,' he said.

My aunt took Naomi's hand to regain her attention. 'Is George your friend?' she asked.

'What?' Naomi asked.

'Not what, pardon,' my mother said, her old self fighting to emerge.

Aunt Lizzie threw Mum a look that said that this was not the time to be correcting Naomi's speech. 'Is George you're friend?' she repeated.

Naomi thought for a moment before declaring, 'I know George, but he's Mummy's friend.'

'Mummy's friend?'

'Yes,' she nodded.

'And he's here?'

'Yes.'

My mother seemed confused and my aunt proceeded cautiously.

'Where?'

'There.' Naomi pointed to the corner of the room. Aunt Lizzie looked directly at George and I was surprised when he waved at her. Naomi laughed.

'What?' Aunt Lizzie asked. Apparently my mother didn't feel the need to correct her sister's speech.

'He's waving at you, Auntie Liz,' Naomi told her.

'Really?'

'He was but he's stopped now.'

Aunt Lizzie nodded.

'George is funny,' Naomi leaned towards her to share this as if it was a secret.

'Is he?'

'Yes.'

'Why is George funny? What does he do that's

funny?'

Naomi had to think for a moment. 'He doesn't do anything really, he's just funny. He looks funny,' she said finally. George pulled a face and Naomi giggled. 'And he wears funny clothes.' George looked down at what he was wearing and Naomi laughed some more.

My mother managed to find her voice but her words came slowly. 'You said he was Mummy's friend.'

'He is.'

'I've never heard of him. I knew all your mummy's friends.'

'He's her new friend.' Naomi's answers came naturally.

'Her new friend?'

'Yes, he's always with her.'

'What do you mean he's always with her?'

Naomi seemed confused. 'He's always with her,' she said again.

'And you say he's here now?'

'Yes, he's over there.' She pointed once more to the corner of the room.

'And your mummy?' my mother asked, her eyes, darting around the room.

'There.' Naomi pointed directly at me.

My mother looked but did not see.

'Can I have a word with you, Marc?' my mother said under her breath.

I knew my mother would not be able to leave the house without having 'a word' with Marc.

'Course.'

• • •

'How long has Naomi been like this?'

'Like what?'

'You know,' she said cautiously, as if she was afraid

190

of being overheard.

'I haven't got a clue what you're talking about,' he said, shaking his head.

My mother looked around to make sure she couldn't be overheard. She needn't have worried because Naomi and Aunt Lizzie had their heads together and were sharing a secret of their own. Just to be certain, my mother turned her back to the pair. 'Naomi says she can see Ellen,' she whispered.

'What?' Marc squawked. 'I thought she was over that.'

'Over it?'

Marc waved the question away. 'What else did Naomi say?'

My mother took a deep breath. 'Naomi says there's a man called George with her.'

'George who?'

'I don't know, just George. Apparently he looks after her on the other side.'

'What do you mean? Why does she need looking after?'

Did my husband sound jealous?

My mother shook her head. 'I don't know and I don't think that's the issue.' They stared at each other. 'The point is, Naomi thinks she can see her mother.'

Marc looked over my mother's shoulder to where Naomi was trying to pick up Aunt Lizzie's huge handbag. 'Are you sure?'

'Of course I'm sure, I wouldn't have mentioned it otherwise. Haven't you noticed anything?'

'No,' he admitted, 'not recently.'

Marc sat in the corner of the sofa and rested his feet on the middle seat. Naomi nestled against his chest. He stroked her hair and I sensed that he was waiting for the

191

right moment.

'I miss her too, you know,' he said softly. 'And I know you do.' Naomi made no response and he continued tentatively. 'Sometimes I wish I could talk to her. Well, more than sometimes, all the time. Every day I wish I could talk to her. I wish I could ask her how to plait your hair.' Marc looked straight ahead as he spoke. He was looking at me. 'I wish I could ask her how to iron the pleats in your school skirt. I wish I could ask her what she used to do to make spaghetti taste the way you like it.'

I wondered why those three things still bothered him so much.

Naomi lifted her head. 'Granny Peg told you, didn't she?'

Marc nodded. 'Yes, darling, she did.'

'She doesn't believe me, does she?'

'Well ...' Marc was evasive.

'And you don't either.' She put her head back on his chest. 'I'm not lying, Daddy.' Naomi's voice was low, barely above a whisper.

Marc looked like he was trying to find something to say but failing. He stroked the top of her head. 'I didn't say you were,' he said sadly. 'I just wish I could see her too.'

He closed his eyes.

* * *

Marc sat in the pistachio room with only a small lamp for illumination. Two fingers of whisky sat in the glass he held in his hand.

'Oh, Ellen,' he said as he looked into his glass. The sound of my name startled me. 'What am I going to do?'

'About what?' I asked.

He took a large drink from the glass and threw his head back. He closed his eyes and I noticed how tired he looked.

'She says she can see you,' He took another mouthful of whisky and swallowed. 'Why can she see you?' he asked with his eyes still closed. 'Why can't I see you? Why do you come to see her and not me? Do you really have a friend called George?' He opened his eyes and focused on his glass. He laughed.

George and I exchanged a look that told me he didn't know why Marc was laughing either. Marc emptied his glass and stretched for the bottle to refill it. He'd never really been much of a drinker .

'Can't believe you've got another bloke already,' he said as he poured more whisky into his glass.

He would never know how much that hurt.

CHAPTER TWENTY-SEVEN

'She thinks she can see her.'

'Who?' Dad folded the newspaper he had been reading.

'She thinks she can see her,' my mother repeated.

'Who thinks they can see who?' He put the newspaper on the table.

'Whom,' my mother corrected and Dad shrugged his acceptance. 'Naomi thinks she can see Ellen.'

'What?' Finally, she had his attention.

Mum leaned forward and sat on the edge of her chair. 'Naomi says her mummy comes to visit her with a man called George.'

'Who's he?'

'Her friend, Naomi says he looks after her.'

'Why?'

'What do you mean?' Mum snapped. 'Does it matter?' Dad shrugged again. 'What's important,' she said, 'is that Naomi needs to see someone.'

'Like who?'

'Like a doctor,' Mum said as if she were telling a two-year-old the simplest thing in the world. 'She needs to see a doctor. I told Marc...'

Dad as usual chose his words carefully. 'Do you think that was wise?' he asked.

I thought the same myself.

'Of course.' Mum looked at him from under furrowed brows and made it sound like he had asked a ridiculous question.

'Well,' Dad started cautiously. 'I'm just thinking he might not welcome you interfering.'

'I'm not interfering.'

'Marc might think you are. Naomi is his daughter.' Dad reached his hand out to her.

'And her mother was mine,' Mum said as she pulled away.

***

'Mum seemed better,' I commented. The world slept and George and I walked the silent streets. George did not answer so I pressed, 'Don't you think?'

'What?' George pulled himself from wherever his mind had wandered to.

'Mum,' I said. 'She seemed better.'

'Yes,' he conceded, 'she seemed more focused.'

'What you would call "focused",' I laughed, 'the rest of us would call controlling.' There was no response from George. We had walked on a while before I asked, 'What's wrong?'

'Nothing.'

'Really?' I know I sounded as sceptical as I was.

He paused for a moment and seemed to be considering something. 'There's something that you should know,' he said.

'What?' I asked suspiciously. George was acting oddly and it made me nervous. 'What?' I repeated, more earnestly this time.

George beckoned to a woman who had suddenly appeared beside him. She was an elegant, grey-haired woman wearing a long, grey skirt and a white blouse buttoned to the top. She walked slowly and purposefully.

'Who's that?' I asked.

'Hello, Constance.' George held out his hand to the woman.

The woman turned her attention from George to me.' Hello, Ellen,' she said in a voice as sweet as treacle. 'I'm Constance.' My eyes flittered from her to George and back again. 'You must be wondering who I am.'

'Yes,' I said nervously. I looked over her shoulder to George. He was looking at his feet.

Constance took my hand and I instinctively knew that whatever her reason was for being here, it couldn't be good.

'It's your grandfather's time,' she said with the air of someone who was used to delivering bad news.

'What? What do you mean?' I looked to George. 'What does she mean?' His head was still lowered but he was looking at me from the corner of his eyes.

Constance reached out and took my hands. 'I mean,' she said, her voice calm and soothing, 'your grandfather will be making his journey very soon.'

'His journey?'

George stepped around Constance and stood in front of me. 'He's going to die, Ellen,' he said.

'When?' I asked.

George looked at Constance and so did I.

'Soon,' she said, 'very soon.'

'How soon?' I wasn't sure if I spoke the words or just thought them.

'Tonight.'

Tonight? How could that be? How could he die tonight? But I knew as well as anyone that anybody can die at any time. I remembered what my gran had said at my funeral about how ill he was.

'Are you here to greet him?'

'Yes,' she said gently.

George took hold of my hand. 'Don't worry,' he said. 'Your granddad'll be all right. She'll make a better job of it than I did.' He tried to smile.

'Does Gran know?' I asked.

'Yes,' Constance said.

'How is she?'

'She's happy.'

'Happy!' I said in a half shriek. 'How can she be happy?' I challenged them.

'She's been on her own for a long time,' George explained.

'Yes but …'

'And she knows that he's in a lot of pain and has been for a long time.'

'I know but …'

'And he's ready.'

'How can you know that?' I could hear the tension in my voice.

'We just do.'

'How?' I repeated. I know my voice was louder than it needed to be.

'Because it's someone's job to know that sort of thing and report it.'

'Someone's job? Whose?' Now it was not only loud but aggressive too.

'Gerald's.'

'Gerald?'

'Yes.' George was using that voice that usually calmed me down. 'Gerald. He's not been in the job very long but I'm told he's very good.'

'And it's his job to know when someone is ready to die?' George must have been having an off day because I wasn't getting any calmer.

'Pretty much.'

'Well, he got it wrong with me, didn't he?' I shouted.

I could feel Constance looking at me. She took my hand and pulled me towards her. 'That was someone else's decision, child,' she said. She smiled at me and I felt better.

Constance left us shortly after that. I didn't need to ask where she was going.

'You alright?' George asked. I nodded. 'Really?'

'Yes.' I paused a second. 'But why does it have to be now?'

'Why not now?'

I looked the way Constance had walked but she was long gone. The only answer to his question I could come up with was, 'Because Mum was just starting to pull herself together.'

* * *

I was sulking.

I sat on a wall with my feet several inches from the floor. I banged my heels against the brick.

George sat beside me plucking non-existent lint from his trousers.

'I'm sure it would help,' I said.

'Never has before.' He stopped the plucking. 'You'll see him soon enough,' he said.

'When?' I asked.

He gave me a crooked smile. 'When do you think?'

'I don't know,' I replied, without giving it any thought.

He shook his head and laughed.

'When?' I pressed. I jumped down from the wall and stood in front of him.

'You'll need to pay your respects.'

'What?'

'The funeral.' He set his head on one side.

'Oh,' I nodded slowly. That made sense. 'Gran came to me on the day of my funeral,' I told him, as if I was

199

telling him something he didn't know.

'And you thought there was no method to any of this,' he said with a hint of mockery.

'When is it?' I asked.

'He's only been dead a couple of days so they haven't decided yet.' He put his cigarette in his mouth. 'Last I heard, your mum and Lizzie were arguing about a coffin.'

'A coffin?'

'Yeah, your mum wants oak but Lizzie wants cardboard.'

'Cardboard?'

'Apparently they're all the rage with the eco-friendly types.'

'And since when was Aunt Lizzie an eco-friendly type?'

'Since your granddad said he wanted cremating and scattering on his compost heap. Lizzie says it's wrong to kill a tree to burn her dad in if all they're going to do is throw him on a pile of rotting vegetables.'

I smiled for the first time since I'd seen Constance.

'Are they really going to scatter him on his compost heap?'

'Why not?' George jumped down and we started to walk. 'Lizzie says he spent more time with his roses than he did anywhere else.'

We turned into the cul-de-sac that had been my grandfather's home for over sixty years. There were a lot of people gathered outside the house. My gran stood at the gate of the house with my great-aunt Maggie, who was Granddad's eldest sister. They were both laughing.

'Why're they laughing?' I asked.

'Why do you think?'

'I don't know.'

He stopped walking.

'You still don't get it, do you?'

'Get what?'

'How it works.'

'He's dead,' I said lamely.

'Yeah,' he nodded. 'So am I, so are you and so's your gran.' He turned to look at her and so did I. She laughed out loud at something Aunt Maggie had said. 'Do you still love Marc?' he asked.

'You know I do.'

'So why should it be any different for your gran?' He put his cigarette into his mouth and inhaled. 'Listen,' he said exhaling the non-existent smoke, 'how would you feel if you knew that today, you were going to see Marc? That you were going to be able to talk to him and kiss him and hold him. And you've been here hardly any time at all compared to your gran.'

My granddad was happy to see her. He looked half the age of the man I had seen on the day of my funeral. The wrinkles weren't so deep, the hair wasn't quite so grey, and there was a smile on his face.

I found that I laughed too as I saw the pair of them hug and kiss like lovesick teenagers.

'Children present, Betty,' George shouted in a raucous manner.

My gran turned to look at me and beamed. She held out her arms to welcome me into her embrace. 'Hello, love.' She kissed my cheek and pulled me close to her chest. When she let me go I turned my attention to my granddad and threw my arms around his neck. As he hugged me I was surprised by the strength in his arms.

'It's good to see you, love,' he whispered into my ear.

'I've missed you, Granddad,' I said through the lump

in my throat.

'We missed you too,' he said as his lips brushed my cheek. He held me at arm's length. 'You look lovelier than ever.' Then he looked over my shoulder. 'You must be George.'

The men shook hands.

'Yeah.' George was as surprised as I was. 'Pleased to meet you.'

'How do you know about George?' I asked.

'Naomi told me.'

'What?'

He took a deep breath. My gran came to his side and they linked arms.

'I knew what was going to happen,' he said, 'and I wasn't afraid. Naomi's a bright girl and she knew too. She asked me if I was going to live with her mummy and I said yes, I thought I was. Naomi ...' He started to laugh. 'Naomi told me not to worry because things weren't so bad when you died. She said I would get a friend to look after me. Have you met Constance?' I nodded and waved a greeting. 'Naomi told me you had a friend called George.' He looked at George and laughed.

'What?' George asked with a smile.

'She described you perfectly.'

'Told you I was a good-looking bloke, did she?'

'They weren't her exact words.'

If it had been weird attending my own funeral, it was weirder attending my grandfather's with my grandfather at my side. At my funeral, the front of the church had been almost full and the back relatively empty. This time, the situation was reversed. Row after row of my grandfather's friends who had gone before him packed the back of the church.

The living made a much smaller group as they made their way to my parents' house for what my mother called 'light refreshments'.

For his part, my granddad seemed to be having a good time. He was treating his funeral like a school reunion. He waved from one person to the next, shook hands, and pointed out to me people I had never known.

'Not a bad turn out,' George commented, looking towards the living mourners.

'Suppose,' my granddad agreed. 'Not as many as there could've been. I've been to a few of these things myself in the last year or two.'

A look was exchanged between George and my grandfather. They moved away with their heads together. I wondered what they were saying to each other that they didn't want anyone else to hear.

I watched my mum and her sister hand out sandwiches and cakes. They exchanged the odd glance but nothing more.

'Mum's taken it badly,' I said to Gran.

'It's come so close after yours,' she said sadly. 'And she thought the world of her dad.'

'And you too.'

She smiled. 'Maybe. Anyway, I'd best go and say goodbye to him.'

'To who?'

'Your granddad.'

'Why?'

She sighed heavily and for the first time that day she looked sad. 'Because I don't live here.'

'But ...'

'But nothing, love. There are procedures that need to be followed, things that need to be done. But it's all right. I don't suppose it'll be too long before he can join me. By the time you get to his age you're more or less expecting

203

it so you've made your peace with most people.'

'Why am I still here, Gran?'

'I don't know, love. But you were taken suddenly. You weren't ready for it. You still need to make your peace.'

'But I'm not sure who with.'

'Hello, Mummy.'

'Hello, darling.'

Naomi stood in front of me and once more I answered her instinctively. I looked around nervously, worried that Naomi was seeing a room full of dead people.

'Where's George,' she asked.

'He's over there,' I told her, nodding to the corner of the room. She waved to catch George's attention. Thankfully, the living seemed too preoccupied with other things to notice Naomi.

'Why's he talking to himself?' she asked.

'What do you mean, darling?' I asked.

'Look,' she said. 'George is talking to himself.' I was grateful that it appeared George and I were the only dead people she could see. 'Why is George talking to himself?'

I was just wondering how to answer when Aunt Lizzie came to my rescue. 'Naomi,' she asked. 'Are you alright?'

Naomi seemed puzzled. 'Yes, I'm just talking to Mummy.'

My aunt nodded sagely. 'Is your mummy alright?' she asked.

Naomi turned to me and asked, 'Are you alright?' I nodded. 'She's fine,' Naomi announced with a smile.

My aunt crouched down onto her haunches so her head was almost level with Naomi's. Without knowing it she was also inches from her own mother's knees. Gran held out her hand and moved it over her daughter's hair.

Aunt Lizzie made a similar movement over my daughter's head. 'Naomi,' she said quietly. 'Will you tell your mummy that I miss her?'

204

Naomi opened her mouth but I spoke first. 'Tell her I miss her too.' Once more, Naomi opened her mouth but I hadn't finished. I had seen an opportunity and I was going to take it. 'Naomi,' I said. 'Tell Aunt Lizzie that she has to make Granny Peg understand that it wasn't her fault.'

'What wasn't her fault?' Naomi asked.

I looked at my aunt. 'Just tell her,' I said. 'She'll understand.'

Naomi repeated what I had said and Aunt Lizzie's eyes widened. She seemed surprised. 'I'll try,' she said quietly, looking to where she thought I was.

'What's the matter?' I hadn't noticed my mother's approach.

'What?' Aunt Lizzie appeared startled by the sound of my mother's voice...

'What's the matter with Naomi?' Mum's voice was tetchy.

'Nothing,' Aunt Lizzie said, forcing herself to stand. She took Naomi's hand. 'There's nothing wrong with Naomi, is there?' She patted the small hand.

'People are starting to leave,' my mother said as she looked around the room. 'We'd best see them out.' Mum walked towards the door where an elderly couple were putting on their coats.

'Will you come and see the people out too, Naomi?' my aunt asked.

Naomi looked at me and I nodded. 'If you like,' she replied, and they walked away together. Naomi stopped after a couple of steps and turned around. 'Bye, Mummy,' she said with a wave. Only my Aunt Lizzie had heard but when she shouted, 'Bye, George,' it was a different matter. Conversation stopped and George looked as self-conscious as a schoolboy caught with his trousers down behind the bike sheds.

With barely any hesitation, my aunt retrieved the

situation. 'Bye, George,' she shouted. 'See you later.'

On the assumption that George was one of granddad's friends from the leek club or an old relative no-one had seen for years, the low hub of conversation started again.

CHAPTER TWENTY-EIGHT

My grandfather and I sat on the sofa in my mother's living room and watched her tidying things.

'So it's right that Naomi can see you.' he said.

'Yes.'

'Only you?'

'And George,' I gestured to where George sat on the arm of the sofa.

'Why?'

'I don't know.'

Silence.

'She's been through a lot, that little 'un,' he said. 'I often wondered how she was coping so well with losing you. I didn't believe your mother when she told me.'

'Told you what?'

'That Naomi thought she was seeing you.'

'She was … is.'

He paused and looked once again at his daughter as she collected plates from the table.

'She wanted Marc to take her to see a doctor.'

'Yes,' I said, 'I know.'

He looked at her again. The room was now clear of the wake's debris and she looked around with sad, tired eyes.

'She'll never get over it,' he said. 'You were the only thing she had that really mattered to her.'

'She's got Dad.'

207

'But he's not you. Did you know that today is the first time she's been in a church since your funeral?'

I nodded. 'Yes, I'm surprised. I thought that the church would be the one place that she would find comfort. You know, God's will and all that.'

'If she loses any more weight,' he said, 'she's going to fade away.'

For the first time I realised he was right. I was ashamed that I hadn't noticed it before.

'She is thin,' George commented.

But she was beyond thin, she was gaunt.

We watched as she sat on a chair. She leaned forward and rested her elbows on her knees. She held her hands to her eyes and started to weep as she rocked gently back and forth.

My dad, who had just seen the last of the mourners out, found her like that. He sat on the arm of the chair and put his arm on her shoulder.

'Come on, love,' he said.

The weeping had progressed to sobbing and her shoulders locked.

'Oh, Brian,' she said, throwing herself back in the chair. Dad had to grab the edge of the table to steady himself.

'Your dad's better off,' my dad said, 'you know that.'

'Are you?' I asked my grandfather's opinion.

'Probably,' he said.

'I know he is.' Mum blew her nose. 'It's just that it's brought everything back.' The tears flowed effortlessly.

Aunt Lizzie, who had been in the kitchen washing dishes, appeared at the door briefly before retreating.

'I know,' Dad said, patting Mum's hand.

'It's not five minutes,' she said, wiping tears away

with a crumpled tissue, 'since we were doing this for Ellen.'

'Seven months,' my grandfather spoke. 'It's been seven months.' I was surprised to hear it had been so long. 'You died in April and I died in the middle of November.'

◦ ◦ ◦

My grandfather had said he wanted to see a man. 'Unfinished business,' he had said. He and Constance had left but I couldn't tear myself away from my parents' house. George and I watched my aunt finally leave the kitchen. Uncle Paul was at her shoulder.

'They're all done now,' Aunt Lizzie announced.

Mum looked at her sister and nodded slowly.

'You alright, Lizzie?' Dad asked.

Lizzie nodded and wiped her wet hands on her skirt. 'Yeah,' she said. 'Just glad it's all over.'

'Yeah,' the men agreed in unison.

'And I know Dad's at peace now. He was ready to go.' She looked at her sister nervously. 'Would you like a cup of tea. Peg?' she asked. 'You've been so busy looking after everyone else I'll bet you've not had anything yourself.'

◦ ◦ ◦

Uncle Paul had taken a silent lead from his wife and disappeared to the pub with my dad. My mum and her sister sat on opposite chairs and each rested a cup and saucer on their knees.

'You did well today,' Aunt Lizzie said.

Mum forced a smile onto her face.

My aunt was staring deep into her cup. I think she was searching for the right words. Mum seemed to notice how uncomfortable Aunt Lizzie looked.

'They're together again at last,' Mum said,

misinterpreting the signs.

'What? Oh, yes, they are.' Aunt Lizzie put the cup and saucer on the table with purpose. 'But that's not what I was thinking about.' It appeared that she had decided that what needed to be said was going to be said, so she settled on, 'Peg, I don't really know how to say this.'

'What?' Mum's hand went to her chest. 'What's wrong?'

'Nothing.' Aunt Lizzie held her hand out in a gesture that told my mother to calm down. 'Nothing's wrong. It's just that something happened today at the wake.'

Aunt Lizzie took a deep breath and locked eyes with my mother. She spoke slowly, as if she was choosing each word carefully.

'I saw Naomi in front of the sofa in the other room. She was talking to someone.'

'Oh my God,' Mum lifted her hand and covered her mouth. 'I told Marc he should take her to see a doctor but …'

Aunt Lizzie interrupted her. 'I believe her.'

Mum said nothing with her mouth but plenty with her eyes. Aunt Lizzie persisted.

'I do.' She ran her tongue back and forth over her lips. 'Naomi had a message for you from Ellen.'

The silence was deafening.

My mother couldn't maintain the eye contact. 'What did she say?' Mum croaked.

'She told me that her mummy said I had to make you understand it wasn't your fault.'

Mum's eyes widened. 'Naomi said that?'

'They were her exact words.'

'You're making it up,' Mum dismissed.

'I'm not,' Aunt Lizzie insisted. 'Why would I do that?'

'To make me feel better.' Mum almost spat the words out. 'To give me hope.'

'Hope for what?'

Mum sighed heavily. 'I want to believe you,' she said. 'I can't tell you how much I want to believe you, how much I want to believe that Ellen still exists somewhere. I want to ... but I can't.' She stood up, collecting her cup and saucer up on the way. 'I can't.'

She walked into the kitchen, leaving my aunt looking deflated.

'We have to make her believe,' I announced.

George inhaled deeply on his fake cigarette and said, 'Yep,' before exhaling equally fake smoke.

CHAPTER TWENTY-NINE

Aunt Lizzie had seemed surprised when Marc rang, and even more so when he asked her to babysit Naomi.

'Of course,' she said, 'I'd love to.'

'It's just that Liam has been on at me for weeks to go out with him for a drink.' He sounded like he was apologising.

Having once hated the fact that Marc often spoke on speaker phone when he rang from work, I now loved it because it meant that I could hear both sides of the conversation.

'Tell you what,' my aunt said. 'If you like, bring Naomi to my house and she can stay here. That way you and Liam can make a night of it.' Marc started to make reluctant noises. 'Go on,' she insisted, 'give yourself a night off.'

'OK,' he conceded, 'that'd be great. Can I bring her round about seven?'

'Bring her whenever you like.'

'Thanks.'

Naomi had packed clean underwear, her toothbrush, and Jaspar into her tiny suitcase, which she carried into the spare bedroom at my Aunt Lizzie's house. She placed

Jaspar on the pillow, left the case on a chair, and skipped back downstairs, where there was a glass of orange juice and a plate of biscuits waiting for her. Aunt Lizzie used to do the same for me when I was a child and I smiled.

'Just like old times,' I whispered to George.

Aunt Lizzie took a drink from the cup she was holding and studied Naomi over its rim.

'Do you remember what you said to me last week, Naomi?' she asked. 'You said I had to make Granny Peg understand.'

'Yes,' Naomi replied in a matter of fact way.

'Why did you say that?'

Naomi furrowed her brow and a crease formed between her eyes. 'Because Mummy told me to tell you.'

My aunt caught her breath and put the cup to her lips again. Maybe there was something stronger than tea in there.

'I do see her,' Naomi said. Naomi's eyes sat wide. 'Granny Peg doesn't believe me, but it's true, honest … I'm not making it up.'

Aunt Lizzie's eyes were compassionate as she reached out her hand to my daughter. 'I don't think you're making it up,' she said.

Naomi had fallen asleep almost as soon as Aunt Lizzie had finished the story she had been reading. With my daughter tucked up safely in bed, my thoughts turned to my husband.

'Can we go and see Marc?' I asked.

'If you like,' George said, 'but why do you want to?'

He had never asked why I wanted to see Marc before but I knew this time was different. I would see … what would I see? I didn't know, but I knew I wanted to see it.

'I just do.'

'If you're sure,' George said as he prepared to do whatever it was he did that moved us around so quickly.

Marc and Liam sat at a table close to the bar. Marc was playing with a beer mat, turning it and tapping it on the table.

'You OK?' Liam asked.

Marc looked at him blankly for a second then forced a smile. 'Sorry,' he said.

'Don't be sorry, just relax.'

'Yeah.' Marc shook his shoulders and threw the beer mat onto the table. He picked up the pint he had barely touched and took a drink. The froth formed a moustache on his upper lip and he wiped it away with the back of his hand.

'That looks good,' I heard George say and when I looked at him I saw he was gazing lustfully at Marc's glass. He was holding his substitute cigarette between his thumb and middle finger and moved it towards his lips. 'There are days, when I'd sell my soul for a real pint and a proper ciggie.'

I couldn't help laughing, but the best George could manage was a smile.

Four pints later, Marc was finally starting to relax. He was also starting to talk, which I suspect had been Liam's plan all along.

George leaned on the bar sniffing up the fumes while I stood closer to the table Marc and Liam sat at.

'I know people think I should be getting over it,' Marc said, his pint halfway between the table and his mouth. He took a sip and I moved closer. 'But … oh, I don't know.' He started to play with the beer mat again. 'Do you know,' he said with a sigh, 'even though I think about her every day …' Marc struggled to find the right words. Eventually, he lifted his head and looked into the space behind Liam. 'Sometimes I can't remember what she looked like.'

I looked at George and wished I wasn't there.

I was thoroughly miserable and George let me wallow as we sat together. The pub had long since closed and the landlord gone to bed. Marc and Liam had been amongst the last to leave and had both walked out on unsteady legs.

'He said he couldn't remember me,' I said.

George screwed his mouth to the side. 'That's not exactly what he said.' The look I gave him must have been aggressive because he held his hands up defensively. 'I'm sorry,' George said, 'but he didn't'

'What did he say then?' I challenged.

'He said that sometimes he couldn't remember what you looked like.'

'So he's forgetting me.' I knew it sounded like an accusation.

'No.' George sighed and tapped his fingers on the table. 'He just hasn't seen you for nearly nine months.'

'I haven't forgotten what he looks like.'

George lifted his head and looked into my eyes. 'You've seen him almost every day.'

'How could he forget me so soon?' I asked, losing the battle with the tears.

I don't know how long I cried for but George let me do it for as long as was necessary. He did nothing and said nothing.

Eventually, the tears stopped and I wiped the last of them away with my fingertips. I sniffed and coughed.

216

George watched me.

I felt self-conscious.

George continued to watch me.

'What?' I asked.

George put his head back and took a deep breath.

'You've got to let go,' he said, lowering his head to face me.

'Let go of what?'

'Him.'

'How can I?' I asked weakly.

'Because you have to. You have no choice. You're dead and he isn't.'

I knew tears were forming again. I could feel them grow and well up in my eyes but I didn't have the strength to fight them.

I cried because I knew George was right.

* * *

We stayed in the pub for most of the night. George seemed to be enjoying the sights and smells that he apparently missed so much and for my part it was as good a place as any to think.

I had thought in silence for much of the night and when George sat down beside me I was surprised to see the early morning glow of approaching dawn.

'You all right?' George asked.

I forced myself to nod but I don't think I convinced either of us.

He watched me for a moment and asked. 'Do you remember Barry Hutton?'

'Yes,' I said.

'OK.' George nodded slowly. 'And he was ...?' He held his head to one side.

'An ex-boyfriend.' I said the words slowly and couldn't help a smile from spreading across my lips.

'Well, he was a bit more than that, wasn't he?' George said with a smile.

'He was my ex-fiancé.'

'That's right,' George nodded. He leaned forward until his elbows rested on his knees. After a moment he pushed himself upright. 'What colour was his hair?'

'Blond,' I said without hesitation.

George moved his head from side to side and crinkled his lips together. 'You say blond, I'd say mousy,' he smiled, 'but what's in a couple of shades? What colour were his eyes?'

'Green.'

'Hazel,' George corrected.

'How tall was he?'

I had to think about that. 'Five foot eleven?' I suggested.

'He was more like five foot nine,' George said with a chuckle. He stood up and started to walk around the table where I sat. He was like a television detective interrogating a suspect. 'What did his tattoo say?'

I winced at the memory. 'Mum and Dad.'

'Incorrect,' George said. '"Mother and Father".'

I stood up too and stopped his movement. 'Why all the questions?' I asked.

'Because you loved him.'

I sat back in my seat.

I had loved Barry. I had loved him with all my heart from the moment I met him when I was eighteen. And he loved me back. For two years we were inseparable.

'That was a long time ago,' I said with bravado.

'But you still enjoy his memory.'

I didn't like to admit that I did.

'They were good times.' I thought for a moment. 'Did it really say "Mother and Father"?'

George nodded.

'Are you sure his hair wasn't dark blond?'

George gave an exaggerated shrug. 'It doesn't matter.' He let his shoulders fall back into position. 'What matters is the way that his memory makes you feel.'

His memory did make me feel good. They had been happy times.

'Do you remember how you felt when he told you he was going to live in Canada and marry the girl he'd met there on holiday?'

I didn't say anything but George appeared to be waiting for an answer. 'I was devastated,' I said.

'What did you do?'

'I begged him to stay with me.'

'What was the last thing he told you?'

'He said he was sorry to hurt me but he had no choice. He said that he had to go.'

'And?'

'What?'

'What were the very last words he said to you?'

'He told me to be happy.'

CHAPTER THIRTY

'Did you have a good time at Auntie Lizzie's?' I asked.

'Yes.' Naomi had no idea how good it made me feel to see her smile. 'She read me a story and did the voices and everything'

'Yes, I saw,' I said laughing. 'I thought her Billy Goat Gruff was very good.' Naomi was staring at me. 'What's the matter?' I asked.

'I didn't see you,' she said.

She looked puzzled.

'I have been with you lots of times when you didn't see me,' I told her.

'How?' she asked.

'I don't know,' I admitted.

'How?' she asked George.

He pursed his lips. 'Do you know,' he said leaning forward, 'I don't know either. I think it must have something to do with science.'

'Science?' She made a face.

George laughed. 'Most things are down to science. And, as I left school when I was fourteen, I don't know much about science.'

'I'm good at science,' Naomi announced and I shared her pride.

'Naomi,' I said, trying to get her mind off science and other things concerned with why she hadn't seen me. 'I need your help.'

'What do you want?'

'I need you to give Granny Peg a message.'

'Like the one I gave Auntie Liz?' she said excitedly.

'Yes,' I said, 'just like that.'

Naomi seemed excited and I had to make sure she was paying attention.

'I need you to tell her it doesn't matter about the ballet lessons.'

'It doesn't matter about the ballet lessons,' she repeated.

'Yes, that's right.'

'Will she remember that she told Lizzie about the ballet lessons?' George asked after we had left.

'Hope so,' I said, 'because I won't be able to tell her the bra didn't matter.'

I told Naomi to ask Marc if she could ring her grandmother just before bedtime. George and I sat in my parents' living room and waited for the phone to ring. I was pleased to see that my mother seemed more like her old self. She had ditched the jogging bottoms and baggy T-shirt in favour of a blouse and skirt.

The television was on but neither of them were watching. Dad was reading the sports section of the evening paper and Mum was doing a crossword.

I looked at the clock and gauged when Naomi would ring. Marc seemed to have stuck to the routine that had been established before my death and, that being the case, the phone should ring at any minute.

Although I was expecting it, I still jumped. Dad reached over and picked up the phone.

'Hello,' he said. 'Oh hello, sweetheart, I'm very well, thank you, how are you? That's good.' He mouthed the word 'Naomi' to my mother. 'Granny Peg? Yes, sweetheart, she's here … All right, night night.'

He handed the phone to my mother.

'Naomi?' She sounded surprised. 'Is everything all right?' Mum listened to Naomi and her eyes started to move around the room nervously. Her hand went to her mouth.

Dad had gone back to reading the paper, but noticing my mother's reaction he put the paper down. 'Peg, what's wrong?' he whispered.

She shook her head and waved his concern away. As she took her hand away, I could see that she was smiling.

'Yes, darling,' she said. 'I understand. Thank you for ringing.' She nodded as she listened again. 'All right. you'd best get off to bed. But before you go, is your daddy there?' There was a delay while the phone was passed over. 'Hello. Marc,' Mum said. 'Can I pick Naomi up from school tomorrow and bring her here for tea?' She listened to what Marc was saying. 'I know, it's been too long. Goodnight.'

She handed the telephone back to my dad. There were tears in her eyes but for once they were not tears of sadness.

'What's wrong?' Dad asked.

'Nothing,' Mum said, 'everything's fine.'

'Is Naomi coming for tea tomorrow?' There was a hint of surprise in Dad's voice.

'Yes.' There was a smile on her face. 'I thought I'd ask Naomi if she wanted ballet lessons.'

Dad looked puzzled before picking the newspaper up again. He'd become used to Mum's erratic behaviour and tried to play it down.

Mum thought about picking up the crossword where she'd left it but changed her mind as her hand hovered over the magazine. Instead, she reached over and picked up the telephone again.

'Who're you ringing now?' Dad asked as he turned the page.

'Lizzie.' She drummed her fingers on her knee as she waited for the connection to be made. 'Lizzie,' she said excitedly, 'it's Peg … No, everything's fine.' I had grown to hate one-sided conversations. 'Lizzie, listen.' Mum lifted her head slightly and took in a deep breath which rattled in her throat. 'Do you remember me telling you I wished I'd let Ellen have ballet lessons?' Mum was nodding like a wise old sage. 'Naomi's just called and told me that Ellen says it doesn't matter about the ballet lessons.'

I turned to George to share my excitement but he wasn't there. He had moved to stand behind my dad and was reading the newspaper over his shoulder. Mum and Aunt Lizzie carried on chatting. When their conversation was over, Dad asked, 'Did you leave the window open in the kitchen?'

Mum glanced briefly into the room. 'No,' she said, 'why?'

'There's a draught coming from somewhere,' he said as he turned another page.

Mum seemed startled. She looked around the room eagerly. 'She's here,' Mum whispered.

'Who's here?' Dad asked without really paying attention.

'Ellen.'

'Peg?' Now she had Dad's complete attention.

'She's here,' Mum said, still looking around the room. Her eyes rested on George for a second.

'What do you mean? What did Naomi say to you? What's all this about ballet lessons?'

Mum sat down and leaned towards Dad.

'No, no before that,' she said to herself. She took a

minute to put things in order. 'After Dad's funeral Lizzie told me she'd found Naomi front of the sofa in the other room talking to someone.' Mum looked at her hands as she spoke. 'There was no-one there.'

Dad took a deep breath and put the paper on the coffee table. Mum looked at him.

'She was talking to Ellen,' Mum said breathlessly.

'Is that what Naomi said?'

Mum nodded and Dad lifted his eyes to the ceiling and sighed.

'Lizzie said that Naomi had told her that Ellen had said she had to make me understand it wasn't my fault.'

Dad looked confused.

'Ellen told Naomi that Lizzie had to make me understand it wasn't my fault,' Mum emphasised.

Dad nodded slowly. 'And Naomi said that to Lizzie?'

'Yes,' Mum insisted. 'At the time I thought Lizzie was making it up. You know Lizzie and I have never been close. But since Ellen went, Lizzie's been there for me and we've become so much closer.' She had that glazed look in her eyes again. 'Anyway,' Mum came back from that distant place, 'like I said, I didn't believe her. I thought she was making it up.'

'Why would she make it up?' Dad was still confused.

'To make me feel better,' Mum said. Dad accepted that with a tilt of his head. 'But when Naomi rang just now she gave me another message.'

'From Ellen?' I thought Dad sounded a little sceptical.

'Yes. Naomi said that her mummy had told her to tell me it didn't matter about the ballet lessons.'

'Ballet lessons?'

'Do you remember how when she was ten she wanted to have ballet lessons? Well, I was talking to Lizzie about how I wished I'd let her have them. Ellen told Naomi that it doesn't matter. Don't you see, Brian? Ellen must have been there when I told Lizzie. She must have heard me say I was sorry.' She looked around again, searching. 'And she's here now.'

'But I thought you didn't believe that Naomi could see Ellen,' Dad said.

'I've changed my mind.' Mum was still searching the room.

Dad chose his words carefully. 'And now you believe Naomi can see Ellen?'

Mum looked at him and almost resisted the temptation to roll her eyes. 'Of course she can. How else would she know about the ballet lessons?'

I was surprised it had been so easy to convince my mother, and I said as much to George.

'She's at that stage of her grief,' he said.

We left Mum looking through the telephone directory for dance studios and Dad saying that maybe she should talk to Marc first. I hoped she would take his advice.

'George,' I said, 'please tell me I didn't die so Mum and Aunt Lizzie could finally start acting like sisters.'

'Would that be a bad reason to die?' he asked, turning his head to one side.

'Too bloody right it would,' I exclaimed.

'Why?'

'Because ...' I couldn't think of a reason.

'There would be worse things to die for,' George said.

CHAPTER THIRTY-ONE

I was grateful that for once Mum listened to Dad's advice. She'd called Marc while Naomi was sitting on her granddad's knee, listening to him tell her story of when he was a little boy.

'I should have done it for Ellen,' Mum told him. 'Let me do it for her daughter.'

For the first time in a long time, Marc agreed without argument.

My death seemed to be bringing the whole world closer together.

I think that was when I finally understood about my issues, and said the same to George.

He breathed in through his nose and nodded his head as he let the breath out the same way.

George and I were there when Mum got the phone call from Marc asking if Naomi could stay overnight with her and Dad in a couple of days' time.

'He's going out with Liam,' she explained to Dad.

But it wasn't just Liam. Liam's wife Catherine was there. And alongside her was another woman.

'Marc, this is Amy,' Catherine said. 'Amy, this is Marc.' She waved her hands between them in the way people do when they introduce strangers to each other.

'Hi.' Marc looked like a schoolboy again and could only meet Amy's gaze for the briefest of seconds.

'Hello.' Amy's voice was more controlled.

I walked around the group slowly, eyeing the stranger. Finally, I settled beside George again.

Catherine and Liam moved through the doors of the restaurant they had met outside. Marc and Amy looked at each other.

'Shall we?' Amy asked after a few seconds.

'Oh, yes.' Marc gave a short, embarrassed laugh and moved towards the door. He pulled it open and allowed Amy to walk through before following her at a distance.

Catherine and Liam were already seated at a table and Marc quickened his step so he could pull Amy's seat out for her. As she pulled her seat in, Marc took his own beside her.

George started to move towards the table but I put my hand out to stop him. I preferred to watch from a distance.

'You can't go in there.' George said, trying to keep up with me.

'Too late,' I said triumphantly. 'I'm already here.' I looked around the gents toilets, taking in the three cubicles on the left and row of urinals to the right. Marc and Liam stood side by side on our right. I marvelled at how easily they could keep up a conversation.

Their voices were low and, along with the other sounds that were going on in there, meant that I couldn't hear a thing. I gave up.

'You all right?' Liam asked as they re-entered the restaurant.

'Yeah,' Marc replied a little too quickly.

'What's wrong?'

'Nothing,' Marc tried to laugh it off.

'OK,' he said. 'And United are going to win the league this season.'

'In your dreams.' Marc looked at the table where Catherine and Amy were deep in conversation. 'It's nothing.'

Liam grabbed Marc's arm to stop him. 'What's wrong?'

Marc looked straight into Liam's eyes. 'Nothing wrong,' he said deliberately. 'And that's what wrong.' He stared at his feet as he spoke. 'Amy's a really nice person and I'm enjoying her company. I'm having a really good time ...' The end of the sentence disappeared before it came out of Marc's mouth.

Liam looked from his friend to their companions.

'It's OK to have a good time,' Liam told him.

'I know,' Marc said.

'So don't beat yourself up about it.'

'I know, but ...'

'No buts, Marc,' Liam said. 'It doesn't mean you love Ellen any less just because you're having dinner with another woman.'

'I know.' If he knew so much, why was he having so much trouble? Marc pushed his hand through his hair. 'I'll never stop loving Ellen,' he said.

'Of course you won't,' Liam told him. 'Nobody thinks that.'

'It's just that ...' Marc took in and let out a huge breath. 'I need to feel loved.' He looked at the floor again. 'I've got Naomi, who is the most precious thing in the world ... but she can't give me the love I need.'

'It's alright to feel that way, its natural.'

'Is it?'

'Yes, it is,' Liam slapped Marc's arm. 'Now, come on before they send out a search party.'

Liam led the way with Marc a couple of steps behind. We stayed long enough to see Amy's face light up when Marc smiled at her.

George and I walked in silence. The people we passed were snuggling into their coats against the cold night air. Fortunately for me I didn't feel the cold as I had no coat to snuggle into. I snuggled into myself anyway.

I put my head down to avoid seeing anyone, concentrating on my feet as I moved them one in front of the other.

I had George by my side but I was alone with my thoughts. I replayed the conversation between Liam and Marc. I heard Marc's words over and over again.

He needed a woman's love. He wanted a woman's love.

I knew he deserved a woman's love.

I wondered if another woman would taste Marc's lips this evening and realised I minded a little less than before.

I was tempted to go back to the house that had been my home. I wanted to see Marc. I wanted to talk to him. I wanted to tell him it was all right for him to feel the way he did. But I was scared I wouldn't find him alone.

I spent much of the night in silence. I walked and thought all through the long, dark hours with George at my side. He didn't prompt me to tell him what I was thinking. Maybe he had thoughts of his own. I never took the chance to ask.

Hearing Marc express his needs to Liam made me realise how selfish I was being. Marc was alive and he needed things. He needed to feel things again, things that were beyond the capabilities of a dead woman. Marc needed another woman to do that for him now. I had no right to expect it to be any other way.

I tried putting myself in his position, imagining what I would do if he had been the one who died.

I stopped looking at my own feet for a moment and looked at George's as they kept pace with mine. Our steps were synchronised as we moved at a comfortable pace. The whole thing about George was comfortable. With George, I didn't have to pretend. He seemed to know me almost as well as I knew myself. But of course he would; he'd read my file.

George had come to mean more to me than I thought any man other than Marc could and it wasn't until that moment that I realised how much I would miss him if he was gone.

'What will happen when this is over?' I asked.

'When what's over?'

'This.' I turned full circle with my arms spread out.

'The end of the world?' George looked puzzled.

'No,' I laughed. 'I mean when I move from here.'

'Beyond the light?'

'Yes.' I looked into his sapphire eyes and marvelled at their intensity. 'Will you go with me?'

He lowered his long lashes briefly. 'If you want me to.'

'I can do this,' I told him. 'I can deal with these issues, but only if you're there.'

George took a step towards me. He put his hand on my shoulder and gave it a gentle squeeze. 'I'm your Greeter,' he said in a deep voice. 'You can't get rid of me that easily.'

My lips formed the start of a smile and I looked sideways into his face. His smile was in his eyes rather than on his lips and the first glow of dawn rising above his head caught the tips of his hair and formed a halo.

His eyes were sparkling even brighter and I felt myself moving towards them. His hand still rested on my shoulder and I slid my own hand inside his jacket to rest on the waistband of his jeans. I don't know who pulled who, probably it was us both. Suddenly our bodies were touching. George lowered his head and I rose on my toes until our lips touched. His lips felt warm and tasted sweet.

When our lips parted we held each other with our eyes for a few moments. The corners of his eyes formed deep creases as he smiled.

Slowly, I lowered my feet to the floor. We both turned in opposite directions, George straightening his jacket and me smoothing my hair.

'That'll be me sacked,' he said.

'What?' I turned back. 'Why?'

Surely he wouldn't have to go away because of one kiss?

George took his cigarette out of his pocket and put it in his mouth. His cheeks formed holes in the side of his face as he sucked. He took the cigarette away and let the air out through his nose.

'I'm pretty sure it says something in the manual about not kissing the Client.'

'Client?' I screwed up my eyes.

'It's just a word.'

'Client?' I repeated with mock annoyance.

'Yes, Client,' he said, pinching the end of the cigarette and putting it in his pocket. 'I'm the Greeter, you're the Client.'

'Is that how they refer to dead people in the manual?' I asked.

George looked at me and took a deep breath in through his nose. 'It's just a word.'

'Will you really get the sack?'

'Don't know, maybe. Who cares anyway? I'm crap at

232

it and the pay's rubbish.'

It felt natural to be holding George's hand as we walked along the street towards the rising sun.

Later, I would wonder why what happened did but at that moment I revelled in how good it felt.

I knew I wanted Marc to feel the same way.

CHAPTER THIRTY-TWO

I wanted to see Marc. I wanted to see how I would feel when I saw him. We waited for him in his office.

Stephen was already there even though it wasn't yet eight o'clock. Judging by the dark rims around his eyes, he hadn't had much sleep. As he stood to go to the coffee machine I could see the heavy creasing on his shirt and wondered if the little sleep he had got had been in the chair he was returning to.

By the speed that Stephen drank the coffee it was far from hot. He finished it quickly and tossed the plastic cup towards the bin. It hit the rim and fell down on the wrong side. Stephen eyed it but didn't pick it up. He returned to whatever was on the screen.

I watched the hands of the clock turn, eager in the knowledge that Marc would soon be here. Now and again, George and I looked at each other nervously.

The door opened and Marc walked in, looking more relaxed than I had seen him since I'd been dead. He looked different and he walked like a man who'd found reason to live.

The plastic cup that Stephen had tossed was still where it had fallen. Marc scooped it up and dropped it in the bin.

Marc looked at his colleague and perched himself on the edge of Stephen's desk.

'I know, I know,' Stephen said. 'I look like crap.'

Marc gave a non-committal nod.

'Baby keeping you up?'

Baby? When did they have a baby? Why didn't Marc tell me? Was I was dead when it was born? Of course, you silly cow. More and more each day I was realising the world didn't stop when a person died.

'Five times last night,' Stephen sounded weary.

'It'll get better.'

'That's what they all say.'

'It will.' Marc picked up a file from Stephen's desk and started to flick through it. 'Listen,' he said. 'Are you and Linda going to the Christmas party?'

Christmas party? I hadn't realised it was so close.

'Wasn't planning on it.'

'You should,' Marc urged. 'It'll do you good. And more to the point, it'll do Linda good. Look,' he said, 'Linda had a baby six weeks ago and she's spent all of those six weeks looking after this screaming demanding ...' His hands moved in small circles. '... thing.' Perhaps not the best way to describe a baby but Stephen seemed to get the point. 'But who's looking after Linda? Ask her if she'd like to go. I'll bet you she says yes. She'll jump at the chance of a night out.' Stephen was taking the bait. 'You've got to show her that you see her as a woman and not just the mother of your child.'

'Do you think?'

'I don't just think. I know.'

'Are there any tickets left?' he asked.

'Hope so,' Marc said, pushing himself into an upright position. 'I'm going to need a couple myself.'

Stephen spun his chair round to look at Marc, who winked before disappearing behind his own computer screen.

'How come he knows so much about women?' George asked after we had left Marc's office. 'All that about still seeing her as a woman and not just the mother of his child. Where'd he learn that from?'

'He's a modern man,' I explained. 'He's in touch with his feminine side.'

'His what?'

'Modern men are different,' I said.

George didn't disagree.

'Bit early for this, isn't it?' George said as he looked around the hall that was decked to the rafters with garlands and balloons. In the corner, a six-foot Christmas tree was decorated in red and gold. Beautifully wrapped boxes were stacked at the base.

'They always have it on the first Saturday in December,' I told him. 'I don't know why.'

Waitresses moved around the tables, serving a traditional turkey dinner to the merrymakers. George and I wandered around the room, searching out the table that Marc and Amy sat at. George pointed them out to me. Their heads were close as they spoke to each other in between mouthfuls.

I watched them for a moment.

'See her?' I pointed out a brunette in a low-cut red dress. 'Last year she got rolling drunk and showed everyone her knickers when she was dancing.'

George nodded and probably wished that he had been there to see it.

'And him.' I squinted to see a man raising a pint glass to his mouth. 'I think he's the bloke who started a fight with someone he thought was ogling his wife.'

'What are we doing here?' George asked before I

could start telling him about the Production Manager's wife.

'What do you mean?'

'I mean that if you came to see Marc and Amy, they're over there.'

'I know.'

● ◆ ●

With the speeches over it was time for dancing. It started slowly with just a few brave souls on the dance floor. Gradually, as the night progressed, more joined the brave. After half an hour, the party was in full swing. Never much of a dancer Marc stayed firmly in his seat until Suggs yelled the immortal words.

'One step beyond ...'

I nudged George. 'He'll be up now.'

We looked and sure enough, there were Marc and Stephen racing their way to the dance floor along with practically every other man in the room. Linda and Amy giggled as they followed.

I laughed. I mimicked the dance that nearly everyone was doing.

'What's that?' George asked.

'The Sand Dance,' I said. He laughed at me, spinning on the ball of his foot so he could follow my movements.

'If you say so.'

'It's Madness,' I shouted above the music.

'I know.' George shouted back without realising the joke he was making. He lifted the collar of his jacket and copied my moves.

It was followed by a slow one and the men were obliged to shuffle awkwardly with wives and girlfriends.

George followed their lead and drew me towards him. I liked to dance and he took tiny steps that led me in a gentle circle. He was a good dancer.

I glanced at Marc and Amy doing the side to side shuffle and smiled. Amy was resting her head against Marc's chest and his cheek lay on the top of her head. I was surprised to realise I felt happy for him. Even a week ago I couldn't have imagined feeling that way if I saw him with another woman in his arms. I allowed George to lead me, but somehow my eyes always found Marc.

Then suddenly, I think Marc found me and our eyes met. Marc lifted his head. Amy looked up to see what had caused his movement and she followed Marc's gaze. She said something. He shook his head and after a few seconds they resumed their position.

The music stopped and the lights went up. The DJ wished everyone a Merry Christmas and told them to take care on the way home. George and I stood amidst the bustle of people preparing to leave. Some were putting on coats, others searching for handbags, and more than one was draining the dregs from their glasses.

Marc was holding out Amy's coat and she was climbing inside it. Marc moved his head towards hers as he lifted the coat onto her shoulders. He said something and she laughed.

I felt George's breath on my cheek as he spoke. 'You alright?' he asked.

'Yeah,' I gave a nod without taking my eyes from Marc and Amy.

He looked at them. 'Sure?'

'Yes,' I insisted, pulling my eyes from them. 'I am.' I patted George's chest to reinforce my point but I didn't meet his eyes.

'He looked happy,' I said.

George and I sat among the debris of the Christmas party. Everyone had gone home a long time ago.

'Yeah, he did,' George said as he flicked a stray balloon away. He waited a second before adding, 'They both did.'

I stood up and kicked balloons and party hats out of the way. I walked for ten or fifteen feet before I turned to look at George.

'He's part of a couple again, isn't he?' I took a few backward steps. 'They're a couple.' I spun around and continued taking a turn of the room. Eventually, I made it back to my starting point and returned to my seat. 'It's OK.'

'Really?'

'Yes.' I dropped my hands and lifted my head. 'I mean, she seems very nice.' I laughed, to myself as much as anything. 'Thank God he didn't fall for Rosie.'

George laughed too. 'Oh I don't know,' he said with a smile. 'Rosie's a very pretty girl.'

I gave him a glare, grabbed a discarded paper napkin, screwed it into a ball, and threw it at him. He ducked and it flew over his shoulder.

'Come on,' he said, pushing his chair back and standing up. 'Let's get out of here.'

'Where are we going?' I asked.

'For a walk.'

Which is what we did, we walked and walked and then we walked some more. All the while we walked, we were silent.

'What's wrong?' I asked.

There was no reply and I wasn't sure if George had heard me so I asked again.

George looked startled, as if he'd forgotten I was there.

He gave me a soulful look and tried to force a smile. 'Sorry,' he said almost under his breath.

'Don't be sorry,' I said, closing the gap between us. 'Just tell me what's wrong.'

'Nothing. Everything's fine.'

'So why have we walked for the last hour without saying anything?'

'It's not been that long.' He started to walk again.

'I know there's something wrong,' I insisted.

He looked like he was going to say something, but the words failed him. He shook his head. 'It's nothing,' he said again. He gestured down the street with a nod of his head. 'Come on, let's walk.' I let him take hold of my hand and fell into step beside him.

CHAPTER THIRTY-THREE

Although it was only five o'clock, the sky was as black as midnight. The streets were busy with people rushing around, most of them carrying bulging bags.

It was raining again and the drops formed miniature rainbows as the lights from the Christmas decorations passed through them on their way to the ground. I'd never noticed anything like it before, and the people rushing around seemed oblivious to its beauty. Maybe they couldn't see it the way I did. Maybe it was one of the perks of being dead.

My walk became a trudge as we milled with the happy and not so happy shoppers and George got ahead of me. He must have noticed because he stopped to look for me and as he did I was stopped in my tracks by a woman loaded with bags and struggling to control an umbrella. A box fell from one of her bags but she carried on, leaving the box lying on the damp floor.

'Excuse me,' I shouted. 'You've dropped something.' Of course it was no good and the woman disappeared into the crowd. The box was kicked by a man, then by another, and finally a woman before coming to a halt in the gutter.

I crouched down and fingered the box where a porcelain face with blonde curls looked out from a now-broken plastic window. The rain fell through the gap and landed on the doll's face, making it look like she was crying. I felt like crying with her.

I saw George's shoes appear by my side and stood up slowly.

'I love … loved Christmas,' I said, giving the doll a final glance before crossing the road.

I stood before the window and looked in. Row after row of earrings, brooches, and bracelets shone under the lights. Marc had bought me a Christmas gift from this jeweller every year we had been married. The old man that used to own it had done us a deal on our wedding rings because he said we reminded him of him and his late wife. The old man had retired now and the business had been passed on to his son but buying my gift from here was one of those traditions that made Christmas so special.

But not this year.

I hoped they wouldn't go out of business because of the lost trade. I doubted they would if the queue was anything to go by.

Another of our traditions was taking Naomi to see Santa in his grotto.

I stood at the back and watched as Naomi climbed onto the fat man's knee. Marc was standing beside the chubby elf and I noticed a hint of a smile that rested on his face. He looked happy and relaxed as he stood with his hands pushed into the back pockets of his jeans.

'Have you been a good girl this year?' Santa asked.

'Yes,' Naomi replied earnestly.

'Has she, Daddy?' Santa turned to look at Marc, who nodded his head. 'Good.' He turned back to Naomi. 'So what would you like me to bring you on Christmas morning? No, let me guess. A doll?' Naomi shook her head. 'A game?' Again she shook her head. Santa looked to one side, as if he was thinking hard. I was impressed, he was much better than last year's Santa. 'No,' he said, 'you're going to have to give me a clue.'

'I want my mummy to not be dead.'

●◄●

Marc sat across the table from Naomi and stared into his coffee cup. Naomi was sipping orange juice through a curly straw.

'Naomi,' Marc said cautiously. 'What you asked Santa for, you know he can't bring you that, don't you?'

'Yes,' she said with the straw between her teeth. 'But he asked me what I wanted and I told him.' She didn't take her eyes off her glass.

●◄●

Marc had taken Naomi home and George and I browsed through the department store. We were like any other couple searching for Christmas presents except we were dead and the store had been closed for two hours. The only other people here were the security guards, who had done a cursory tour of the store before disappearing to a secret place where they probably spent the night drinking coffee and playing cards.

I stroked the teddies in the toy department. I stopped by a chocolate-coloured bear. 'This is the one Naomi wants,' I said. George seemed unimpressed. 'It talks,' I told him.

'Does it?' He wasn't really paying any attention to the bear, he was more interested in the train track set up in the centre of the room.

'Yes,' I said, 'it tells you stories, and helps you to read

if you buy the accessories.'

'Good.' I doubted he heard a word I had said. I moved to the train track. 'What is it about boys and train sets?' I asked.

'Same as girls and teddy bears,' he said.

I walked off, letting my fingertips touch whatever was sitting on the shelves that I passed.

Marc was standing in almost the same spot I had stood in the night before. He was stood in front of a teddy two along from the one I had told George was the one Naomi wanted. He picked up the one in front of him.

'That's not the right one,' I told him.

Marc was examining the underside of the bear for a reason that only he knew. He put it down and picked up the one beside it.

'That's not the right one either,' I said.

Marc examined it in the same way. He put it back and picked up the first one again. He started to make his way to the cash desk.

'It's the wrong one,' I shouted as I ran after him. When I was a couple of steps ahead of him I turned and walked at his pace. 'It's the wrong one,' I said again. 'Oh, what's the point?' I said, peeling away. I watched as Marc put the bear on the counter beside the till and reached in his pocket for his wallet.

'You give up too easily,' George said.

Behind Marc was a man with a small boy. The man was carrying a large box. 'Let me hold it, Dad,' the boy said and put the bottle he had been holding onto the counter so he could take the box in both hands.

George stood beside the bottle and leaned down so his eyes were inches from it. I was about to ask what he was doing when the bottle flipped and fell.

246

'Sorry,' the boy's dad said, quickly righting the bottle. However it was too late to stop the river of fizzy liquid from running along the counter top. Marc took a step back to avoid the waterfall that it became and the assistant reached under the counter for a wad of tissue to dry it up with. The man and his son looked embarrassed.

With the damage cleaned up, the assistant threw away the wet tissues and turned her attention to Marc.

'Sorry.' She smiled and picked up the bear. As she did, drops of whatever had been in the bottle dripped from it. The assistant turned the bear over and a soggy brown patch covered its base. She put it to one side. 'I'll get you another,' she said.

'That was the last one on the shelf,' Marc told her.

I hadn't noticed but I hoped he was right.

'Oh,' the assistant said. 'I'm really sorry then, that means we're out of stock until we get our delivery tomorrow.' She stood on her tiptoes and looked to where the rest of the bears sat. 'I see we have the white one,' she said, 'or I could put one of the tan ones away for you tomorrow if you'd like.'

'No, it's OK,' Marc said, 'one of the others will do.' The assistant moved from behind the till to fetch it. 'But not the white one,' Marc said. 'I don't like the white one. I'll take the dark one instead.'

'The chocolate one?'

'Yes,' Marc and I said in unison.

With the right teddy paid for and in his bag, Marc left the shop. I threw my arms around George's neck and hugged him. 'Thank you,' I said.

We were both a little embarrassed by my outburst.

CHAPTER THIRTY-FOUR

With Naomi staying with my parents overnight, Marc took the chance to wrap the presents he had bought.

He held his hand in the air and looked at the ribbon of sticky tape that had wrapped itself around his finger.

He ripped the tape off and screwed it into a ball, which he tossed towards an already overflowing bin. He pulled another piece free from the roll. He held it at arm's length and looked horrified as it started to curl at the bottom.

George stood behind Marc, watching his struggles from over his shoulder. George scratched his head and I laughed.

Marc dropped the roll of tape as he bolted upright. He looked around like an animal that had heard a strange noise. Had he heard my laughter?

After a few seconds, he sat on the edge of the sofa. I reached out my hand and it rested just inches from his shoulder.

Slowly, Marc bent down and picked up the tape. He turned it round in his hand, trying to find the end.

'I don't believe this,' he said, tossing the tape away. 'Now I know why I left wrapping the presents to you. That stuffs bloody ridiculous.' He slouched back on the sofa.

Marc sat like that for ten minutes before collecting the

presents and wrapping paper together. His tread sounded heavy on the stairs. I wondered if he would hide Naomi's presents in his wardrobe this year.

Shortly after, I heard him switch the shower on, and fifteen minutes after that he closed the front door behind him.

'Nice,' I said as I looked around Amy's living room. The truth was I meant it. There wasn't a lot of furniture but what there was looked as if it belonged there. Everything was in the right place and the soft furnishings perfectly complimented the decoration. It was a bit too perfect, the sort of room that I had always aspired to but had never been able to achieve.

'I don't know what we're doing here,' George said.

Neither did I, I just knew it had seemed like a good idea. I'd finally realised what my issues were and if I was to ever move on I had to deal with them.

This was my way of dealing with the issue of Amy, or rather of Marc and Amy. When he'd left the house after the present-wrapping fiasco I'd known instinctively where Marc had been going and it was clear Amy was expecting someone. I just hoped for his sake that Marc was that someone.

There was a knock at the door and she almost ran to answer it.

'She's keen,' I said before I could stop myself.

George didn't say anything. He just put his arm around my shoulders.

She welcomed Marc with a light kiss on the lips and he followed her into the room. He took a seat without being asked, and clearly felt comfortable. Amy poured two glasses of wine and gave one to Marc.

They sat in silence for a few minutes. I noticed that

Amy looked nervous.

'I was surprised when you rang,' she said. 'I hadn't expected to hear from you today. What was it you needed to tell me?'

Marc took a drink from the glass he'd spent those minutes looking into.

'Doesn't matter,' he said.

Another period of silence followed.

'Marc, please.' She inched forward on her seat. 'On the phone you said you had to see me, that there was something that you had to tell me. What is it?'

'I can't,' he laughed. Amy looked hurt. 'You'll think I'm mad,' he explained.

'What is it?'

He drained his glass. 'OK, you asked for it,' he said. 'Ellen was laughing at me.'

'I was not,' I protested.

'You did,' George mocked.

'When?' Amy asked.

'Tonight, just before I rang you.'

Amy looked puzzled. She opened her mouth but no words came out. She reached for her own glass and took a drink. 'Tell me exactly what happened,' she said.

'Do you mind?' Marc asked, eyeing up the bottle of wine. Amy nodded her approval. Marc filled his glass and carefully put the bottle back. He looked at the glass in his hand.

'Just tell me,' Amy urged.

Marc took a deep breath and kept his eyes on his wine as he spoke. His words came slowly. 'I was wrapping Naomi's present. The tape wasn't playing the game, it kept wrapping itself around my fingers.' He took a drink and I exchanged a look with George. 'I heard her laughing.'

'I wasn't laughing at you,' I said, inching closer to

him.

'She wasn't laughing at me, though.'

I was shocked when Marc repeated what I had said. A noise escaped as I gasped but apparently only George heard it.

Marc set his glass on the table. 'It wasn't like she was laughing at me … she was just laughing. She thought it was funny that I was struggling with the sellotape.'

Marc and Amy looked at each other. Amy was the first to look away.

It took me a second or two to realise that I had moved towards Amy, as if I were giving her my support.

'He'll explain himself in a minute,' I told her. 'Just give him a minute,' I urged. 'It's not what you're thinking.' I looked towards Marc and willed him to speak.

'How did you feel?' Amy's voice was hoarse.

'What do you mean?'

'When you heard Ellen … laugh.'

Marc's head tilted. 'I did hear her,' he said.

'I know you did.'

Marc seemed agitated. 'I heard it like I've heard it a thousand times before.'

'I believe you,' Amy said, reaching her hand out.

'I didn't imagine it,' he insisted.

'I didn't say you did,' now Amy was agitated too.

'Oh, for God's sake!' I exclaimed. 'Will the pair of you just grow up?' I turned to Marc. 'She's asked you a perfectly good question,' I said. 'Tell her how it made you feel.'

Marc shook his head, 'I'm sorry,' he said.

'It's OK,' Amy answered for both of us.

'No, it's not,' he said. 'I haven't explained myself very well.' He reached for his wine. 'At first I thought I was imagining it,' he said, looking deep into his glass. 'You know, like it was something I wanted to hear. But I wasn't, it was real.' He looked up from the glass. 'It is something I wanted to hear, but I didn't imagine it.'

'I believe you,' Amy said, but I wondered if she did.

'I never got the chance to say goodbye.' Marc was looking in Amy's direction but his eyes had a glazed, vacant look. 'I kissed her goodbye when I left for work and promised I wouldn't be late because we were going out with her friend.' He paused while he pushed his hair back. 'I never saw her alive again.' I noticed that Amy was plucking at a fingernail. It broke. She ripped it off and threw it to the side. She started on the next nail as she listened. 'When I got home there was a police car outside. By the time I found out, Ellen had been dead for two hours.'

I saw a tear falling down Amy's cheek as she reached for the wine bottle and refilled her glass.

'Naomi has said right from the start she could see her mother, but I didn't believe her.' Marc's words came slow after careful choosing. 'Ellen's mum wanted me to take her to a doctor but I thought it was Naomi's way of coping and I was just glad she had found a way to do that. I mean, if anyone could see Ellen it would be me … surely.'

'You would think.'

'And then tonight, I heard her laugh.' I felt Amy's pain. Marc's words must have felt like a knife in her back … until he added, 'And the one person I wanted to tell was you.'

Marc smiled that smile that used to melt my heart and I sensed Amy's relief.

It was just after that that Marc told Amy he thought he was falling in love with her. I was pleased for them. Marc didn't go home that night.

'You all right?' George er we had seen the light

go out in the bedroom.

'Yeah.'

That night I felt truly at peace

CHAPTER THIRTY-FIVE

I knew my time in this place, wherever it was, was coming to an end. It had taken me a while but I had finally come to terms with my issues.

Naomi, my beautiful child, would know that I was always going to watch over her, no matter where I was.

My mother had realised she wasn't to blame for my death and she was making up for what she didn't give me as a child by doing it for my daughter. I just prayed that Naomi would be able to withstand all the attention.

And Marc, my darling Marc was moving on with his life.

Of all my issues, this was the one I found most difficult. I had to go beyond my feelings of jealousy at the thought of him with another woman in his arms, in his life. I should have been that woman. It wasn't fair that I was dead.

I had discovered that neither life nor death was fair.

George. What can I say about George? He started out as an annoyance and turned into a companion and then a friend. In recent weeks, he had become more. I had come to need him and had been horrified at the thought of moving on without him. Who would have thought being dead could be so complicated.

'What are you thinking about?' George asked.

'You,' I answered.

He gave that familiar shrug. 'What about me?'

I contemplated my fingernails. 'Who are you?' I asked. 'Why are you here?'

He kicked an imaginary stone as he walked along. 'You asked me those questions once.'

'A long time ago,' I said as I fell into step.

'So you've had your answers.'

'No.' I pulled at his arm to stop him. 'That's not enough. Who are you? Why did you come to me? Why didn't I get the other person I was supposed to get?'

'Would you rather have had them?'

'No.'

'Then why question it?'

'Because I need to know.'

'You can't.'

'Why?'

'Because you can't.'

It sounded like a conversation I used to have with Naomi. George laughed.

'If you ever get into the Big Bloke's office you can ask him yourself. I don't know why you got me, you just did.'

'I'm glad I did.' The words came out without any effort. 'This Big Bloke you mentioned,' I said, 'do you mean God?'

'He's got lots of names.'

'So he really exists?' The disbelief in my voice surprised me.

'Yeah.' George had a similar amount in his voice.

'What?' I said. 'There's one person up there who decides what's going to happen to us?'

'You don't think all this happens by accident, do you?'

I had to think about that one. 'Suppose not.'

Being one of life's eternal doubters, however, I knew I would probably have to see him before I believed it.

We had walked a while when I said. 'It's nearly over,

isn't it?'

'Yes.'

'When?'

'Soon.'

'How long?'

'I asked them to let you have Christmas Day.'

* * *

'Are you coming to my concert?' Naomi asked as we sat on her bed together. George was looking out of the window.

'Of course. When is it?' I felt bad that I didn't already know the answer. But why would I? I didn't read the letters she brought home from school any more.

'Tomorrow night.'

'Can I come?' George asked.

'Yes,' she smiled. She looked at me and her face became serious. 'Daddy said he's bringing a friend.'

'Really?' I looked at George, who had turned to look at me.

'Yes. I think her name was Amy.'

'Oh.'

Naomi looked at me. 'Who is she?'

'Daddy's friend.'

'Why's she coming to my concert?'

'For the same reason I am,' George said. 'Your daddy and mummy can't go together so they're each taking a friend. And everyone loves a Christmas concert. What are you going to be?' he asked.

'A snowflake.'

* * *

My parents would also be at the concert.

Marc and Naomi stood hand in hand in the corridor outside the classroom where children were getting changed. Amy was with them. Apparently they were waiting for my mother, who had been putting the final touches to Naomi's costume. George and I stood a short distance away and watched Naomi eye Amy with suspicion. Marc had introduced the two of them and Naomi stood quietly while the adults chatted. Marc's hand moved towards Amy's, which didn't go unnoticed by Naomi. Amy pulled her hand away but Marc reached further and took hold of it. He bent down to talk to Naomi but I couldn't hear what he was saying.

The doors at the end of the corridor opened and my dad appeared. He held the door open and my mother followed, carrying what I assumed was Naomi's costume. Her eyes were on the cargo she was carrying. My dad said, 'Sorry we're a bit late, Marc. The traffic was terrible.'

When she looked up, Mum's step faltered just a little as she saw Amy and Marc holding hands. I could see that Amy was trying to pull away but Marc just held on tighter. Eventually, Amy gave up trying.

'Hello, Marc,' Mum said before turning her attention to Naomi. 'Hello, my darling.'

Naomi smiled. 'Did you finish it, Gran?' she asked.

'Just like you wanted it,' she said with obvious pride.

'I need to get dressed,' Naomi announced, 'come and help me, Gran?'

The two of them disappeared and I pulled George's arm to follow them. 'How much do you want to bet, the first thing Mum asks is who's that woman with your daddy?'

'Nothing, because there's never been a bigger certainty.'

We arrived just in time.

'Who's that lady with your daddy?' Mum asked.

George and I laughed.

258

'Amy.' Naomi was more interested in getting her shoes off.

'Who's Amy?'

'Daddy's friend.'

To my surprise, Mum left it at that.

❦

I realise I am biased but without a doubt Naomi was the best snowflake on the stage.

Marc and Amy stood in the corridor with my parents and waited for Naomi to change out of her outfit. There was a conversation going on but my mother wasn't really participating. She was watching Amy.

'I need to see Naomi,' I said.

❦

I held my finger to my mouth to tell Naomi that she must be quiet. It was one thing to talk to your dead mother in the privacy of your own bedroom, but a class full of six year olds was a different thing altogether. She understood and started to get dressed.

'Naomi,' I said. 'First of all, you are the best snowflake I ever saw.' She looked like she was going to speak so I quickly put my finger to my lips. 'When you go outside, I want you to hold hands with Amy.'

She questioned me with her look and I nodded to show she had heard me right. I thought of how to best explain it.

'Daddy likes Amy a lot,' I said. 'And that's all right because I like Amy too. Amy feels a bit awkward because your gran is here and she doesn't know how your gran will feel about her being Daddy's friend.'

Naomi leaned down and pretended to fasten a shoe that was already fastened. 'Is she Daddy's girlfriend?' she whispered out of the corner of her mouth.

I smiled. 'Yes, I think she is.'

259

'Don't you mind?' Her face was going red and I motioned with my hand that she should sit up.

I tried to smile. 'No, darling,' I said. 'I don't mind. Like I said, I like Amy and she makes your daddy happy and that's the main thing.'

She nodded wisely and carried on with the business of getting dressed.

'So,' I continued. 'When you go outside I want you to show that Amy is your friend too. If your gran knows you like Amy, she will like her as well.'

Naomi had finished dressing and gave me a smile before saying goodnight to her teacher and going to find her family.

'Why'd you do that?' George asked.

'It's not Amy's fault I'm dead.'

We found them in the corridor, walking towards the exit. Marc and my father were walking ahead with the women following a few paces back. Naomi was between Amy and my mother. She was holding hands with both of them.

'Clever girl,' George said and I agreed with him.

CHAPTER THIRTY-SIX

I still had to talk to Naomi about going away. Christmas was in only a week so it would have to be soon.

'Don't leave it too long.' George advised. 'Don't leave it until the last minute.'

I knew he was right.

'Naomi, darling,' I started. 'I have to talk to you and I need you to listen carefully.'

She looked at me with those eyes that were so precious to me and I couldn't speak.

'It's time for you to go, isn't it?'

'Yes,' was all I could say.

She reached over and plucked Jasper from where he lay on her pillow. She put him on her knee and started to stroke him. 'When?' she asked with a break in her voice.

'Soon.'

'Why?'

Naomi's head was down and she continued to stroke Jasper in silence. I didn't know what to say. I looked over to George for support. He nodded slowly. He reached into his pocket but came out empty handed. He looked at his hand and wiped it over his mouth.

'OK, Naomi,' he said. 'I'm going to try and explain this to you because I understand it a bit better than your mummy does.' He crouched down and looked up at Naomi. Her eyes were still settled on Jaspar but eventually George managed to secure her gaze.

'Just tell me why,' she murmured.

'Because it's time,' George said. 'It's as simple as that, it's time for your mummy to go to a different place.'

'What place?'

'It's got a really long name that I can't say but people call it the Other Side.'

'The other side of where?'

George laughed. 'That's a really good question,' he said.

'And what's the answer?'

'It's not really the other side of anywhere, it's just a name.'

'So Mummy's not really going anywhere?' Naomi looked at me for the first time since I told her I had to go away.

'Let me put it this way. It'll be like you're on television.' Naomi appeared confused. 'Mummy will be able to see you and check on how you're doing. She won't leave you completely. It's just that she won't be able to come and visit you.'

'Not ever?'

'Not often,' he said sadly.

'But there have been times,' I told her, finally finding my voice. 'When I've been watching you and you've not known I was there. It'll be just like that.'

Naomi looked at George and then me. 'Will I ever see you again?'

I found it hard to hold her gaze. 'I'm going to see you on Christmas Day.' I forced myself to look at her. 'That will be my present to you. I wish I could give you something else but I can't. This is all I have to give you.'

There was another short period of silence before

Naomi asked, 'Is Amy going to be my new mummy?'

I thought for a moment. 'I will always be your mummy,' I said.

'But what if she marries Daddy?'

'I wouldn't worry about that yet,' I said. 'But if one day your daddy does get married again, his new wife will be very lucky, because she'll get to look after you.'

'But will she be my mummy?'

The idea of Naomi having another mummy was even worse than that of Marc having another wife. I found it a struggle to control my breathing.

'You can only have one real mummy.' George came to my rescue. 'So if your daddy does get married again, his new wife would be like a mummy to you. She would look after you and help you with things.'

'But she wouldn't be my mummy?' I realised how confusing this must be for her.

'Not your real one,' George said.

'But you can call her Mummy if you like.' I took a deep breath and reached out to my child. She wasn't looking at me and I wished she would. 'I know this is really hard for you to understand,' I said. 'But there are some things that happen and there's nothing we can do about it. I would give anything, *anything*, for things not to be the way they are. I want nothing more than to be alive and taking care of you.'

I looked at my hands and they were trembling. I looked at Naomi and saw her also looking at my hands.

'But it can't be that way and no matter how much you and I both want it, it will never be that way again.' I tried to sound upbeat. 'But we've had this time together. We've been able to talk. You've been able to help Granny Peg ...' I took a deep breath. 'But now, the time has come when that's got to change. I have to go away, so I won't be able to come and visit you. But I'll still be able to see what's happening to you.'

'Will you watch me on the television?' I thought for a second she was going to look at me.

'Yes.' I tried to sound excited. 'I'll tune in to Channel Naomi every day.' She almost smiled. 'Please look at me, Naomi.'

Eventually, she did.

'I will always love you.' I spoke slowly. 'No matter where you are and where I am, I will never stop loving you.'

A tear formed in the corner of Naomi's eye. It grew and grew until it could no longer be contained. It rolled down her cheek. She and I went to wipe it away at the same time and for a second our fingers touched.

'I'll always love you too, Mummy,' she said through a sniff.

My own tears I kept until after we had left Naomi.

'Is it really like watching television?' I asked when the tears had stopped. I tried to imagine myself queuing up for my turn in front of a bank of television screens so I could pick up the latest episode of Naomi's life.

'The whole world's a television,' George said.

CHAPTER THIRTY-SEVEN

It was Christmas Eve and I watched as Naomi helped Marc put the final touches to the presents they had bought. I would have had them wrapped weeks ago but Marc had always been a last-minute bloke so I wasn't surprised that he had left them until now.

First they had wrapped a jumper for my dad and now they worked together to wrap my mother's favourite perfume. I knelt with them and watched as Naomi held the edges in place and Marc secured them with tape.

I felt like part of my own family again and realised it would probably be for the last time.

As I walked the streets that night for what would be the last time, on this side at least, I wondered what the Other Side was like. Would I feel different? I had so many questions going round in my head but there was one that cropped up more than the rest.

Would I see Matthew?

As I passed a church, it felt natural to follow the crowd heading in its direction. Midnight Mass was about to start.

We had always gone to Midnight Mass when I was a child and I remembered it fondly. I wondered where my mother was and if she would be attending this Christmas. I hoped that she could find it within herself to return to the church at some point. It had always meant so much to her. Her faith had been so strong. I realised it was one of the things I had always admired about her.

I hadn't planned on staying long but before I knew it the communion procession had finished, the priest had given the Christmas Blessing, and the congregation was leaving.

I felt the gentle crush of frost forming as I walked along. It was a cold night and although there was no hint of snow, the ground would be white on Christmas morning.

I sat in the pistachio room in the semi-darkness. The only light came from the Christmas tree that stood in the corner.

We'd always left the Christmas tree lit on Christmas Eve and I was happy that the tradition was still going. We'd started doing it the year after Naomi was born. Marc had laughed at first when I suggested that Santa might trip over something if we didn't leave a light on but he played along. We'd left the tree lights on that Christmas Eve and each of the five since then.

I was smiling when I heard footsteps on the stairs.

A minute or two later, the door opened and there stood Marc and Naomi.

Marc flicked a switch and the lights came on. I saw Naomi and she saw me. We smiled at each other.

'It's cold in here,' Marc said, pulling his dressing gown tighter around himself. He ran his hand along the radiator.

'It's not cold, Daddy.' Naomi looked at me and gave

her head a shake as she pulled on Marc's sleeve and dragged him towards the presents. I couldn't help but smile. Despite everything, she was still a little girl on Christmas morning which was exactly as it should be.

And so the ritual present opening began. One by one, Naomi opened her gifts. She seemed to have more than usual this year but I guessed that was Marc's way of compensating. Each present was inspected carefully before being put to one side while the paper was discarded onto a pile. Eventually, Naomi reached for the last present. I knew it must be the talking teddy.

Marc looked on with a smile on his face as Naomi opened the top of the present carefully and then, once she realised what was inside, she ripped the paper frantically. She pulled it out and held it aloft triumphantly.

She jumped up and threw her arms around Marc's neck

'Thank you,' she said as she climbed onto his knee.

'Is it the right one?' he asked, kissing the top of her head. She nodded as she pressed the bear's stomach and forced him to speak. 'You wouldn't rather have had the white one?'

'No,' she said. 'I told Mummy it was the chocolate one I wanted.'

Marc lowered his head until it rested on Naomi's. She turned her head to look at me.

I knew it was now or never. This was the chance I had been waiting for. My last chance, my only chance.

I coughed to clear my throat. 'Naomi,' I said. 'Will you tell Daddy I'm here?' She looked at me but said nothing. 'Please.'

Naomi pulled her head out from under Marc's and looked at him. 'Daddy,' she said cautiously. 'Please don't be mad at me because I'm not making this up.'

'Making what up, sweetheart?'

'Mummy said to tell you she's here.'

Marc's head shot up and his eyes searched the room.

'She's over there.' She nodded her head in my direction.

'Is that why it's so cold?' His words were slow and nervous.

I told Naomi what to say. 'She says she's sorry about that but she's been here all night.' She sounded very serious as she told him, 'She has to go away.'

'What do you mean? Away where?'

'The Other Side,' Naomi said, sounding like the fountain of knowledge. 'But she'll still be able to watch us, and she'll never stop loving us.'

I realised then as I listened to Naomi's babbling that she was just a child and maybe the reality of what had happened in the last few months wasn't real to her at all.

'Naomi,' I said, 'I need you to tell Daddy ...'

'Ellen.' I turned as I heard Marc say my name. He was looking straight at me. The difference this time was that I knew he could see me. 'Ellen.' He eased Naomi off his knee and stood up.

'Marc.' My voice was a whisper.

'What's happening?'

'I don't know.'

'How can you be here?'

'I don't know.'

We looked at each other in silence. But silence wasn't a luxury I could afford. 'Marc, there's so much ...'

'Oh God, Ellen, I've missed you so much.' He covered his mouth with his hands.

I looked at him and felt his love as strongly as ever before. 'I know,' I mouthed.

'Are you alright?' He laughed at his own question.

'Yes,' I laughed too. 'I'm fine. It's not so bad when you get used to it.' I pushed my hair behind my ears. 'It's

268

the getting used to it that's the challenge.'

'I can't believe this.' Marc shook his head. 'I'm going to wake up in a minute and Naomi's going to be asking me who I'm talking to.'

'You're not asleep, this is real.'

'I don't understand …'

'Nor do I but I've learnt not to question things.'

There was something I had to say before it was too late.

'I'm happy for you,' I said.

He shook his head. 'I don't understand.'

I rubbed the end of my nose, the way I always did when I was preparing to say something difficult. 'I'm happy for you … about Amy.'

He opened his mouth but it was a few seconds before any words came out. 'Amy?'

'Yes, I like her,' I smiled. 'And I think you like her too.'

He looked a little sheepish. 'You don't mind?'

'No.' It wasn't a lie, 'I don't mind. You have to move on.'

'You're sure you don't mind?'

How well he knew me.

'I did at first,' I admitted. 'But the more I thought about it, the more I realised that all I really wanted was for you to be happy.'

Marc looked away. 'I thought I'd never be happy again.'

'Are you happy?'

'Yes.' He made it sound like an apology.

'Good,' I smiled.

There was another silence.

Marc ran his fingers through his hair in the way I adored. 'I'll always love you,' he said. I think he sensed that we didn't have a lot of time.

I nodded. I could feel tears forming in the corners of my eyes.

'I know … and I'll never stop loving you.'

The tears fell from my eyes and rolled down my cheeks and off the end of my chin. 'Marc,' I said. 'There are some things I need to tell you before I have to go.

'You're doing a fantastic job with Naomi. We made something beautiful together. Our love made something beautiful. Just keep doing what you're doing. She's a good kid and if you show her that you love her, you'll be fine.' I paused. 'Try not to cut my mother out. I know things have never been easy for the pair of you but she needs the contact with Naomi and Naomi needs that too.' I paused again. 'Oh, and if you can ever drop it into conversation, tell her I once told you I loved her very much and wished I'd shown it more.'

I looked over at Naomi, who was playing happily with her new teddy. She was lost in a world of her own.

'About Amy,' I said, looking deep into his eyes. 'I don't know if she's the right one for you, only you know that. All I ask is that you can find someone who makes you happy and who can love Naomi at least half as much as I do.'

Naomi looked at me and smiled. Maybe she wasn't as far away as I'd thought.

'Just promise me you'll be happy,' I said.

'I promise.'

I beckoned to Naomi and she came towards me slowly. She stood at my knees. 'You know I've got to go now,' I said and she nodded, looking at me through eyes that seemed larger than normal. 'But remember what I said about how I'll be able to see you. So you must be a good girl, because if you aren't then I'll know.' Her head bobbed up and down. 'And I want you to remember that no matter where I am, I still love you. That is never going to change. Can you do that?'

This time she nodded her head slowly.

'Why do you have to go away, Mummy?' she asked.

'I don't know, darling,' I said. 'I don't understand it. I just know that I do … and I have to go today.'

I could sense something happening and I knew my time was almost over. I reached out a hand and ran it down Naomi's hair. I reached the other out to Marc. He moved his hand towards mine and our fingertips brushed against each other. There was no need to speak but I couldn't have if I'd wanted to.

It was time.

'Goodbye, Marc,' I said, sniffing back a tear.

'Goodbye,' he croaked.

'Bye, Naomi,'

She looked at me through serious eyes. 'Goodbye, Mummy.'

As I turned, I noticed the light again. It was just as bright but this time my eyes didn't need to adjust to it. I knew that was where I was going and took a step towards it. I wondered if Marc and Naomi could see it too.

'Oh,' I said turning around. 'Do you remember the park where we used to take Naomi?' Marc nodded. 'Do you remember the pond where we used to feed the ducks?' Again, he nodded. 'Would you see if the council will let you put a bench there for me?' Marc nodded one last time.

After a final look and a deep breath I walked beyond the light.

CHAPTER THIRTY-EIGHT

It was Christmas Day on the Other Side too. My Gran and Granddad were there, each sporting a paper hat. And I could have sworn I could smell a turkey cooking. My grandparents held out their arms and took me into their embrace.

When I stood back from them I looked over to George. I followed his eyes to the left, where a child played with some building blocks. I felt myself stumble. George moved to support me but I regained my composure and held up my hand. I looked at my grandmother but couldn't force the question out of my mouth. She answered with a nod.

I moved to the child and knelt down. At first, he didn't notice me. He bashed two blocks together and giggled, his soft curls bobbing. I picked up a block from the floor and offered it to him.

He looked up at me warily through the same dark eyes his father had. At first he just looked. Then a smile formed on his lips and he set the blocks aside. He had to half turn and use his hands to force himself up onto his tiny feet with his back to me. Those tiny feet supported his chubby legs as he carefully manoeuvred himself round and took the steps needed to move to me.

'Ma-ma?' It sounded like a question.

'Yes,' I said as I scooped Matthew into my arms and held him tightly.

I had been in this new place for what was probably a few hours. This new place that looked remarkably like the living room of my grandparents' house when my grandmother had been alive. I sat on the lumpy sofa with Matthew asleep on my lap. I stroked his face and his hair. George was sat close by and I looked at him from time to time. He was looking at me with a smile on his lips.

Granddad appeared with someone dressed from head to toe in white. Their clothes were in stark contrast to their hair, which was jet black.

'You've got a visitor,' Granddad said to George.

George stood up. 'Arthur,' he said by way of greeting.

Arthur did not greet George. Arthur was busy studying some papers he held in his hand. Arthur didn't look at me but he did wave his pen in my direction. 'Is this Ellen Reed?' he asked.

'Yes,' George said, looking over at me.

Arthur finally looked at George. 'Better late than never,' he said.

George dropped his head to the side. 'Yeah, sorry about that.'

It was clear that Arthur was trying to intimidate George. He was looking down his nose, through tiny slits of eyes. I didn't like this newcomer and didn't like the way he was talking to my friend. I slid Matthew onto the sofa and stood by the men.

'What are you apologising for?' I asked George.

George was still looking at Arthur, who flicked to the second sheet of paper. I could sense the contempt that George was feeling.

Arthur looked up from the papers. 'There were certain

procedures you failed to follow correctly,' he said.

'I know, but I did the best I could,' George offered with an edge in his voice.

'Your best, eh?' Arthur looked at George from under what were ridiculously bushy eyebrows. 'Do you think it was good enough?'

'She's here, isn't she?'

'Hang on a minute. Who is he?' I asked.

'Arthur,' he said.

'I heard his name,' I said glancing at the newcomer, 'but who is he?'

'My supervisor.'

'Oh.' I spun round. 'Hello, Arthur, I'm Ellen. Is there anything I can help you with?'

Arthur was unnerved and looked down at his papers. 'No thank you, Ellen,' he said. 'I've just come to have a word with George.'

'What about?' He flicked over another sheet. 'What is this you're looking at?' I asked, straining my neck to see. I saw my name in bold print.

'Nothing you should be concerned about,' Arthur said.

'They're about me, aren't they?'

'No,' he denied.

'I saw my name at the top.'

Arthur looked at me and said through pursed lips, 'If you don't mind, I need to debrief George.'

'Of course I don't mind,' I said. 'But what was this about procedures not followed? I'd like to know if I didn't get the full service'

'Maybe you should come to the office later?' Arthur suggested, flicking the sheets over and straightening them. George was nodding without making eye contact.

'No,' I said. 'Do it now, that's what you came for.'

Arthur looked at George, who shrugged his shoulders. Arthur lifted his nose into the air and took a deep breath.

275

'Very well,' he said, looking round for somewhere to sit. He chose a chair at the table and brushed some imaginary crumbs from the oil cloth before putting his papers down. He shuffled through the papers and pulled out a sheet from halfway down and placed it on top. He pulled a silver pen from the inside pocket of his jacket. He held the pen poised over the paper as he asked George, 'On a scale of one to five, where one is the lowest and five is the highest, how would you evaluate the job that you did?'

'Four,' George said. Arthur raised an eyebrow but said nothing.

'On a scale of one to five, where one is the lowest and five is the highest, how competently would you say you followed procedures as laid down in section four sub-section seventeen of the Greeters code of conduct?'

'Four.'

'Four?' Arthur not only lifted his head, but threw the pen onto the table. 'Four?' he repeated. 'How can you possibly give yourself a four? Where in the manual does it say you take a client to see someone who has received their organs?'

I tried to object to use of the word 'client' but I didn't get the chance to speak.

'Not only do you take the client to see their organ recipient, you allow the client to speak to said organ recipient.' Arthur pushed the forefinger of his right hand against the thumb of his left as if to mark off the number one. 'Then,' he said moving onto the next finger, 'there was all that with her kid.'

'Naomi could see her,' George protested.

'But did you have to let her pass messages on to her grandmother?' Arthur waved his arm out to the side.

'Alright,' George conceded, 'maybe I shouldn't have allowed it, but it helped Ellen's mum to come to terms with Ellen's death.'

Arthur's cheeks hollowed as he pursed his lips. 'We have means of dealing with that.'

'I didn't think they would work,' George said.

'You never even tried.' Arthur moved to the middle finger of his left hand. 'Then there was that nonsense today.' Arthur's voice got louder and Matthew stirred on the sofa. I made a shushing noise. 'Where,' Arthur asked barely able to conceal his anger, 'does it say you allow the client to be seen by someone other than those the committee has chosen should see them?'

'Committee?' I finally found my voice. 'What committee?'

George either did not hear me or chose to ignore me. He stood face to face with Arthur.

'I thought it was the best way to proceed,' George seethed through gritted teeth.

'And since when were Greeters paid to think?' Arthur sneered.

George moved away and ran his hand over his hair. I could see the anger in his face.

'Excuse me, Arthur,' I said, moving to George. 'Is there some sort of problem here?'

Arthur looked at George and laughed. 'Yes, you could say that.'

'Something about procedures?'

'He doesn't follow them.'

'OK,' I said as I straightened the lapels of Arthur's jacket. 'And can I just say I love the cut of this jacket.' Arthur's face softened as he nodded his agreement. 'Anyway, about those procedures. Wasn't this George's first time as a Greeter?' He nodded. 'And wasn't the plan that he help me to resolve my issues?'

'Yes,' Arthur agreed reluctantly.

'Well, here I am. So what's the problem?'

Arthur lifted his nose again and took another deep breath.

'He didn't follow procedures.' Arthur took a step away. He stood with his hands in his pockets and a smirk on his face. 'And I have to tell you,' he said. 'They took a very dim view to the relationship the pair of you have formed.' George and I looked at each other. 'A very dim view indeed.' Arthur walked to the table and separated the top sheet from the rest. He put it to one side and tucked the rest under his arm. 'I'll leave that with you, George,' he said. 'Fill it in at your leisure and drop it into the office.' He held out his hand to me, 'It was nice meeting you, Ellen. Welcome to the Other Side.'

I shook his hand without saying anything. As he moved towards the door Arthur stopped and added, 'When you do drop it off, George, you might also want to pick up your cards. The boss won't be using you again.'

The door closed behind him.

'Sorry.' I didn't know what else to say.

He shrugged. 'Doesn't matter.'

I moved a step closer to him. 'For what it's worth,' I said, 'I'm glad I got you.'

George put his arms around me and spoke into the top of my head. It sounded like, 'And I'm glad I finally found you,' but it couldn't have been. That wouldn't have made any sense.

Acknowledgements

A lot have people are responsible for getting me where I am today and I am indebted to each and every one of them.

John, John and Andrew – aka my men – thank you for your love and for not laughing at my dream.

My dear friend Jan Weiss, thank you for your encouragement over the decades. Only you truly know what it has taken for me to get here.

My parents and my siblings, thank you for always making me feel special. I just wish Mum and Dad could have lived another month so I could have told them about this book.

I have to give a special thank you to the staff of Sunderland Royal Hospital, especially those in ICCU, the renal unit and ward B28. You saved my life and then returned me to health and I will never be able to thank you enough.

Last be not least, thank you to everyone at Accent Press. I would like to give special mentions to Hazel Cushion for creating a beautiful place, Rebecca Lloyd for her guidance and to Alex Davies for making this book the best it could be.

If there is anyone that I have forgotten, please accept my apologies but know that you are forever in my heart.

'Engaging and lively, empathetic and addictive...
I was hooked from the off' *Sarah Rayner*

Redemption
Song

LAURA WILKINSON

If you lost everything in one night, what would you do?

Saffron is studying for a promising career in medicine until a horrific accident changes her life for ever. Needing to escape London, she moves to a small coastal town to live with her mother. Saffron hates the small town existence and feels trapped until she meets Joe, another outsider. Despite initial misgivings, they grow closer to each other as they realise they have a lot in common. Like Saffron, Joe has a complicated past ... one that's creeping up on his present. Can Joe escape his demons for long enough to live a normal life – and can Saffron reveal the truth about what really happened on that fateful night? Love is the one thing they need most, but will they – can they – risk it?

Redemption Song is a captivating, insightful look at what happens when everything goes wrong – and the process of putting the pieces back together again.

For more information about **Colette McCormick**

and other **Accent Press** titles

please visit

www.accentpress.co.uk